AN IMPOSTER WITH A CROWN

EMPIRE OF TALENTS BOOK TWO

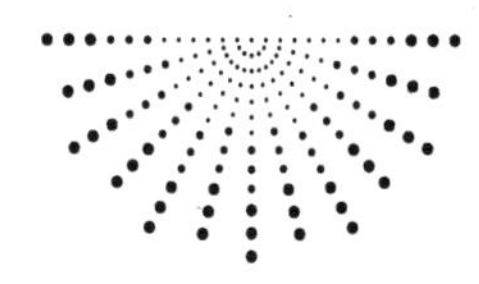

JORDAN RIVET

Contact the author at Jordan@JordanRivet.com

For updates and discounts on new releases, join Jordan Rivet's mailing list.

Cover by Deranged Doctor Design

Edited by Red Adept Publishing

Map by Jordan Rivet

❀ Created with Vellum

This book is dedicated in memory of my grandpa,
Keith Frederick Young.
1922-2017

CONTENTS

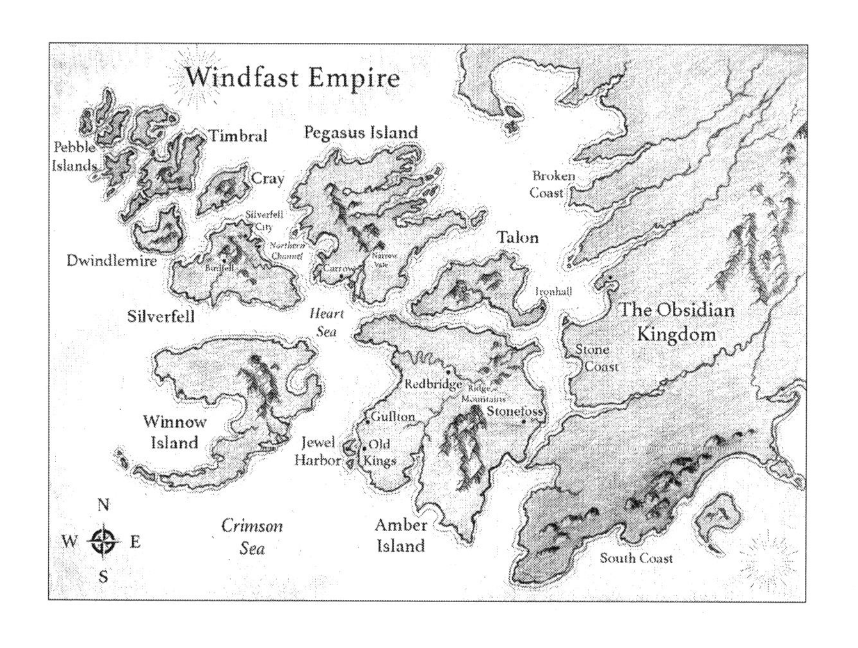
Windfast Empire
Pebble Islands
Timbral
Pegasus Island
Cray
Broken Coast
Silverfell City
Northern Channel
Birdfell
Carrow
Narrow Vale
Talon
Dwindlemire
Ironhall
Silverfell
Heart Sea
The Obsidian Kingdom
Stone Coast
Redbridge
Ridge Mountains
Stonefoss
Winnow Island
Gullton
Jewel Harbor
Old Kings
N
W
E
S
Crimson Sea
Amber Island
South Coast

CHAPTER ONE

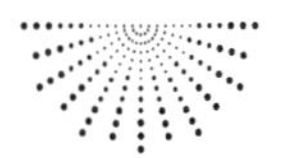

Mica ran her fingers through her dark-red hair. It fell in perfect waves over her shoulders, shimmering in the light of a thousand candles. She wore a midnight-blue gown and a silver tiara, which shone as bright as if a star had come down from the heavens to grace the ballroom. From her sumptuous attire to every detail of her face, Mica looked like a princess.

It was the two hundredth anniversary of the formation of the Windfast Empire, and Mica was hosting the celebratory ball—one of her many duties as the full-time Impersonator for the real princess.

Mica had never been to such an extravagant party. It felt as though half the population of the city filled the Silver Palace's main ballroom. Black fabric draped the walls, and the candles arranged at different levels gave the impression of a starry firmament enveloping the dancing couples. Tables piled with decadent cakes and savory delicacies lined the room, each surrounded by a horde of chattering guests. Flowers had been shipped in from warmer climes, and the smell of jasmine mingled with the perfumes of the ladies and the sugary aroma of winter wine.

Mica glided across the polished dance floor, searching for a woman she had never seen before. Hundreds of faces whirled by, painted lips, oiled mustaches, and flushed cheeks on display. Spirits were high among the revelers, but Mica ignored the frivolity and concentrated on her mission.

She was looking for a spymistress.

The islands that made up the empire had sent their most prominent nobles and governors to the capital for the anniversary ball. One of these noble ladies could hold the key to a mystery Mica had been trying to solve for nearly two months, ever since she assumed the role of imposter for Princess Jessamyn Styldier, the emperor's daughter.

Mica had urged the princess to attend the ball herself in the days leading up to the celebration.

"It would be the perfect time to tell everyone what happened to you."

"Don't be ridiculous, Micathea," Jessamyn had said. "The two hundredth anniversary is far too important for such a distraction." She handed Mica a list of demands to relay to the palace steward on her behalf, including the request for thousands of candles of varying heights. "Now remember: the stars will represent the individuals that make up the Windfast Empire. Even though they're all from different islands, the effect is more beautiful when everyone is united."

Mica scanned the list, written in Jessamyn's elegant hand. "Will the guests know that?"

"They'd better. Otherwise, those lovely wall hangings will go to waste."

"Maybe you should be there so you can tell—"

"I don't have all day, Micathea. Let's discuss the entertainment for the cocktail hour."

Mica had gritted her teeth as Jessamyn yet again refused to disclose she had been poisoned. Her insistence on maintaining the imposter charade was beginning to worry Mica. Jessamyn seemed to think her disfigured face would return to normal, leaving no one the wiser, but she had shown no signs of improvement in two months. Even Emperor Styl still didn't know that Lord Ober had nearly killed his daughter.

Mica found Jessamyn's stubbornness especially frustrating. As long as she insisted on keeping this crime a secret, catching Lord Ober was harder than it should be. He and his wife had fled the capital, and Mica still hadn't been able to discover their whereabouts. She hoped to make progress on that front tonight.

Heads turned to watch as Mica crossed the ballroom, her lively steps moving in time with the dance music. She wore the princess's old face—which was stunning. Glowing skin. Big brown eyes. Expressive eyebrows. Rose-red lips. In addition to taking on her features, Mica had worked hard to perfect the energetic mannerisms and charisma that contributed to Jessamyn's unique allure. The impersonation had to be perfect. She couldn't make a single absentminded gesture without it being noticed by a dozen pairs of eyes.

Just keep this up for a little while longer, she told herself. *When the empire is stable again, Jessamyn will take back her crown, and you can get on with your mission.*

Being the center of attention made it difficult to connect with her spymistress, but Mica hoped to get a report from her anyway before the night was over. Based in Winnow Bay, the noblewoman and her network of informants had helped track Lord Ober's movements. He had kept busy since he left Jewel Harbor, and Mica feared she was running out of time to bring him to justice.

As Mica maneuvered through the candlelit room, she ran through the list Jessamyn had given her of everyone she needed to greet in addition to the elusive spymistress. Mica had studied hard in the weeks leading up to the imperial ball so she could recognize the visitors from across the empire and welcome them with the appropriate levels of enthusiasm or disdain, depending on what Jessamyn wanted to accomplish.

She spotted two of the ladies on her list of targets by the entrance to the palace gardens, chatting with strained smiles on their faces. Ingrid and Elana hated each other—a fact that was well known at court—but they kept up the façade of courtesy that was second nature to all the nobles.

I suppose they're guests, not targets.

Mica swept toward them. "Lady Elana, Lady Ingrid. How lovely to see you both!"

The women greeted her enthusiastically, both looking grateful for the interruption.

"Princess Jessamyn, you must allow me to borrow your dress-maker one day," Elana said after she kissed Mica on both cheeks. She had a sharp nose and red hair, like the princess, but where Jessamyn's hair was a dark mahogany red, Elana's was bright and coppery. "Where *ever* did you get that lovely velvet?"

"Now, now." Mica smiled coyly. "I couldn't possibly reveal all my secrets." Also, she had no idea where the velvet came from.

"It's magnificent on you." Elana couldn't quite hide the envy in her voice. Her dress was a silver material designed to shimmer like starlight. She had good taste, but Mica's midnight-blue gown looked richer and more effortlessly elegant against the starry backdrop of the thousand candles.

"We'd expect nothing less of our princess," Lady Ingrid said.

Ingrid wore her customary black, which matched her hawkish features and black hair. She was from Talon, a harsh, rocky island where the people didn't go in for the frivolities of fashion—as she loved to tell people. Despite her disdain for luxuries, Lady Ingrid spent an awful lot of time living in the Silver Palace instead of in her family's austere fortress.

"You both look positively effervescent," Mica said. "I *do* hope you're enjoying the evening. I so wanted this to be a night for all my dearest friends to remember."

"The ballroom looks marvelous," Elana said.

"Yes, it's stunning, and the food is exquisite," Ingrid said. "You've outdone yourself this time."

"You are *ever* so kind." Mica resisted the urge to point out that it was the steward and the palace cooks who had outdone themselves. She had learned that nobles liked to take credit for whatever their employees did. They could also compliment each other for hours on end.

Time to make my escape.

She scanned the jewel-bedecked couples swaying around the dance floor, seeking out her spymistress or her next target—*guest*. "Have either of you darlings seen Lady Lorna?"

"She was dancing with Lord Fritz a while ago," Elana said. "They probably snuck off somewhere for privacy."

Ingrid snorted. "They've been doing that a lot lately."

"Lorna likes his scar," Elana said. "It makes him look less like a little boy."

"It's not just his scar she likes," Ingrid said. "The boy worships the ground she walks on. Lorna can't resist flattery."

"I think they make a *delightful* couple," Mica said.

"Never mind them," Lady Ingrid said. "*You* still haven't danced with Lord Riven tonight, Princess. Bellina told me her maid overheard his Shield telling a girl she thinks was a Mimic spy that Lord Riven is losing hope he will ever be chosen as your consort. Has he fallen out of favor?"

"Ingrid, you are too bold!" Elana said in a faux scandalized tone while leaning in to hear the princess's answer.

Mica was still trying to follow the convoluted path that particular rumor had taken to get to her.

"Well, we're all wondering," Ingrid said. "You used to pay more attention to him, Princess."

"I haven't decided whom I'll chose as my consort," Mica said airily. Jessamyn had been playing her suitors off each other since she reached marrying age, and Mica didn't intend to settle that particular arrangement on her behalf. "I am young yet, and there are so many spectacular men in the empire."

"Well, if you don't want Lord Riven, a few other ladies wouldn't mind the alliance."

"Really, Ingrid," Elana said with a sniff. "Must you be so tactless?"

"Better tactless than witless."

"Excuse me," Mica said as the two ladies began giving each other very polite death stares. "I *must* say hello to the Lord of Old Kings over there. It was ever so nice to see you."

Mica hurried away from Ingrid and Elana, weaving amongst silken skirts and trying not to trip over polished boots. She still catalogued interesting features out of habit: an attractive freckle pattern, a shapely brow, a set of long gray nose hairs. She'd had precious few opportunities to impersonate anyone but Jessamyn lately. She couldn't wait to be her old self again, when she would no longer have lords and ladies pretending to hang on her every word while scheming behind her back.

Mica hadn't been idle over the past two months, even though she'd worn a single face for most of that time. She had used the princess's vast resources—including her carefully cultivated relationships with the nobility—to root out the corruption in the City Watch, where Lord Ober had recruited partners for his scheme to kidnap Talents—those born with one of four supernatural abilities. Ober and his potioner had then conducted experiments on their captives, all in the name of instilling new and better Talents in those who'd been born without any special capabilities whatsoever. As far as Mica could tell, their most recent breakthrough was that the best way to make a potion effective was to brew it out of Talent bones.

No matter how she felt about her current role, Mica intended to keep using Jessamyn's influence for as long as it took to stop Lord Ober from continuing his grisly work. The nobles' conversations might revolve around fashion and affairs and decorations, but she couldn't forget that the dandies and simpering ladies waltzing across the ballroom in their finery were the most powerful men and women in the empire.

"Princess Jessamyn. It's about time you welcomed me."

Mica turned. An old lady she'd never met was marching toward her through the crowd. She had steel-gray hair tied in a bun and a wrinkled face as gaunt and pale as a crescent moon. Her black gown had a high neck and long, lace-trimmed sleeves holding back the chill of the winter evening.

"Lady Maren," Mica said, perhaps a beat too slowly. "I am so pleased you could make it. How was your journey?"

"I am too old to be long at sea."

"We simply could not have the celebration without you."

"Humph. Let me look at you."

The woman took Mica's face in her hands and gave her a squeeze somewhere between affectionate and severe. Mica held her breath. Jessamyn had warned her this would be a serious test of her abilities. Lady Maren and the princess's mother had been close, and Jessamyn had spent many summers visiting Lady Maren in Winnow Bay.

She also happened to be the spymistress.

"You have grown more beautiful than even your mother," Lady Maren said, releasing Mica's face at last. "You must visit me in the Bay."

"That would be delightful," Mica said. "I remember how I loved the pomegranates on my last visit."

"How could I forget?" Lady Maren chuckled. "You covered my entire courtyard with those infernal seeds."

"They were delicious." Mica had never tasted a pomegranate in her life, but the details the princess had made her memorize before the ball served her well.

"I shall send a Blur with some when I return."

"Thank you, Lady Maren." Mica glanced around to make sure

none of the revelers were listening in. "Have you an answer to my latest query?"

"You want to know about Ober again? He and that fruit pastry of a wife only stayed a short time on their last visit to Winnow."

"Did they go straight back to Timbral?"

"For a time. They have been prancing all over the western islands, as you know, but I have heard naught of them for over three weeks." The old woman put her hands on her ample hips. "Now, where is your father? I must speak with him about the Twins. Trouble is brewing."

Mica frowned, taking care to use the charming wrinkle that appeared between Jessamyn's eyebrows when she was concerned. "What kind of trouble?"

"The mountain folk always have one complaint or another." Lady Maren waved toward the west, the lace on her sleeves floating around her wrinkled hands. "This time there are whispers of secession. Your father must stamp out such talk before it turns to violence."

"Is it likely to get that bad?"

"We can almost be certain of it with the Twins," Lady Maren said. The Twins referred to two small islands called Dwindlemire and Cray. They were approximately the same size and shape, and their people alternated between fighting each other and partnering up to create problems for the rest of the empire—much like Mica's twin brothers, now that she thought about it.

"Are the people of Dwindlemire and Cray working together this time?"

"One report says they are. Another says they've skirmished amongst themselves already." Lady Maren harrumphed, and a passing serving man in palace livery jumped at the sound. "Perhaps I need new spies. My Mimics have been saying the most outlandish things of late."

"Like what?"

"Something about Talents behaving strangely."

Mica gripped her velvet skirts, keeping her voice calm. "Oh?"

"They're sleeping on the job and claiming illness to shirk their duties. It's just laziness if you ask me." Lady Maren paused, looking closer at Mica. "Is something wrong?"

"Not at all." Mica fought to keep her features from shifting out of shape. "I saw my father speaking with Lord Dolan over by the statue of the first emperor, the one with the gold overlay."

"Being spoken *to* by Dolan is more like it," Lady Maren muttered. "All right, run along and enjoy the dancing, Princess. We'll speak again before I sail out of this congested chicken coop of a city."

Lady Maren stomped away, leaving Mica to mull over this rumor, which was more concerning than the old spymistress knew. Talents exhibiting signs of illness and fatigue could mean Lord Ober was trying out his potions on new victims. He had rarely been seen on his own Timbral Island of late. She had never doubted he would continue his experimentation, but she still couldn't determine the exact location of his headquarters. Her spies had sighted him in so many different places over the past few months that she was beginning to suspect he had sent out an army of Impersonators to throw her off.

The lords and ladies by the nearest dessert table were watching her, whispering behind hands dusted with sugar and cake crumbs. Mica smoothed the worry lines out of her forehead, knowing Jessamyn wouldn't display such weakness, nor would she stand still for so long. She turned on her crystal heels—and bumped right into the person who had the best chance of recognizing her for the imposter she was: Lord Ober's nephew, Lord Caleb of the Pebble Islands.

"Jessa, you look radiant, as always." Caleb bowed, an easy smile on his face. The young nobleman had skipped the blues, blacks, and silvers many of the others had chosen to match the starry-night theme. He wore a deep-green waistcoat and a white silk blouse. His brown hair was as unruly as ever, falling around his slightly pointed ears and square face. He somehow looked earthier and more real than anyone else here.

"You . . . you look good too," Mica said.

"Careful, or I'll let your extravagant compliments go to my head."

Mica jutted out her lip in her best Jessamyn pout. "You shouldn't tease your favorite princess."

"Wouldn't dream of it," Caleb said. "Apologies for not coming by for tea the other day. I wasn't feeling well."

"Are you okay?"

"It's the same old story." He lifted his broad shoulders in a shrug and went on in a lighter tone. "Listen, I have a favor to ask you. Fritz is working up the nerve to propose to Lady Lorna this evening. I was hoping you could reassure him that she's definitely going to say yes."

Mica grinned. "Where is he?"

"Hiding on the promenade. Shall we?" Caleb offered his arm, and she hesitated for a second before taking it. He was on Jessamyn's list of people Mica was supposed to pay attention to tonight, but she had avoided dancing with him so far. In truth, she'd avoided him as much as possible over the past two months. Maintaining the impersonation around him was difficult when a huge part of her still wanted him to realize who she really was. It had been a mistake to allow her feelings for him to grow.

Unfortunately, she couldn't change her feelings as easily as she could change her face.

They climbed a stone staircase to the promenade overlooking the ballroom, passing the spot where Mica had learned Caleb's name—and lordly title—so many months ago. The first time they'd met, she had thought he was a commoner like her. He had always treated her as an equal despite his noble status, but now that she was acting as the princess, there were more barriers between them than ever.

"Fritz is over here," Caleb said as he escorted her along the promenade.

Deep plush cushions had been piled along the balcony railings, creating large couches where guests could lounge when they wanted a break from dancing. Serving men and women traversed the promenade, carrying trays of spiced wine and chocolates. A single musician strolled behind them, offering to perform violin solos for the couples perched on the cushions.

Lord Fritz slumped on one such pile of cushions, a dark-green bottle clutched in his hands. The young lord had sandy-blond hair and a youthful face marred by a scar on one side. He had been hit by a burning piece of wood at the disastrous harbor cruise a few months ago, giving him a slightly debonair new look. Fritz's scar wasn't as bad as Jessamyn's, but it didn't seem fair to Mica that *his* social clout had improved with the imperfection while Jessamyn felt the need to stay hidden in her room.

"Had enough liquid courage yet, Fritz?" Caleb asked, dropping onto the pillows beside his friend.

"I'm not going through with it." Fritz's voice slurred slightly.

"Yes, you are," Caleb said.

"What if she says no?"

"She won't." Mica pried the bottle out of Fritz's hands and set it aside. "You know good and well what Lady Lorna's answer will be. Now pull yourself together, my lord."

"But what if her father objects? Or my mother! Silverfell is far away. She might not want me to marry a lady from way out there."

"Silverfell isn't that far away," Caleb said.

"You both spend all your time here anyway," Mica said. "You can continue to live right next door to your mother."

"Lorna will *love* that," Caleb said.

Mica shot him a look, and he grinned. Lord Fritz's mother was formidable, and she coddled him worse than ever since his injury.

"I can see Lorna right now," Mica said, glancing over the balcony at the dance floor below. A buxom young woman with pouting lips and curly dark hair was bouncing on the balls of her feet as a serving girl attempted to fill her wine goblet without spilling. "She's looking for you."

"How do you know it's me she—"

"Are you questioning me, my lord?" Mica gave a longsuffering sigh. "I've had quite enough of this foolishness. Get down there and propose to that pretty lady before I do it for you."

Fritz looked up hopefully. "Could you—?"

"Go!"

"Yes, Princess."

Lord Fritz leapt to his feet and hurried toward the stairs, forgetting to bow as he took his leave. Mica couldn't help smiling. Fritz and Lorna were two of the nobles she actually liked, and she was starting to think of them as friends.

They're Jessamyn's friends, not yours, she reminded herself. *They would never look twice at the real you.*

"Care to join me, Jessa?" Caleb took a swig from the bottle Fritz had abandoned and patted the cushion beside him. "I know you have people to see, but I bet your feet could use a break."

Mica hesitated. She couldn't afford to let down her guard around Caleb right now, but he and Jessamyn were real friends. He would notice if she kept avoiding him.

"I guess I can stay for a minute." Mica sat beside him—not too near—and arranged her velvet skirts exactly as Jessamyn would if she ever allowed herself a moment's rest.

"Tell me, darling," she said, fiddling with her skirt and not quite meeting Caleb's eyes. "Have you made any progress on your mystery lately?"

"Afraid not. I've been interviewing potioners now that I know my extra abilities came from an experimental potion, but they haven't been as much help as I'd hoped."

"You're still having frequent . . . episodes?"

"Same as ever," Caleb said. "I've been training with Stievson and my men more often to work on control. I'm not sure if it's helping."

"If Mimics can learn control, so can you."

"Maybe, but it's dangerous to carry on like this," Caleb said. "It's only a matter of time before one of my Talents manifests at the wrong moment and I hurt someone."

Mica looked up. "Don't they come through when you need them most?"

"Unfortunately, that's not how it works." Caleb rubbed a hand through his hair, a shadow falling over his eyes. "I'd rather not have the abilities at all. I'm starting to wonder if another one of my uncle's potions might get rid of them."

"I wouldn't trust him to pour me a glass of wine," Mica said fiercely.

Caleb chuckled. "I don't trust him either. I wouldn't seek him out without an exit strategy."

"There has to be another way."

"Maybe." Caleb looked a little closer at her, a frown wrinkling his brow. "You're awfully serious this evening."

Mica's stomach lurched as he leaned toward her. Why did he have to be so handsome? He even smelled nice. Her gaze dropped to his lips.

Stop.

Mica vaulted to her feet. "Whatever makes you say that, darling?" she sang. "I'd better return to my guests. Lots of people to see. I do love a good party." She smoothed her skirt over her hips and checked that her assumed face had stayed in place. "We shall talk later. May you thrive."

She started to walk away when Caleb called out, "Do you have your new Impersonator yet?"

She froze. "I beg your pardon?"

"Since Mica—excuse me—Miss Micathea left. Shouldn't the Academy have assigned you a new Impersonator by now?"

"I certainly think so," Mica said airily. "I *must* send a Blur to see what's keeping them."

"I could always ride up there for you," Caleb said. "I was thinking of visiting her."

"You were? Why?"

"It's nothing. Sorry to keep you."

Mica didn't move. She desperately wanted to know what Caleb had to say about her—the real her. As far as he knew, Mica had quit her job as the princess's Impersonator and left Jewel Harbor without saying goodbye. And that was after they had rescued dozens of captive Talents together, she had saved his life, and he had kissed her. She wished she could talk to him about it, but the princess didn't know about the kiss—or about the connection that had been growing between her Impersonator and her best friend.

"Jessa? Is something wro—"

"Don't go anywhere without talking to me first, darling," she said a little too cheerfully. "I'm sure Micathea is busy with her next assignment by now."

Caleb frowned. "If that's what you—"

Screams erupted from the dance floor, startling them both.

CHAPTER TWO

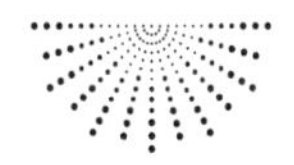

"What is that thing?"

"Oh, it's grotesque!"

"Someone make it stop!"

"But what *is* it?"

The dance music ceased as the shouts reverberated around the ballroom. Mica and Caleb exchanged fleeting glances and hurried to the balcony together. The stone railing was cold under Mica's hands as she leaned over it to see what was happening below.

The dance floor was in chaos. People surged backward from a single point, as if a stone had been dropped in a pond and the guests were the ripples. Ladies stumbled over the hems of their gowns, and lords dropped wine goblets in their haste to retreat. All wore expressions of fear and disgust.

At the center of the tumult stood a solitary figure. Mica couldn't tell if it was a man or a beast. The figure was morphing and writhing in nightmarish forms, like a wax statue dropped into a fire. For one horrible moment, Mica had feared that Jessamyn had arrived at the ball and everyone reacted exceptionally badly to her condition. But this figure was male and far larger than the princess. He had to be a Mimic. No other human could change like that.

The figure barely looked human now, though. His skin slipped and surged, roiling like oil. His hair shifted through varying shades of blue, from a midnight shade that matched Mica's dress all the way to the pale sky-blue of an Obsidian's eyes. The figure was obviously in pain, and his screams were bloodcurdling in their intensity. But his words were coherent.

"You striking criminals!" he shrieked. "You live in luxury, growing fat with the spoils of your people. You ignore the suffering you cause. Dine and dance while you can, for a reckoning is coming!"

Shield guards were moving forward, approaching the writhing figure cautiously, as if afraid to catch a disease. The strange man was unarmed, and he wore the livery of a palace servant.

"You have become traitors to your own," he wailed as his limbs grew longer and thinner, flailing like the antennae of some demented sea creature. "An abomination grows in the empire, and you are blind to it."

Some of the nobles were fleeing the ballroom now, trampling each other to get away from the disturbing display. Many of the ladies were crying, and the lords seemed split between their own fear and a desire to impress the ladies by coming to their defense. They settled for stepping back slowly, mouths agape, dessert plates raised like weapons.

"I came to warn you, but your vanities know no bounds. The danger growing in the West will destroy you all!"

The first of the Shield guards reached the madman, but when they attempted to grab him, he threw them off as easily as if they were little children.

"He's a Muscle," Caleb said.

"A Mimic too," Mica said. "But he can't control it."

The man's features and coloring continued to change as he

lurched around the ballroom, shouting reproaches at the gathered nobles. The light of a thousand candles flickered grotesquely in his mad eyes.

"The suffering has become too great!" he wailed. "It started in the barren fortress, festering in the abominable cesspit. But it will end in the silver halls of Jewel Harbor itself!"

Agony drenched the man's voice, and his contortions looked torturous, uncontrollable. He held off the palace guards with unnatural strength, and tears leaked from his ever-changing eyes. The scene was alarming, but it was pity rather than fear that filled Mica at the man's cries.

"Torment!" he howled. "Misery and lies! The Windfast claims to protect us, but you nobles refuse to listen. You would not help us, and soon it will be too late."

The Shields renewed their approach, this time waving for Muscle guards to assist them. They attempted to wrestle the figure into submission, making no effort to be gentle despite his distress. Mica winced. They should be trying to alleviate his suffering somehow, not fighting him. She had to help.

But as Mica turned for the stairs, a guard raised a truncheon and slammed the end into the man's head. A sickening crack echoed through the ballroom.

"Stop!" Anger flashed through Mica like lightning. *This man needs help, not a beating!*

"Wait, Jessa." Caleb seized her arm before she could take off running. "There might be more of them."

"He's ill," Mica said. "They can't treat him that way."

Another crack sounded, and the man's cries faltered.

"Release me."

"Have you forgotten you're the future empress?" Caleb's eyes were wide with surprise, but he kept a firm grip on her arm. "Stay here until it's safe, Jessa. The Shields will handle it."

"Have *you* forgotten I'm the future empress?" Mica hissed. "I'll go where I please."

She wrenched her arm free and raced for the stairs leading down to the main dance floor. Caleb followed close on her heels, but he didn't try to stop her again. He drew a knife from his coat sleeve as they plunged down the steps. Mica had a knife hidden in her velvet sleeve too, but she left it alone.

Neither one needed their weapons. The strange figure lay unconscious on the polished wooden dance floor by the time they reached the lower level. Even though he was no longer a threat, the palace guards were tying him up tight enough for three Muscles. More guards gathered in close, as if they still expected him to leap up and start attacking the lords and ladies.

"Out of my way!" Mica snapped.

"Princess!" said one of the Shields. "Are you injured? This madman—"

"I am fine, thank you." Mica waved him aside. "Let me see him."

She approached the man on the floor. His face had stopped shifting, and he'd been left with a strange amalgam of features, none of them correctly proportioned: flat nose, huge eyes with lashes long enough to brush his cheeks, skin that seemed to be a different shade on every visible body part, tiny ears, and aquamarine hair. His arms were different lengths, and his legs were roped with excessive musculature. It was as if his body couldn't stay in a single shape long enough for a full impersonation to form.

Mica had heard of Impersonators completely losing control before, especially if they tried to stretch themselves beyond their abilities. The students at the Academy had whispered about such things to scare each other. This man's contortions weren't far off from the worst of the stories. But impersonations didn't usually remain when people had been knocked unconscious. Something was very wrong here.

The guards had tied the bonds on their prisoner so tight his skin puckered, and a deep cut on his forehead was spreading blood down his mottled face. Mica turned to the nearest Shield, too angry to see his features clearly.

"In the future," she said, her voice stiff with fury, "you will refrain from unnecessary force when dealing with the ill and unstable."

"But, Princess, he was—"

"He was ill. Not dangerous."

The Shield bowed deeply.

Mica waved him away and studied the unconscious stranger. The cut on his forehead meant he didn't have a Shield's impervious skin. Shields weren't completely invulnerable, and they could be killed with poison and suffocation, among other methods, but they couldn't be cut. This man had displayed both Muscle strength and a Mimic's impersonation abilities, though, which made him the second person she had met with more than one Talent.

She addressed the nobles, who had emerged from behind candelabras and dessert tables to gather in a wide circle around the dance floor. "Does anyone know where this man came from?"

Shocked faces stared back at her.

"Did anyone see him start to change?"

"I did, my princess."

The lord governor of Silverfell, whom Mica had met earlier that evening, stepped out from the crowd. Corpulent, with shiny hair and flushed cheeks, he wore a rich coat embroidered with heavy silver thread. She searched her memory for his first name.

"Please tell me what you saw, Lord Bont."

"He poured a drink for me, Your Eminent Majesty. He said he hoped this was the last fine wine I ever tasted. That's when his face started changing. Before I knew it, he was screaming about a cesspit of abomination and corruption."

Murmurs spread through the crowd. Corruption was hardly the type of accusation a room full of nobles and wealthy merchants liked to hear, especially when draped in their most fabulous jewels and silks. They hadn't all come by their wealth honestly.

"What did he look like at first?"

"I can't say I noticed, Your Most Excellent Highness," Lord Bont said. "He was pouring me a drink. I didn't look too closely at him until his face started twisting like that."

"Did *anyone* see the face he wore to get in here?"

The lords and ladies looked at each other blankly. Mica bit the inside of her mouth to keep from chastising them. She shouldn't be surprised that the nobles hadn't given a man in a servant's garb a second look. She'd taken advantage of that habit more than once to pass unnoticed among them.

"Take him to a cell, and have a healer see to his head," Mica said. "Notify me the moment he is awake. I must speak with him."

"That will not be necessary." The voice that spoke from behind her was crystal clear and as deep as a mountain lake.

His Imperial Majesty Emperor Styl was striding across the ballroom, the nobles parting to make way for him. He had white skin, black hair, and a visage as grave as a stone gargoyle.

"Father! I wanted to ask—"

The emperor's thin lips twisted faintly, and Mica broke off at once, aware she wasn't acting entirely regal.

"You needn't fear," the emperor said smoothly. "I shall question this man when he awakens."

"Yes, Father." Mica dipped into a curtsy, blushing slightly. Emperor Styl and his daughter shared a subtle code of expressions that Jessamyn had taught Mica over the past few months. With that slight twist of the lips, he had communicated extreme disapproval of the way she'd handled the situation. This wasn't the sort of thing the princess should concern herself with openly.

On the other hand, Jessamyn had a temper. Mica hoped the onlookers would attribute her involvement to that well-known trait. Maybe she shouldn't have rushed into the fray, but Mica couldn't stand to see the poor man mistreated. She could only imagine how difficult it would be to suddenly discover the Impersonator Talent later in life or, as was more likely, have the Talent foisted upon him.

Could this be another victim of Lord Ober's experimental potions? Mica had always known Caleb couldn't be the only one. The madman had mentioned a "barren fortress" where his suffering began. Could Lord Ober have moved his operation there after she and Caleb cleared out the warehouse? Hope surged within her. This mysterious Talent could solve the mystery that had consumed her for months!

I'll talk to him as soon as—

A palace guard stood up from examining the bound figure. "I beg your pardon, Emperor Styl," he said gruffly. "It looks as though we hit him too hard. He's dead."

Anger quickly replaced Mica's hope. The man hadn't deserved to die. He had been trying to warn them! She rounded on the guard.

"You killed—"

"Remove him at once," Emperor Styl interrupted, snapping his long, pale fingers. "We will have words about this later."

The guards bowed deeply and dragged the poor Talent away. Mica wanted to follow, but the emperor's severe look warned her not to do more damage than she had already.

The chatter began the instant the body disappeared through the ballroom doors.

"Can you believe he dared disrupt the anniversary ball?"

"How scandalous!"

"And did you see Princess Jessamyn darting in as if she were a common guard?"

"Yes, so shocking!"

Emperor Styl gave Mica another dark look and marched off to begin containing the situation. She winced, wondering if she could avoid reporting that part of the evening to Jessamyn. But she had bigger concerns than the princess's disapproval.

"I came to warn you . . . a danger growing in the West."

She tried to replay the man's words in her mind, but lords and ladies kept coming up to see if she was all right, even though she hadn't been anywhere near the Talent until he was unconscious. Why couldn't they have shown him the same human decency? That man shouldn't have been killed—and now his warning would be wasted if she couldn't figure out what he'd meant.

Mica's own thoughts mixed with the madman's words. *They treat us commoners like we're nothing, like we're animals.* She fought to contain her rage, to hold onto the words he'd said before he died.

"A barren fortress," he'd said. *"Torment. Misery. Corruption."*

She felt sick. She couldn't let her mask slip, not in front of all these people.

The nobles had resumed their revelry as if nothing had happened, as if a man hadn't been killed right in front of them.

"A reckoning is coming."

His pained cries echoed in her memory, far louder than the music that once again filled the ballroom.

Ober is to blame. I'm sure of it.

Lady Maren had said Talents were behaving erratically, complaining of illness and fatigue. And now the mad Talent had appeared. It was too soon after Lord Ober's exodus to be a coincidence.

Caleb approached cautiously, as if he sensed the storm of fury raging inside her. "Did you see what I saw, Jessa?"

Mica nodded grimly. "He was a Muscle and a Mimic."

"Do you think my uncle gave him his double abilities?"

"He's the only person I know of who's tampering with Talents," Mica said. She searched for something Jessamyn-like to add, but the words wouldn't come.

Caleb didn't seem to notice that she didn't sound much like Jessamyn right now, too absorbed in this new mystery. He stood over her as if they were about to dance so no one would interrupt their conversation, keeping his voice low.

"Why would he send one of his 'experiments' here after working so hard to keep his project secret?"

"Even if Ober gave the poor man the two Talents—two that we know of—" Mica said, "he didn't necessarily send him here." *And if the guards had been gentler, he would be alive to tell us himself.* She struggled to master her anger over the Talent's treatment, to regain control of her voice.

"He warned of a danger in the West," Caleb said. "And he mentioned a barren fortress too."

"Doesn't Ober have a fortress on Timbral Island?"

"I'm not sure I'd call Timbral Castle barren, though it is quite far west," Caleb said. "Maybe I should visit him there, see what I can find out."

Mica raised an eyebrow. "You want to turn spy?"

"We need to find out what he's doing somehow."

"After what you did to his warehouse?" Mica gave a humorless laugh. "He'll never let you in, darling."

"I'm not so sure about that," Caleb said. "Ober is not stupid, but he knows I've been trying to figure out why I am this way for years. He misled me intentionally, steering me away from the idea that my special skills came from a potion. But he knows I want to control my erratic Talents—or even get rid of them."

Mica ran her fingers through her hair, weighing the risks. Lady Maren's Impersonator spies had reported no sign of nefarious activity on Timbral so far, but Caleb might be able to access places her spies could not. She was worried Ober would figure out how to give someone multiple Talents *without* the side effects that hampered Caleb.

"It started in the barren fortress, festering in the abominable cesspit. But it will end in the silver halls of Jewel Harbor itself."

All these revelers dancing in the candlelight and drinking wine in the shadows wouldn't stand a chance against multi-

Talented attackers without limitations. The threat of such an attack was why Jessamyn had been afraid to openly arrest Lord Ober in the first place. But they had to take risks, or the danger would grow.

"Let's say he invites you in," Mica said. "Would you let him try another potion on you if he claimed he could cure you?"

Caleb hesitated. "I can't ignore the way he does his research, Jessa. If he has to chop people up in order to fix me, it's not worth it."

Mica shuddered. She'd had countless nightmares about the warehouse filled with mutilated Talents over the past few months. That and the princess's face melting as poison spread through her body. Lord Ober had a lot to answer for.

"He's an evil bastard, isn't he?" she said.

Caleb raised his eyebrows, and Mica realized that "evil bastard" wasn't an especially ladylike turn of phrase. She had also been leaning toward him, drawn in by the prospect of tackling this puzzle together. She pulled back and began fussing with her hair and silver tiara in the most Jessamyn way possible.

"It sounds *dreadfully* dangerous, darling."

"He has to be stopped." Caleb looked at her with his particular sort of certainty. "It's worth any risk if I can prevent him from hurting anyone else."

Mica couldn't argue with that, even though she didn't want Caleb to put himself in peril. In truth, nowhere was safe. The princess had been poisoned in her own sitting room, and Talents found dangers wherever they turned.

She looked around the ballroom, where the dancers once again waltzed in circles of colorful silks. Emperor Styl stood by the entrance to the gardens, still soothing the guests after the excitement with the mad Talent. Mica wished he would take a stronger stance sometimes. The biggest lesson she'd learned in the Silver Palace was that the Windfast Empire wasn't as stable and easy to rule as she had once believed. Jessamyn and her father worked hard to keep the islands in line, but Mica couldn't help wondering if they were going about it the wrong way.

"Maybe it's time my father sent the army to deal with this directly," she said. "The subtle approach is giving Ober too much space to scheme. He hardly seems to fear the emperor's justice."

"Perhaps." Caleb hesitated. "I'm not sure sending the army to the western islands would go over well. We need better intelligence first."

You've got that right, Mica thought. *But you're not the one who's qualified to gather it.*

"You mustn't go gallivanting about the empire just yet, darling," she said in her very best Jessamyn voice. "Lady Maren gave me some interesting gems of information tonight. Let us see what comes of them first."

She would leave the politics to the emperor and his daughter. Investigating Lord Ober's fortress, on the other hand, was a job for an Imperial Impersonator. Mica had spent years training to be a spy, and she'd had enough of dances and silk dresses. If Caleb went off to spy on his uncle, Mica intended to go with him. Princess Jessamyn would just have to tell everyone the truth.

CHAPTER THREE

Mica was so tired she could barely maintain her impersonation as she trudged back to the princess's chambers. Midnight had struck long ago, and the guests had dispersed to their beds gradually, fading like stars. Mica lost track of how many times she twirled around the dance floor with a different lord or complimented a different lady's dress, hair, or jewels. She'd renewed her efforts to be charming, but the incident with the strange Talent would overshadow all the gossip from the ball anyway. Jessamyn wasn't going to be happy about that.

At the princess's doors, Mica dismissed the Shield guard who had escorted her from the ballroom, a young fellow called Rider (bald, with crooked teeth and blue eyes). Banner was waiting to take over from the younger man. The princess's loyal Shield was one of the only people in the palace who knew what had happened to her—the other being a healer—and he always insisted on guarding the real thing.

"Good evening." The middle-aged guard had a drooping mustache and a melodious voice. "I am glad to see you unharmed."

"Thank you, Banner," Mica said wearily as he pulled open the large door for her. "You heard what happened?"

"News travels fast in these halls."

"I'm sorry you missed the excitement."

"I cannot say I mind, though *she* may say otherwise. She is in a rather excitable mood."

"Thanks for the warning." Mica bid him good night and entered the candlelit sitting room, bracing herself for a tempest.

"Finally!" Jessamyn bounded toward her and grabbed her arm. "I have been going crazy in here, waiting for you to return."

The princess pulled Mica over to a couch by a low mahogany table, where it looked as though she'd been drinking tea and stress-eating ginger biscuits all evening. She wore a thick woolen dressing gown and had applied a sticky brown ointment to her scarred face, some of it smearing in her dark-red hair.

"You must tell me every word that was said to you tonight. Don't leave out a single detail."

Mica slumped back against the cushions. "Do you think I could rest before—"

"Remember what happened the last time I let you sleep before giving your report? I swear the details drained right out of your head in the night. Quickly now. What was everyone wearing?"

Mica sighed and began relaying the details of the evening for the princess. While she spoke, she pulled off her crystal-trimmed dancing shoes and undid the ties on her velvet dress. She helped herself to some of the princess's tea and biscuits, stealing bites between Jessamyn's follow-up questions. They had acted more casual around each other since Mica became a full-time imposter, mostly out of necessity. Mica had precious little time to actually rest, and she had to be permitted to sit and eat around the princess, or she might drop dead. She imagined what Jessamyn would say if that happened.

"This is terribly inconvenient for me. Honestly, Micathea, it's not as if I ask for much."

Mica understood now why the princess had relied so heavily on expensive energy tonics and health potions before her poisoning. She lived her life at a furious pace that Mica found difficult to replicate. But they couldn't trust any potioners after Quinn had betrayed them, so Mica had to grit her teeth and soldier on. In truth, her soldier brothers probably got a lot more sleep than she did these days.

Mica considered the dramatic appearance of the mad Talent the leading news of the evening, but the princess was more concerned about the report from the Twins.

"Are you certain Lady Maren said secession?" Jessamyn demanded for the third time.

"That's the word she used." Mica thought back to the conversation with the elderly spymistress. "But she said the Twins are always making trouble."

"Of course they are." Jessamyn put her hands on her hips. "Have you even read a history book? Dwindlemire and Cray have been unusually quiet over the past year or so. I had half a mind to look into it myself. If they've kept the secession talk from reaching me for this long, either they are more organized and careful than they have been in the past, or the spy network is not as effective as it once was."

"Master Kiev is still focused on the Obsidian threat, as far as I know."

"I daresay he is, but defending ourselves from Obsidian requires keeping the rest of the empire strong."

Jessamyn paced around the sitting room, tapping her finger on the less damaged part of her lips. The princess was often in pain, but she tried hard not to show it. She had presented herself as a superhuman force of nature for so long that she found it difficult to reveal any weakness. She would have to get over that now that Mica intended to depart in search of the barren fortress.

Timbral Castle might not be the fortress of suffering the madman mentioned, but that seemed like the best place to start. She didn't want Caleb to go in alone. He was a good fighter, but any use of his Talents rendered him borderline comatose. She would have tried to impersonate him herself if they were close enough in size to fool his uncle.

We'll have to go in together.

She tried to ignore the anticipation—excitement even—that flared like tinder in her chest.

It will be strictly professional, of course.

The question was how to present the idea to the princess. All Mica's previous efforts to convince her to end this imposter charade had failed. Perhaps she could sway Jessamyn to her way of thinking more subtly. She *had* spent a lot of time around diplomats by now.

"What do you think about what's happening to the Talents, Princess?" she began.

Jessamyn blinked her large brown eyes. "What about them?"

"Well, that strange man definitely had two abilities. And Lady Maren said other Talents have been acting strange. She attributed it to laziness, but if they're showing signs of madness or getting ill like Caleb—"

"*Lord* Caleb."

"Yes, him." Mica hurried on. "If Talents are getting ill so close to Timbral Island, I think we can conclude that Lord Ober is involved."

"I do not jump to conclusions, Micathea," the princess said. "We should certainly monitor the situation, but we can't assume he's going around poisoning *everyone* in the empire."

"Maybe not," Mica said, "but we have to deal with him. What if—"

"*I* will deal with Lord Ober in my own time. *You* will follow orders. I believe the unrest in the Twins is a more immediate problem. You must speak to my father about it when you go riding tomorrow morning."

"About that—"

"Don't you dare suggest pushing back the time," Jessamyn said severely. "My father and I *always* go riding the morning after a ball while everyone else is sleeping in. He will be suspicious if you cancel."

Mica reached for a leftover ginger biscuit to cover a grumble. She had spent months believing the princess wasn't that close to her father. The forbidding, stone-faced man didn't seem to have a fatherly bone in his body. Since becoming the princess's imposter, Mica had discovered that the distance between Styl and his daughter was yet another layer of subterfuge in the elaborate political game they played to maintain control over their empire. They were incredibly careful about how they spent time together, stealing moments to meet in secret so no one would suspect how aligned they truly were.

"Don't you think it's time you told your father what happened?"

Jessamyn hesitated. "My skin feels a little tighter today. I'd rather not worry him until it isn't so bad."

Mica glanced at the left side of Jessamyn's face, where the poison had made her skin melt like candlewax. It didn't look any different now than it had two months ago, and the right side, where she had smeared the ointment, was still a mess of burn-like patches.

"Princess," Mica said gently, "what if it never gets better?"

"I will not have that kind of talk." Jessamyn waved her hand dismissively then paused, as if noticing the patches on the skin of that hand.

Mica felt a twinge of sympathy, but she stamped down on it. Jessamyn's aversion to being pitied was exactly why she was so determined to maintain this illusion. But she couldn't keep it up forever.

Mica took a deep breath. "I'd like to leave Jewel Harbor to spy on Lord Ober."

Jessamyn paused for a beat. "You are not the only spy in the empire, Micathea."

"But—"

"You have work to do here."

"But you should have heard that Talent." Mica wished she could mute the memory of his screams in her mind. She might not be the only spy in the empire, but she had seen the concerns of Talents pushed aside before. She wouldn't stand by and let it happen again. "He was asking for help, and he made it sound like there are others like him."

"Lady Maren's people will look into it."

"I've learned a lot from the spy network, but I can do more good out there. I can find Ober's fortress. I'm sure of it."

"Your place is here." Jessamyn put her hands on her hips and squared her shoulders, a stance she only adopted when she was feeling particularly stubborn. But her face was as damaged as it had ever been. It might never heal.

Mica met her eyes. "I think we have to discuss the possibility that your face—"

"I don't *have* to do anything," Jessamyn said. "Honestly, I may be in seclusion, but I am still the princess here."

"Then you should actually *be* the princess," Mica blurted out.

Way to be subtle, Mica. But she didn't care. She was fed up with Jessamyn always thinking her way was the best way. She stood.

"I have to leave. Can't you get a different Mimic?"

"The Academy assigned you to me, Micathea. It's your duty."

"But you're just wasting time hiding in here."

"Excuse me?"

Mica knew she'd gone too far by the tension in Jessamyn's arched brow. "I only meant—"

"That's enough." Jessamyn's voice was as sharp as a slap. "Continue with your report, *if* you please."

Mica sighed. "Yes, Princess."

She slumped back onto the couch and resumed her recitation of overheard conversations and carefully worded greetings, feeling frustrated and trapped. While the princess persisted in believing that her appearance would return to normal, Mica couldn't leave her side to capture the man who had hurt her. She would never abandon Jessamyn outright. The princess's condition was partially Mica's fault, and Mica had sworn to atone for her failure.

If only she could convince Jessamyn to rejoin the world in her new face. It wasn't right for such a vibrant and energetic person to stay cooped up for so long. Appearance was important in the Silver Palace, but it wasn't everything.

Hints of dawn had begun to appear at the window by the time Mica drew to the end of her report.

"I've been saving the good news for last: Lady Lorna and Lord Fritz got engaged."

She described how the young lovers had missed the incident with the mad Talent because Fritz had finally gathered the courage to whisk Lorna off to a quiet corner of the winter-bare garden to propose. They'd burst back into the ballroom to announce their betrothal, utterly oblivious to what had happened.

"Was there any talk of where the wedding would take place?" Jessamyn asked.

"Lorna said she wants to do it at home in Silverfell."

"And did you encourage her on that front?" A light had appeared in Jessamyn's eyes, a familiar look that meant her mind was churning like a summer storm.

"I didn't encourage her one way or another," Mica said. "Does it matter where she has the wedding?"

Jessamyn gave a shrill laugh. "Micathea, Micathea. Of course it matters! Weddings are a massive occasion, and they provide positively limitless social opportunities. We must orchestrate this carefully."

"But it's Lorna's—"

"Oh, she'll have a nice wedding no matter what. She's madly in love with that boy."

Mica covered a yawn with her hand, hoping to wrap this up soon. "So you want me to encourage Lorna and Fritz to have the wedding here in Jewel Harbor?"

"Not necessarily." Jessamyn strode over to her window and stared out at the city spreading below her. The early-morning rays were beginning to peek above the horizon across the harbor, where the city of Old Kings sprawled across the hills of nearby Amber Island. Mica sighed. She wouldn't have time to sleep before going out to ride with the emperor after all. Funny how casual she was about such things now. Mica Graydier, soldiers' daughter and working Talent, horseback riding with the Emperor of Windfast himself.

Apparently Jessamyn intended to keep whatever she was mulling over to herself. After frowning at the landscape for a few minutes, she spun around and snapped her fingers at Mica.

"Are you still here? Get moving. My father will be waiting."

"Are you going to reveal your poisoning and let me go?"

"Don't be silly," Jessamyn said. "We will continue our current arrangement until I say otherwise."

"But what if the—"

"I shall do it when the time is right. I'm very intelligent, you know. Now go put on my riding clothes."

CHAPTER FOUR

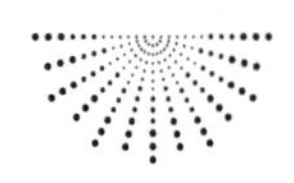

Mica and Emperor Styl met in the stable yard, both wearing cloaks, their frosted breath puffing out from beneath fur-lined hoods. Extra carriages crowded the grounds this morning, evidence of the many guests staying in the Silver Palace's luxurious guest rooms. Sleepy stable boys tended the horses, though no other nobles were likely to call for their mounts before midday. In the quiet of dawn, the emperor and his daughter passed almost unnoticed.

Shields guards surrounded them at respectful distances in case of trouble. Most of the people Mica and the emperor passed as they left the palace gates on matching black mares would have no idea their ruler was among them. The people went about their routines, Muscles hauling deliveries, Blurs speeding by with messages, and heavy-lidded tradesmen hastening to work. The two could talk privately, lost amidst the hubbub of Jewel Harbor.

Riding with Jessamyn's father always felt surreal to Mica. Though grim and forbidding in front of others, he seemed almost cheery on these early-morning jaunts. Their excursions were like private classes in how to manage the complicated relationships of the Windfast Empire. Styl had recognized his daughter's political instincts early on, and he used her as both a sounding board and a foil for his courtly machinations.

On this particular morning, Mica expected a lecture about her actions following the appearance of the mysterious Talent. But the emperor had a different issue in mind. He leapt right to it as soon as they were out of sight of the palace gates.

"Did you speak with Lady Maren?"

"Briefly," Mica said. "She told me there have been rumors of unrest in the Twins."

"It is more than rumor," Emperor Styl said. "Maren and I spoke for several hours after the ball. The agitators for secession are more organized than ever, and they have the support of the local nobility."

Mica was surprised at the apprehension in his crystalline voice. She tried to catch a glimpse of his face hidden in the shadows of his cowl.

"Are you saying there might be a rebellion?"

"Conceivably. We must restore order before the unrest spreads."

"Will you send the army?"

"I don't want to resort to force so soon." The emperor lowered his voice so the Shields shadowing them would have no hope of overhearing. "Our spies in Obsidian have warned me about increased troop movements on the Stone Coast. We cannot afford to deplete our eastern defenses right now."

Mica shifted uneasily in her saddle. "The border should be our priority." Her brothers and parents served in the Imperial Army on the eastern edge of the empire. She wanted them to have all the reinforcements they needed if their enemies in the Obsidian Kingdom tried anything.

"It's a dangerous time for us to be divided regardless," the emperor said. He tugged back his cowl and eyed her steadily. Passersby by didn't even glance at him, focused on their early-morning tasks.

"Tell me," he said. "How would you resolve this if you were already the empress?"

Mica chewed on her lip as she considered the question, stopping just short of contorting her features. Emperor Styl often tested her—his daughter—like this. Mica had grown up among soldiers, but that didn't mean she was particularly adept at suggesting strategies to prevent wars and uprisings. Still, she wouldn't waste these moments when she had the emperor's ear. He spent too much time listening to his noble advisors rather than the people he was supposed to serve.

That gave her an idea.

"What if you sailed to the Twins yourself?" Mica said. "It would do the people good to see you paying attention to the outer islands. You could listen to the rebels' concerns and try to settle things peaceably."

"Hmm." The emperor fiddled with the silver-and-emerald signet ring he wore on his bone-white finger. "That idea has potential. It would send a better message than dispatching soldiers to deal with them. My presence would require a military escort, but it would only take one or two ships. We could use the soldiers to contain the rebels if the rumors prove true."

"Hopefully it won't come to that," Mica said.

"I'm afraid Lady Maren was less hopeful than you."

Mica thought of the sharp old spymistress's warnings that the violence would escalate. An uprising was worrying, but there were greater threats brewing in the West if the mad Talent was to be believed.

They reached a bend in the road, where two carriage drivers were shouting at each other over a collision. One horse had become tangled in the other's harness, and the bellowing of their masters agitated them so much that they were becoming even more intertwined. A mob had gathered to watch the commotion, pressing close and shoving each other for a better view.

At a signal from the emperor's Shield, Mica and the emperor

altered their route to avoid the fuss. As they cleared the worst of the crowds, Mica reined in closer to Jessamyn's father.

"Let me go with you when you sail." She tried not to let the urgency show in her voice. "I'd like to get to know the western islands too."

"I don't wish to disrupt your work in Jewel Harbor," the emperor said. "I am pleased with the way you cleaned up the City Watch, and you are more popular than ever with the nobility."

Mica grimaced. The emperor still prioritized the nobility in the capital and large islands like Amber and Winnow far too much. That could be part of why the people of the Twins were upset. But sailing west would get her much nearer to Timbral Island and the barren fortress. Besides, Jessamyn would be forced to reveal her true face when traveling in close quarters with her father. The emperor couldn't help but destroy Ober then.

I just need an excuse to go along . . .

Then her eyes fell on a curly-haired young woman bobbing up and down on her toes, trying to get a look at the carriage accident—and she remembered.

"There is to be a wedding in Silverfell for Lord Bont's daughter!" Mica said. "Lorna is marrying Lady Velvet's son, Fritz. Many of the nobles will travel to Silverfell for the celebration. We could visit the Twins after the festivities to address the people's concerns."

And find the barren fortress where the mad Talent's suffering began.

Mica could still hear the sickening crunch of the truncheon against the man's head. He hadn't truly been a threat. All she could do for him now was discover the source of his suffering—and see that there were no further victims.

Emperor Styl considered the suggestion in silence, the cowl falling forward to hide his expression. He had to let her sail west. Jessamyn certainly hadn't sounded as if she was planning to give in to Mica's request to leave anytime soon.

Mica fidgeted with her reins, wishing the emperor would think a little faster. She was ready to get moving—and it sounded as if he was needed in the West too.

At last, the emperor nodded. "Very well. It'll be beneficial to acquaint the outer islands with their future ruler. If you play your role there as well as you have here, they are sure to love you."

Mica couldn't help noticing that the emperor spoke of Jessamyn's role as if she were a Mimic herself.

"It's settled then?"

"We shall prepare to sail west. And if things go poorly, we will be well positioned to put a swift end to the rebellion."

"Of course, Father." Mica smiled with Jessamyn's mouth. "The empire must remain strong."

The plan took shape quickly in the weeks after the two-hundredth-anniversary ball. The emperor, the princess, and a select entourage of nobles would sail to Silverfell for Fritz and Lorna's wedding, visiting other Windfast islands on the way. After the festivities, they would journey through the Twins, where the crucial diplomacy would take place. They'd finish their voyage in Winnow Bay, where many nobles kept holiday villas. Thanks to a warm current to the west, the weather was always pleasant, and they could swim in the sparkling, temperate waters and lounge in the sunshine away from the pressures of Jewel Harbor.

Officially, the voyage would be an excuse to enjoy a diverting vacation. In reality, Styl and Jessamyn would remind their subjects—rebels or not—that their rulers weren't so far away after all. A warship would accompany them too, ready to put a stop to any violence that might arise in the waters around Dwindlemire and Cray.

Jessamyn was proud of Mica for suggesting they use the wedding as a cover for the voyage to the Twins.

"I can see you are learning," she said. "Though I'd have gotten my father to think the whole thing was his idea."

"I'll remember that next time."

Mica would sail with Jessamyn at first and launch her own mission to find the barren fortress when they got closer to Lord Ober's territory. She fully expected the princess to tell her father about her poisoning on their journey—she would no doubt insist it had been her intention all along—and take back her crown. The two of them would realize the dangers Lord Ober posed to all of them were even more perilous than a potential rebellion. They would have to let Mica go. Until then, their disparate goals would carry all of them west.

Or so she thought.

The arrangements progressed smoothly until mere days before they were scheduled to depart Jewel Harbor, when Jessamyn's father summoned her for another early-morning ride.

This time, the Silver Palace nobles were sleeping in to recover from a late-night performance by Jewel Harbor's premier theatre troupe. The cast, made up entirely of Academy-trained Mimics, had transformed themselves into elves and sea sprites with pointed ears and iridescent hair. The night had involved more drinking, revelry, and drama than the actual play. Mica was bleary-eyed with exhaustion, but she dutifully assumed the princess's appearance and met her father at dawn.

As soon as they left the palace gates, the emperor once again got straight to business.

"I have just received word that small parties of Obsidian raiders have crossed our borders twice in the past week."

Mica's head cleared in an instant. "Where?"

"They struck settlements on the northern coast of Pegasus Island both times."

Mica released a breath. *Not Stonefoss. My family is okay.*

"Were there many losses?"

"More than a dozen non-Talents were killed. Two Blurs

managed to escape to give the report, but a few Muscle builders and their Shield escorts were captured from a worksite."

Mica tightened her grip on her reins. The Obsidians enslaved Talents, and their work camps were infamous for their brutal conditions. She had spent most of her life wanting to work against the shadowy kingdom to the east because of the way they treated people like her and her family.

"It has never been more important for the empire to be united," Emperor Styl said. "Yet every report I've received from the West this week has mentioned restlessness in Dwindlemire and violence in Cray. People are speaking out against us on both islands. A rumor that they have noble support is spreading. But we must be ready to meet the Obsidians if their aggressions escalate."

"Do you think we'll go to war?"

The emperor grimaced. "I have tried to resist the provocation, but I fear we may have no choice."

They had been on the verge of a conflict with the Obsidian Kingdom only a few months ago, when a group of Obsidian terrorists attacked the princess and her guests in the middle of the harbor. Lord Ober had advocated an aggressive response, and Jessamyn and the emperor had resorted to deceiving the imperial court to avoid rushing into a war they might not win. Such methods might not work this time.

A familiar mix of smells announced that they were nearing Potioners Alley. The scented steam issuing from the doors of the apothecaries made the place feel eerie, like a cursed land in a story. Mica rubbed her nose, feeling slightly nauseous after the night's obligations. Or perhaps it was the prospect of war that made her sick.

"You should know that I have decided not to sail west," Emperor Styl said.

"What?"

"I cannot be far from the capital if the Obsidians invade."

"But what about everything happening in the Twins?" *And everything Ober is doing.*

"Alas, the timing is unfortunate. I may need to forgo diplomacy after all."

Mica stole a glance at Quinn's shop as they passed. An eviction notice had been nailed to the door. Mica had told Lord Ober about the skilled young potioner. If the pair were continuing to use Talents for the despicable work Ober had begun with Haddell, Mica could see no higher priority than stopping them, war or no war. They couldn't call off the trip.

"What if we—I go on the voyage as your representative, and you remain here in case the Obsidians strike?"

The emperor pursed his thin lips. "I don't wish to send you into danger."

"I'll have Talent protectors with me," Mica said. "Besides, maybe I can still settle things diplomatically."

"Perhaps." The emperor rode in silence for a moment. "It would only be natural for me to send a warship manned by my best men to escort my daughter. You would have the resources to put down the rebellion."

Mica summoned her most confident voice. "I can handle the Twins." It occurred to her that she might be getting in over her head by offering to put down a revolution. But that was Jessamyn's job. "It will leave you free to confront the Obsidian problem."

The emperor didn't speak, a stone gargoyle in the middle of the bustling street. Despite his formidable appearance and stiff countenance, Mica couldn't help wondering if he was feeling overwhelmed by the threats growing on all sides.

"Very well," he said at last. "But you must be exceedingly careful as you travel west."

"Yes, Father." It was a testament to Styl's trust in his daughter—and the ship full of soldiers who would travel with them—that he was willing to send her to smooth things over with their dissatisfied subjects. "We will see all these threats contained."

"I hope you are right. The rebels may be numerous, as some reports claim, but they are nothing compared to the Obsidian forces."

"Our armies can stand up to Obsidian," Mica said fiercely, thinking of her brave brothers, who would be on the front lines in an Obsidian conflict. "Free Windfast soldiers won't be defeated by the Obsidian King's poor slaves."

The emperor sighed. "I wish it were that simple."

Their new course decided, they soon turned back toward the Silver Palace, riding beneath the bridges that spanned the gaps between the jumbled buildings. Merchants shouted about their wares, and barefoot children darted among the horses and carriages, laughing shrilly. A Blur courier and a short, round woman got into an altercation over the fee for a delivery, and the woman's hair shifted from red to white and back again as her anger ebbed and flowed. Mica was used to the cacophony by now, but she was looking forward to a break from this overcrowded metropolis. She hadn't seen much of the empire beyond Amber Island.

"I'm disappointed I cannot visit Silverfell with you," Emperor Styl said. "I have fond memories of the place. Your mother and I courted there, you know."

Mica shifted awkwardly in her saddle. She and the princess had never discussed her mother, who died when Jessamyn was young. Mica pictured her own mother instead, a practical, perceptive woman with the strength of ten men and the patience of a hundred.

"I miss her." She didn't have to fake the emotion in her voice.

Emperor Styl bowed his head. When he raised it, he was all business once more.

"You may be more effective on your tour of the islands

without me looming beside you. On that note, have you made any progress toward choosing a consort?"

Mica waved her hand vaguely. "I have several enchanting possibilities."

Emperor Styl barked a laugh. "Yes, you're very convincing, Jessa. In all seriousness, you need to come to a decision soon." He lowered his voice so their Shield escorts would have no chance of overhearing. "With the agitation in the Twins and Obsidian breathing down our necks, a new alliance would help to renew the ties between the islands."

"I'm still young." Mica wasn't sure what Jessamyn would say to her father in these circumstances. "Perhaps in a few—"

"That was an order."

Mica shut her mouth. Her horse tossed its head irritably as she fiddled with the reins. She was tempted to tell the emperor he wasn't really speaking to his daughter, but Jessamyn would have her head for that. She had made the mistake of disobeying the princess before, and she was in no hurry to do it again.

I'm not getting married in Jessamyn's place either.

"How long do I have?"

Emperor Styl gave her a look she couldn't read.

"I expect you to announce an engagement before you return from your trip."

Mica winced. "Yes, Father." *Jessamyn better get well soon, or we're going to have a problem.* Mica had long expected to eschew close ties during her career as a spy. She didn't know what it would be like for Jessamyn to be under pressure to marry early. Noble ladies must be used to this sort of thing.

"It isn't so bad, you know." Emperor Styl's voice softened. "I had some of my happiest years with your mother. You needn't be so averse to marriage."

"I'd love to have what you had with my mother," Mica said, thinking of the happiness her own parents shared. The emperor looked up, and she rushed on so she wouldn't have to say more. "Who do you think would be a wise choice for my consort?"

"Are you asking for my advice?" The emperor chuckled—actually chuckled! "If I didn't know better, I'd think you'd been replaced."

Mica blanched. "I—"

"I've been trying to talk to you about this since you came of age. I'd have given you a deadline sooner if I knew it would sway you!"

He chuckled again, and Mica did her best not to stare. The emperor was downright terrifying in public, and it was beyond strange to see him like this.

"I take it you have someone in mind?"

"You may be determined to snare the most powerful match you can possibly stomach, but I'd urge you to look beyond current political influence and think in larger terms."

"You mean love?"

Emperor Styl snorted. "I'm being serious here, daughter."

"Sorry."

"Any individual lord could fall out of favor with the rest of the nobility, as Lord Ober has so aptly demonstrated recently. You need a match that will represent something larger to the people, regardless of his immediate influence." They passed through the gates of the Silver Palace, safe from prying eyes and would-be assassins, and the emperor tugged back his hood so he could meet Mica's gaze. "Lord Caleb, for example, comes from the farthest island in the empire. A match with him would be a symbolic bond across the entire empire. Besides, he's a fine young man."

"You . . . you want her—me to marry Caleb?" Mica felt her throat constricting. Her horse danced across the cobblestones of the palace courtyard, sensing her agitation.

"I won't tell you what to do," Emperor Styl said. "I am simply saying he's a viable option, even though his family controls a relatively small part of the empire. His status has risen of late thanks to his bravery on the harbor cruise and in the potioner's warehouse."

"Of course, that's, honestly, yes." Mica tried to answer with something flippant and Jessamyn-like, but her response came out garbled.

The emperor dismounted, flinging his stallion's lead at a serving man without looking at him.

"You might also consider a match who ordinarily resides in Pegasus or Winnow," the emperor continued. "It would send a strong message to choose a man who is *not* constantly with you at court. I'd caution you not to make a Silverfell match if you can avoid it, though. Our ties with your mother's people there are still quite strong."

"Yes, Your High—Father."

Mica dismounted too, struggling to maintain control of her features. The emperor might have mentioned several options, but he had only named one lord directly. Caleb was his first choice for his daughter's consort.

It's not like you could have Caleb anyway, she reminded herself sternly. *This isn't a competition.*

Fortunately, Emperor Styl didn't notice her dismay, still pleased she had agreed to the deadline. "This tour will be the perfect time to explore your options outside of Jewel Harbor. And make sure you take Lord Caleb with you on the voyage. I expect to hold an engagement feast in your honor when you return."

Feeling slightly miserable, Mica curtsied, dark-red hair obscuring her face.

"Yes, Father. As you wish."

CHAPTER FIVE

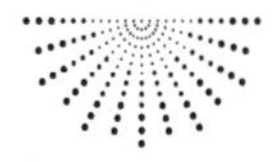

"You told him you'd do *what*?"

Mica rubbed her ear. She had never known anyone who could shriek as loud as Princess Jessamyn.

"It was more him telling me," she said. "He needs you to go ahead and choose your consort by the time we—"

"Go ahead and choose my consort? Are you *daft*?"

"He's the emperor. Did you expect me to tell him no when he gave me an ultimatum like that?"

"Of course not," Jessamyn said. "You were never supposed to let it get to that point. What did you do? Ask him how long you had?"

Mica's cheeks warmed. "It's possible I said something like that . . ."

"*Unbelievable.*" Jessamyn returned to pulling dresses out of one of her wardrobes and separating them into piles on the floor of her opulent dressing room. She had fired her former handmaids, Ruby and Alea, months ago to make sure they wouldn't find out what she and Mica were up to. She was taking to the task of packing for their trip with the seriousness of a hurricane. "My father has been trying to get me to settle on a match for the past year. I can't believe you gave in to him like that."

"He said that with Obsidian and the Twins causing problems—"

"He would say that, wouldn't he? It's just like him to use that to his advantage."

"You don't think the empire is in danger?"

"The empire is *always* in danger." Jessamyn held up a diaphanous silk gown to Mica and studied it critically. "I told you the Windfast is a delicate construct. Weren't you paying attention? But that doesn't mean I want to get married right now."

"Maybe it's time you told him about the poisoning," Mica said. "That could buy you some time."

Jessamyn raised a scarred eyebrow. "Because I'm too hideous to secure a match now?"

"That isn't what I meant."

"No, but it will be an issue." Jessamyn turned to face the mirrors and scraped a fingernail down one of the red patches on her neck, as if testing to see if it would peel away.

Mica's voice softened. "Anyone would be lucky to marry you, Princess, no matter what you look like."

"Of course they would. I am an excellent catch. Honestly, Micathea, you needn't project your self-esteem issues onto other people."

Mica gaped at her. She felt as if she were at sea already, and the deck kept tipping under her feet. She often felt like that around Jessamyn, come to think of it.

"I'm not—"

"It doesn't matter what's real in this situation," Jessamyn said. "That's the whole point. I will be the Empress of Windfast when my father dies. I could have been born looking worse than this, and every nobleman in the empire would still consider me a fantastic match—and that's not even taking my delightful personality into account."

"You *are* delightful, Princess," Mica said.

"Don't be snide, Micathea." Jessamyn moved over to her glass case full of jewels and perused the crowns displayed on velvet. "As I said, it doesn't matter that that's the reality. If I marry someone looking like this, even if he worships me inside and out, others would whisper about how he was taking pity on me. It would take away some of the power that I have worked so hard to build up, never mind the reality."

"That doesn't seem fair."

"No one ever said anything about fair," Jessamyn said. "You know better than anyone that how you look matters in this world. Until it doesn't, I will work with what I've been given. As it happens, I've been given a remarkably skilled Impersonator at exactly the right moment."

"You're not saying—"

"Oh yes I am."

"You want me to genuinely court someone on your behalf?"

"I *order* you to court someone on my behalf." Jessamyn waved a ruby-set crown at her as if it were a mace. "And if it comes to that, you will marry them on my behalf too."

"But—"

"You swore to serve the empire."

"Not like this. I refuse to—"

"You refuse?" Jessamyn took a step toward her, eyes glittering dangerously. "What makes you think you have that right?"

Mica tried to summon some of that pity she had felt earlier. The princess could be even more intimidating than her father.

"You can't stay hidden forever," she said.

"I will do what I have to, and so will you."

Mica stared at the piles of dresses all over the floor, the jeweled crowns, the costumes that would take her farther away from herself. She felt as if Jessamyn were trying to absorb her, swallowing her with dresses and commands and her uncompromising view of how the world worked. She was chipping away at

Mica's very identity, pushing aside her goals, using her face—her *body* to serve her needs. The trouble was that one of Mica's goals had long been to serve the Windfast Empire. She *had* to do what the future empress said, even though the costs weren't turning out to be quite what she expected. And Mica still felt guilty about her part in the princess's suffering. She couldn't walk away until she figured out how to make amends.

It troubled Mica that the princess refused to show any weakness, any hint that she'd been made vulnerable. The emperor was like that too. Some of the unrest in the outlying islands stemmed from the fact that the imperial family was considered too political and too scheming. If they'd only allow themselves to be seen as real people, maybe they wouldn't be in this mess.

You'll be going your own way soon enough, Mica told herself. She would find the barren fortress and figure out how to end the suffering of the Talents at Lord Ober's hand. Jessamyn could worry about marriage alliances and political unrest. At some point, whether the princess's face had healed or not, they would have to part ways.

The evening before their departure from Jewel Harbor, Mica went to see Peet the Blur messenger. She resumed her own face as she climbed the narrow stairs to Peet's flat in a rickety tenement building not far from the Silver Palace. The door opened a split second after her knock.

"Mica! Are you the real Mica or some other Mimic?"

"Hey, Peet. It's me." She shifted through a few impersonations to confirm her identity: her city-woman look, Master Kiev, her favorite scullery maid, and Peet himself.

"That's good enough for me," Peet said. "Do you want some cheese? I picked up the good kind from Redbridge on my last run, and I have some bread around here somewhere."

"Sounds great."

Mica settled back into her own face (hazel eyes, snub nose, nut-brown hair) while the gangly redhead rummaged around his cluttered little flat for the food. She took a seat at the small table, enjoying the chance to be herself for a few minutes.

Peet had been her primary link to the Masters Council from the Academy before the poisoning. As with Caleb, she had told him she was leaving Jessamyn's service for another mission two months ago. Being an imposter took up so much time that it was easier to pretend that Mica the Imperial Impersonator had left the city.

"What're you doing back in the capital?" Peet asked as he set the food on the table and joined her.

"Just stopping by on my way to my next assignment."

"Oh yeah? I haven't heard a peep about it."

"It's confidential, I'm afraid."

Peet didn't press her for more information. He had worked for Master Kiev's spy network for a few years now, and he knew he would never have all the pieces of any puzzle.

"So what brings you to my door?"

"I was wondering if you've heard anything about a place referred to as the barren fortress," Mica said, "or a place where some kind of Talent suffering began?"

"Can't say that I have." Peet tapped a rapid rhythm on his tabletop. "Things have been quiet since that nasty warehouse business. I reckon that was enough Talent suffering for two lifetimes."

Mica nodded, pushing away her memories of the place, as she always did. She should have gotten to them sooner. She'd been busy with the princess's tasks, but following orders wasn't a good-enough excuse.

She cleared her throat. "Have you heard anything about Talents acting strangely?"

Peet took a bite of cheese, chewing thoughtfully. "I saw something odd down at the docks last week, now that I think about it. It was this sailor. He was as fast as a Blur, and he lifted a stack of lumber like it weighed no more than a twig."

Mica put down her bread. "Are you certain?"

"I only caught a glimpse of him unloading a ship. I could have sworn he was a Blur *and* a Muscle. Naturally, I thought of you and what happened to our buddy Danil."

"Which ship was it?"

"A trader called the *Greta*"—Peet raised a hand before Mica could leap to her feet—"but it left that same day. I asked the dockmaster. The *Greta* sails a regular route between the Twins, Silverfell, and Winnow Island, with a stop in Jewel Harbor once a year."

"They start in the Twins?"

"Dwindlemire, I think," Peet said. "Nothing unusual about the ship itself, except this Blur-Muscle hybrid."

"That's strange enough. You didn't speak to the man?"

"He wasn't around when I returned to get another look at the ship. I asked the captain about the fellow—he's from a village called Dustwood in Silverfell, spent ages telling me about their pear orchards—anyway, he told me he keeps the fellow on as a favor because he's a relative. His brain is addled, and he falls sick sometimes too. Gets worse every year, the captain said."

"That's not good."

"I'll say. You hear about the crazy fellow that turned up at that fancy ball?"

"I heard."

"Think Lord Ober is behind it all?"

Mica made her bottom lip grow and shrink absentmindedly, a habit that was hard to avoid when she wore other faces. "Ober worked on that project with Haddell for a long time. It makes sense that others ended up with unwanted Talents to one degree or another."

"What about what the captain said? That this other man is crazy too?"

"I'm not sure what to think." Mica pictured the poor Talent flailing his spindly limbs in the center of the ballroom. That made two people with signs of insanity among the three she had encountered with multiple Talents. Caleb's abilities wiped him out every time he used them, but he had never shown signs of madness. "I heard a noble lady from Winnow Bay talking about Talents suffering from fatigue and illness recently, and we know Ober experimented a lot. The two could be connected."

Peet rubbed at the reddish stubble on his chin. He'd begun a valiant attempt to grow a beard since Mica last saw him. "Could there be different side effects for different mixes of Talents, like you only get the madness if you've got a bit of Mimic in you?"

"Possibly. Or they could vary depending on which batch of the potion Ober used." Or perhaps some of the victims hadn't learned to cope with the strange manifestations of Talent. Caleb had worked hard for the control he had.

"He had his claws in a lot of good Talents," Peet said.

"That he did." Mica thought of Danil, who had lost a leg to Ober's experiments. She hoped to get him work with Lady Maren when he was well enough, but he would be forever limited by what had been taken from him.

Peet leapt up to grab the teapot, bringing it back to the table in an instant. Mica watched the young Blur lean over to pour her tea, his movements deft despite their speed.

"Can I ask you something?"

"Sure."

"If someone offered you the chance to be a Muscle and a Shield as well as a Blur, would you take it? Even if there were some nasty side effects?"

"I'd consider it. I'm not gonna lie. But madness and sickness don't sound like much fun. I'm happy with just one supernatural ability." Peet sipped his tea, thinking for a moment. "I imagine an ordinary man would be striking tempted, though. Lord Ober might win supporters just by promising them a Talent-granting potion, regardless of the side effects."

"That's what I'm afraid of." Mica rubbed her forehead, making her brow change shape as she did. "We should have executed him when we had the chance."

"Or arrested him," Peet said. "Can't say I understand why Her Highness took her time about that."

That makes two of us. Jessamyn seemed to think an army of super soldiers would descend on Jewel Harbor if Lord Ober were arrested. Mica had to hope the potion hadn't advanced that far yet.

"At least he doesn't have his potioner anymore thanks to you and Lord Caleb," Peet said. "That should slow him down. And if he has been tinkering for over a decade, maybe the stuff won't ever work well enough to be dangerous."

"I wouldn't count on that." Mica pictured Quinn's workshop, cleared of all her notes and diagrams. Was Quinn helping Lord Ober perfect his formula at last? If all his men had multiple supernatural powers, Lord Ober might be able to take on the Imperial Army, no matter how many well-trained Talents like Mica's brothers he had to face.

On the other hand, with the same powers, the Imperial Army could march on the Obsidian Kingdom itself.

Mica forced down that thought. As Caleb had said at the ball, if Ober had to chop people up to do his research, it wasn't worth whatever benefits the empire might derive from it.

"Have you heard from Edwina and Rufus lately?" Mica asked. The older couple worked as freelance Mimics, but they had been imperial spies for Master Kiev and Lady Maren in their youth—and Rufus had been another one of Ober's victims.

"Not since they shipped out," Peet said.

"Shipped out?"

"Right, that was after you left. They went to join Master Kiev in Obsidian. Strange doings there. I know your mission is confidential, but can't you give me a hint? Is that where you're headed too?"

"I really can't say."

Peet smiled knowingly, and Mica didn't correct his assumption. If anyone could foil the Obsidian King's plans, it would be Master Kiev and his band of Imperial Impersonators. Mica had coveted the opportunity to join them once, but she still had work to do here.

"Thanks for all the information, Peet." Mica stood to go, preparing to abandon her own face again. "If you hear anything about a barren fortress, can you send a message to Princess Jessamyn? She'll get word to me."

"Will do."

"Thanks. I owe you one."

"Send me a snack from wherever you end up." Peet grinned. "I hear the sugar dates from Obsidian are delicious."

CHAPTER SIX

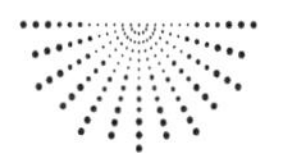

The day of the princess's grand tour arrived with much fanfare. The citizens of Jewel Harbor gathered along the route from the Silver Palace to the docks, eager to catch a glimpse of the nobles as they paraded to their ship on horseback. The commoners waved colorful handkerchiefs in the crisp breeze, calling out for the princess to look their way. Enterprising vendors sold hot buns from carts along their route, and tavern keepers near the docks offered special deals on spiced Timbral wine. The smell of warm bread and cinnamon mingled with the usual sweat-and-refuse-and-seawater aroma of the city.

Mica rode at the head of the entourage on a fine white stallion, resplendent in her Jessamyn impersonation. The horse pranced as if it were enjoying the adulation of the onlookers. Shimmering aquamarine silks hung from the saddle, flowing in the morning breeze, drawing every eye. Mica wasn't sure she'd ever be used to attracting so much attention. She was looking forward to the day when she could disappear into the crowds again.

Princess Jessamyn rode directly behind Mica on a scrappy bay mare, Shield guards flanking her. Banner scanned the crowds vigilantly, his drooping mustache hiding the nervous tension in his mouth. This was the first time Jessamyn had ventured into the city since the poisoning, and Banner was as worried as if she were riding into Obsidian territory. He would have carried the princess to the ship in an iron box if she had allowed it.

Mica almost hadn't recognized Jessamyn when she emerged from her dressing room that morning. She had chopped off her beautiful red hair. That alone might have disguised her from those used to her long tresses, but she had also donned a close-fitting linen cap with a veil that hung down to cover her mouth and nose. Combined with the shorn hair and damaged skin, it made her face look round rather than heart-shaped. As a final touch, she had outlined her eyes in black, subtly altering their shape.

Mica was impressed. She had never seen a non-Impersonator change their appearance so completely.

"Princess, you look—"

"Yes, I know. I'm very talented."

Jessamyn wore well-cut trousers reminiscent of a sailor's garb. The material was fine, but it had no embellishments, nor did it sport the imperial sigil most palace employees wore. A pile of thin gold bracelets adorned one wrist, and a plain brown satchel was slung across her chest, making her look like a well-to-do scholar.

"I thought you were going to dress as a maid," Mica said.

Jessamyn scoffed. "And what excuse would a maid have to attend meetings with the local nobles? My father tasked me with restoring our influence in the farthest reaches of the empire and shoring up the loyalties of the local nobility. I don't trust you to handle every delicate interaction on your own."

"Fair enough."

"I will go by the name Myn Irondier," Jessamyn said. "I am to play your cultural advisor, ostensibly charged with making sure you're aware of local customs on your tour of the islands. I will be at your side the whole time."

"That's a good idea." Mica suspected she would quickly grow tired of Jessamyn whispering in her ear whenever she did something wrong, but she'd been nervous about all the diplomatic duties she would have to perform.

"Of course it's a good idea." Jessamyn put her hands on her hips. "Now, we *must* do something about your hair."

Mica wore an airy white dress with a long sash that would flutter artfully in the wind as they pulled away from the docks—and conceal one of the fine, curved knives she liked to wear underneath her clothes. Jessamyn wanted her to keep her hair loose too, but Mica objected to the prospect of untangling it afterwards. They finally compromised with a thick braid tied with white silk ribbons.

"It won't have the same effect." Jessamyn touched Mica's locks wistfully, as if she regretted cutting her own hair.

"I'm sure every eye will be on you anyway," Mica said.

"No, Micathea." Jessamyn lifted a simple silver circlet and set it on Mica's head. "On you."

As they paraded toward the docks, Mica tried not to look back at the princess, fearful of drawing attention to the similarities in their features. But as she had discovered when she impersonated servants at the princess's side, no one was even looking at her entourage. Jessamyn probably could have skipped the veil entirely, and no one would have noticed her.

Rider, the newer Shield, had been positioned so his impervious body would keep the real princess safe from a thrown knife or a volley of arrows. He still didn't know Mica was an imposter. He was enjoying the parade as much as Mica's horse, preening before the spectators and barely keeping half an eye on his charge.

In addition to the Shield guards, their party consisted of Muscle porters carrying the luggage, nobles who had come along to wish them well, and the chosen few who would join them on their ship.

"I can hardly wait to see Lorna's gown," said Lady Elana, who rode next to Mica in a sea-green dress designed to complement her coppery-red hair. She was among the lucky ladies Jessamyn had chosen for the grand tour. The remaining nobles would make their own way to Silverfell for the wedding festivities later.

"I heard it will be lavender," Mica said. "It'll look *marvelous* with her complexion."

"*I* say it'll be silver." Lady Ingrid reined in her stocky slate-gray stallion on Mica's other side. "Her father will insist on reminding the guests of the wealth Silverfell provides."

"That would be a pity," Elana said. "I've seen Lorna wear silver before. It washes her out in the most dreadful way."

Ingrid snorted. "You're just saying that because you wore silver at the anniversary ball."

"That gown was iconic," Elana said acidly. "I wouldn't want it to upstage Lorna's wedding dress."

Mica murmured something conciliatory, privately wishing Elana had not been among the three ladies Jessamyn selected for her entourage. Ingrid wasn't so bad on her own. Mica appreciated her no-nonsense manner, which reminded her of the female soldiers she had known back in Stonefoss. But the bickering was sure to wear on her.

"Where is Lady Wendel?" Mica asked.

"She went down to the ship early to make sure security measures are in place," Ingrid said. "After what happened on the harbor cruise, she has been terribly nervous about sea travel."

"Her nose will never be the same," Elana said. "Not that it was especially nice to begin with."

Mica winced. She had broken Lady Wendel's nose during the Obsidians' attack on the harbor cruise a few months ago. She had been impersonating an Obsidian lady at the time, and Lady Wendel assumed she had coordinated the ambush.

Wendel had tried to apprehend her—something Mica admired a great deal.

"She's right to worry," Ingrid said. "Especially after those raids on the Pegasus coast."

"The Obsidians wouldn't dare bother us so far inside the empire, would they?" Elana asked, fiddling nervously with her sea-green sleeves.

"They came to Jewel Harbor itself," Ingrid said. "And I hear the Obsidians aren't the only ones we have to worry about."

"I'm sure we'll be safe on this voyage, ladies," Mica said quickly. "My dear father has ordered a warship full of his best soldiers to escort us. We will have far more protection than necessary."

In truth, the reports from the West didn't bode well. The secession agitators had looted a few manor houses in Cray, and they were clashing with the local noble family's retainers. It was looking increasingly likely that they would need to use force to bring the rebels back into the imperial fold. Pretending this was a pleasure cruise was risky. Mica wasn't sure how far these rebels would go to get out from under Emperor Styl's rule. She touched the knife strapped to her thigh beneath her dress. At least if any enemies tried to harm Jessamyn, they'd get her first, giving the real princess a chance to escape.

"Don't forget we'll have Lord Caleb with us." Ingrid gave Mica a sly look. "He has proved himself good in a fight lately."

Elana gave a little sigh. "That *does* make me feel better."

"There will be no need for Caleb or anyone else to fight," Mica said sharply. Her white stallion tossed his head, sensing her agitation. Caleb had been spending more time than usual training with his retainers after seeing the Talent lose control at the ball. He still intended to leave the expedition to seek out his uncle. She would much rather send a Mimic double in his place, if it were possible to imitate his erratic bursts of Talent.

Suddenly, blurry movement caught her eye. A figure shot out

of the crowd toward her white stallion, weaving deftly among the guards. Before Mica could react, someone seized her hand.

"What—"

"My princess." Peet had appeared beside her horse. He closed her hand around a piece of parchment and bowed over it. Then he sped away, narrowly evading the guards once more.

"Did you see that?" Ingrid said.

"What?"

"A Blur! He was just here!"

"I didn't see anything," Mica said breezily. "I do hope you won't become as paranoid as Lady Wendel. I won't have anything ruining our fun."

Ingrid narrowed her eyes, but she didn't press the issue. Elana was too busy preening for the crowds to notice the exchange. Mica discreetly tucked the parchment into her belt to read later. The incident reminded her how easy it would be for a Blur to dart up and stab her before anyone could stop it. Such assassinations had occurred many times in Windfast history, which was why the nobility often made use of Mimic body doubles.

Mica kept an eye out for any signs of multiple Talents among the dockworkers when they arrived at the harbor. The usual commotion filled the docks. Muscles unloaded huge crates from trading ships as if they weighed no more than snuffboxes. Their captains shouted at them to take care with their delicate wares. Blurs dodged through the crowds, delivering messages. New arrivals stared wide-eyed at the tumult. Farther out in the harbor, boats skittered across the sun-drenched waters like mosquitoes, Talents manning their oars.

Mica and her entourage approached the vessel waiting for them at the heart of the chaos. The *Silk Goddess* was a fine trading ship with three sails, a tall prow, and long rows of oars protruding from her wooden belly. Muscle oarsmen would guarantee that their journey proceeded on schedule whether or not the wind was in their favor. A buxom woman was carved on the prow of the ship, and touches of gilt outlined her handsome features. Mica thought she looked a little like the princess herself.

The *Silk Goddess* belonged to Lord Dolan, who would be traveling with them up the coast of Amber Island, across the Heart Sea to Pegasus Island, then on to Silverfell. Lord Dolan wanted to marry Jessamyn, which was undoubtedly why he had offered the use of his best ship for their voyage. The princess entertained his suit because of his influence with the merchants' guild. Mica hoped Jessamyn wasn't seriously considering the dough-faced lord as her consort. Dolan loved to hear himself talk, and he got far too handsy when he drank.

Jessamyn had invited all the front-runners for her hand on this voyage: Lord Dolan, the cold, ambitious Lord Riven, and of course, Lord Caleb. Lord Fritz would also join their party for the first half of the tour, while Lady Lorna went ahead to Silverfell to prepare for the wedding.

Fritz and Caleb were already waiting on the dock near the *Silk Goddess* when the ladies arrived. Both men wore white linen shirts with crisp sleeves that billowed in the sea breeze. Caleb had on a waistcoat the same deep blue as his eyes, and a fine sword was slung low on his hip. With the wind in his hair and the sunlight bringing out the angles in his face, he looked positively gallant.

He strode toward the ladies as they dismounted from their horses.

"Good morning, Jessa. You look stunning, as usual." He leaned in to plant a swift kiss on Mica's cheek. She wasn't expecting it, and the sudden touch left her blushing.

"S-so do you."

"Thanks." He gave her an odd look, and she feared he'd heard the slight hitch in her tone.

Why does he have to be a lord? Why couldn't he be a simple soldier, like my brothers?

A foot trod hard on her toe.

"I beg your pardon, Princess," Jessamyn said. She flashed a warning look over her veil, and Mica shook herself. She couldn't go swooning after Caleb now. He and Jessamyn had always been casually affectionate toward each other, and the real princess would never act starry eyed over a peck on the cheek. She needed to get her head straight.

But why does he look so good?

She rounded on Caleb's companion.

"Lord Fritz, you look positively dashing! I hope you aren't too nervous about your wedding."

"No, Princess. I can't wait to marry Lorna." Fritz bowed over her hand, his blond hair swooping over his scar. His jeweled dagger was tucked in his belt. He hadn't been without it since the Obsidian ambush. "Thank you for inviting me to accompany you on the *Goddess*. She's a beauty."

"This will be a *delightful* last hurrah before your marriage," Mica said. "And we will have a divine time on Pegasus as well. Speaking of which, have you seen Lady Wendel and Lord Riven? It's high time we set sail."

"Lord Riven hasn't arrived yet," Fritz said. "Lady Wendel is speaking with the captain of the HIMS *Arrow*."

"I'd better make sure she's all right."

Mica pranced across the dock, with Jessamyn, Banner, and Rider shadowing her, to where a massive war galleon floated at the opposite mooring. His Imperial Majesty's Ship *Arrow* would serve as their military escort. It was manned by an elite force of Talent soldiers, who would be called upon to contain the agitators for secession if Jessamyn's diplomatic efforts failed. Mica touched the note from Peet in her belt, wondering if it contained information that could help.

At the gangway leading to the HIMS *Arrow*, Lady Wendel stood toe to toe with a uniformed soldier, standing every bit as tall as he did. The noblewoman had thick black hair, which she had tied into a tight bun at the nape of her neck, and her straightforward mannerisms came off as brash despite her nerves.

"How can you be certain none of your men have been replaced by Obsidian Impersonators?" Wendel demanded.

"My lady, the army carries out regular identity checks on our forces." The muscular soldier had brown hair cropped close to his scalp, and he wore a slightly bemused expression on his sunburnt face. "I have a system of code words to make sure the men on my ship are who they appear to be."

"What if someone sneaks on board?"

"I shall verify their identity after every stop. I am sworn to protect the princess and her companions."

"But what if—"

"Lady Wendel, how are you faring?" Mica cut in, hoping to spare the poor man any further interrogation.

"Hello, Princess." Lady Wendel curtsied stiffly. "I am as well as can be expected."

"Princess Jessamyn, it is an honor to serve you." The soldier snapped to attention and saluted. "I am Captain Able Karson."

"At ease, Captain Karson." Mica acknowledged the salute, which made her feel a little homesick. "Is everything ready for our departure?"

"Yes, Princess. As I was telling Lady Wendel, in addition to your escort on the *Arrow*, a rotation of Shields will be posted on the *Silk Goddess* to defend you at all times, and your Muscle oarsmen are trained combatants."

"I pray there will be no need to fight," Mica said.

"If there is, we will not falter."

Mica met the captain's eyes, and they shared a brief moment of understanding. Emperor Styl had personally informed Captain Karson that his men might be called upon to put down a rebellion in the Twins if his daughter's conciliation efforts failed. They couldn't let on that they were fully aware of the threats they faced in the West, but both knew this was no simple escort assignment.

"We are in your hands, Captain," Mica said.

Karson saluted again. "Then you have no reason to fear, my princess."

Mica smiled. She had forgotten what it was like to be around soldiers, with their crisp movements and plainspoken ways.

"I have assigned an Elite Blur fighter to serve at your side with your personal guard," Karson said. "He will be here in a moment. I sent him to run up the waterfront to check for ambushes."

"Ambushes?" Wendel said sharply.

"We can never be too cautious, my lady."

"I am sure we will be well taken care of," Mica said. "These are my personal Shields, Banner and Rider, and this is my cultural advisor, Myn Irondier. Banner should be your first point of contact for all security matters."

"Yes, Princess." Captain Karson nodded at Banner, who stood beside the real Jessamyn, attempting to look in every direction at once. Rider appeared more interested in the ship full of soldiers waiting beside their own. The men had gathered on deck to get a look at the princess they'd be escorting around the empire over the next few weeks. Mica scanned their faces, memorizing as many details as she could: square jaws, cropped hair, young and confident eyes.

How many of those soldiers had been posted to Stonefoss, where her family lived? Talents from all over the empire went to the base on Amber Island to defend their homeland from the dread armies of Obsidian. As the only person in her family with the impersonation Talent, Mica had ended up on a different path. She still wanted to serve the empire, but that was turning out to be more complicated than she had expected.

Jessamyn was tapping her foot again, and Mica knew she should return to her noble guests, but she lingered beside the gangway, learning the faces of the soldiers peering down at her. She wished she could ensure their safety somehow.

"Are you a Talent as well, Captain Karson?"

"Yes, Princess. I am a Shield, trained to position myself to protect my men in battle."

"And us, I hope," muttered Lady Wendel.

"Of course, my lady. My men will—" Karson looked up as a gust of wind ruffled his uniform. "Ah, here is your Blur Elite now."

The Blur fighter halted at his side, arm already raised in salute.

"All is well along the coast, Captain."

It was Mica's brother Emir.

CHAPTER SEVEN

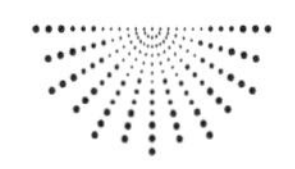

Mica barely stopped herself from throwing her arms around her brother's neck. She made a strangled sound as Captain Karson introduced Emir Grayson, a member of an Elite Blur division based out of Stonefoss Infantry Base. The second-oldest Grayson looked tall and handsome in his uniform, which had a patch embroidered with a winged pair of boots to indicate his status. He was lean and strong, with hazel eyes like Mica's, and his close-cropped hair was dark like their father's. Mica hadn't heard that Emir had been promoted to the Elite division. And now he had been assigned to her!

"It is an honor to serve," Emir said.

"Thank you." Mica swallowed a lump in her throat as she acknowledged his salute. She was so proud of him. "I hope you won't be in any danger in my service, Soldier Grayson."

"I am ready to face any perils, Your Highness."

Mica smiled at his formal tone. "Then I'll be glad to have you at my side."

Jessamyn shifted her position in a rather emphatic way, and Mica stopped short of asking Emir about their family. It took a concerted effort to keep her hair from changing to its real color and her eyes from lightening to match Emir's—even with Jessamyn's glare blasting her like a sandstorm.

"We'd better be on our way, Captain Karson," Mica said briskly, turning back to Emir's commanding officer so she wouldn't have to make eye contact with the princess. "There's Lord Riven now."

The nobleman had just galloped up on a black stallion, forcing the people still gathered along the waterfront to fling themselves out of his way. He dismounted and bowed before her.

"Princess Jessamyn, forgive me for my tardiness." Riven had black hair, a thin nose, and a proud, chiseled face. He wore a black coat trimmed with silver details that made him look like an ancient night god.

"It's quite all right." Mica offered him a delicate hand. "I am glad you could join our little tour of the empire."

"It will be more beautiful than ever for your presence." As usual, little sincerity touched Lord Riven's voice, and less showed in his eyes. "If I may say so, you become more gorgeous by the day."

"Stop, my lord. You are making me blush." Mica gave a high, false laugh, wishing she could morph into an old hag just to escape these sycophantic compliments. Riven was pure artifice. Mica had never seen even a hint of true emotion or personality from him. It felt ridiculous to exchange such empty words in front of the soldiers. "Shall we get underway?"

"As you wish, my princess." Lord Riven bowed, giving his coat an extra flourish, and strutted off to greet the other ladies.

Riven had been a last-minute addition to their party. Jessamyn had originally invited Lord Nobu, who came from the Twins, but he had been called home when secession agitators looted his family's manor house. Jessamyn worried that Nobu's departure meant tensions were escalating too fast in Dwindlemire and Cray, but she'd been quick to invite another powerful—and unmarried—lord in his place.

Mica wondered if Emir recognized Lord Riven from her Assignment Ceremony back in Redbridge. Her brother had been intrigued when she was assigned to Jewel Harbor. Now, he kept stealing glances at the teeming city behind her, as if he wished he could explore before they set off. In other circumstances, Mica could have shown him around the capital city herself.

There was a sharp cough in her ear. "Princess?"

Mica started then swept away from her brother before Jessamyn could step on her toe again. She was eager to set sail. The sooner they finished with all the pomp and circumstance, the sooner she could talk to Emir without so many people looking on.

Mica gathered her entourage of guards, lords, ladies, and luggage carriers and boarded the *Silk Goddess*. The ship consisted of a lower main deck and a raised foredeck and stern deck. The masts, all hung about with sails and lines, took up most of the center of the ship. Suspended above the deck were two longboats, which could carry them to and from the ship in ports too narrow to admit the *Silk Goddess*'s broad hull.

A double line of sailors and oarsmen greeted them on the main deck, lined up as if waiting for a blessing. They wore matching white tunics that looked as if they had been specially made for the occasion, though their faces weren't quite as fresh and eager as the soldiers'.

The captain, a wiry, windblown type, had been talking with Lord Dolan by the forecastle.

"Dolan pays him for information," Jessamyn whispered in Mica's ear as the captain and nobleman rushed over to receive her. "Be wary of your words in his presence."

"Understood."

"Welcome aboard the *Silk Goddess*, Your Highness. Ladies." The wiry man bowed deeply to Mica and her companions. "I am Captain Pol. You do my ship great honor with your presence."

"Thank you, Captain. I am pleased to join you for this voyage.

And thank you for your hospitality, Lord Dolan." She gave the nobleman her hand for the shortest moment possible.

"Nothing gives me greater pleasure than to have you aboard my ship," Lord Dolan said.

Jessamyn gave a faint snort.

Mica pulled loose from his clammy grasp and nodded at the sailors.

"I'm sure your men have work to do, Captain Pol. You needn't stand on ceremony on my account."

"As you wish, Your Highness." Captain Pol bowed again then snapped his spindly fingers. The sailors rushed back to their work, preparing to cast off.

Lord Dolan greeted Lord Riven—his rival for the princess's affection—with a stiff mask of politeness, and the two began discussing their various impressive holdings. Mica took the opportunity to escape to the railing of the ship, where she would bid Jewel Harbor a final farewell.

The other lords and ladies gathered beside her, their bodyguards posted unobtrusively behind them. Mica almost called Emir up so he could get a better look at the city from the water. He was sure to be as impressed as she had been by this chaotic place.

The city shone like crystal in the morning light, the rooftops rising in layer upon layer to the shining dome of the Silver Palace. A multitude of colorfully painted walls, glimmering windows, and mismatched flags filled the little island to bursting. People watched their departure from a hundred windows and balconies. Handkerchiefs flew wild on the breeze, sending them on their way with a revolution of color. A thousand faces looked up at them from the docks, the features impossible to catalogue.

For a moment, Mica thought she saw a certain gangly young redhead with a meager beard, but he was gone when she looked again. She touched the note in her belt.

Trumpets blared, and cries of farewell rose from the crowds

as the *Silk Goddess* and the *Arrow* pulled away from their moorings. The nobles who hadn't been invited on the voyage waved them off with sour expressions, annoyed at having to arrange their own transportation to the wedding. They flounced off to their fine carriages almost immediately. But the common people remained to watch the two great ships set sail.

On impulse, Mica let her hair loose from her braid. Her white gown and flowing red tresses would stand out against the broad blue sky, leaving a strong impression in the memories of her people. If Mica had her way, she would be invisible again by the time she returned.

As the *Silk Goddess* pulled into the center of the harbor, the babble of the crowds gradually subsided. Soon the creaking of the wooden ship and the gentle slap of water against the hull overtook the city noises. Jewel Harbor slipped away, its teetering towers blending together except for that bright-silver dome. The smells of refuse and sweat faded too, replaced by pitch, timber, and salt. They might be sailing toward dangers unknown, but Mica could already breathe a little easier.

Before long, all they could see to the right was the distant coast of Amber Island, its steep cliffs and quiet seaside towns rolling along beside them. To the left was the hulking form of their warship escort and the endless green ocean.

The nobles quickly tired of the views and dispersed to explore the ship. Jessamyn went below, no doubt to make sure all the supplies she had ordered were present.

As soon as no one was watching her too closely, Mica withdrew Peet's note from her belt.

Princess Jessamyn,

I have just learned from a trusted source that one of the nobles on your ship is an imposter. I do not know which lord or lady it is, but the Mimic is an associate of Lord Ober. Please take care.

Your loyal servant.

Mica quickly ripped the parchment into tiny pieces and let them fly loose on the breeze. The tiny white shreds disappeared in the waves like stars in a predawn sky. Heart racing, she gripped the wooden railing until her palms ached.

So there was an imposter in their midst. She had little doubt what their goal must be. Ober had tried to assassinate the princess before. He would surely try again.

So much for breathing easier.

"Are you well, Princess Jessamyn?"

Mica looked up into the face of her brother, who had come up beside her. She wanted to tell Emir about this new threat, but Elana, Ingrid, and Riven were standing only a few paces away.

Someone's always watching.

She scanned the decks. Caleb and Fritz were chatting amiably with Wendel over by the mast, and Dolan was giving instructions to the ship's steward in the stern. One of those seven nobles was an imposter. One of those nobles wanted the real princess dead. Which meant Mica had a target on her back for as long as she wore this face.

Emir cleared his throat. "Princess Jessamyn?"

"I am quite well, thank you." Mica forced herself to adopt her most breezy tone. "That's enough watching the coastline for me. This is a holiday excursion. Let us bring out the food and wine!"

CHAPTER EIGHT

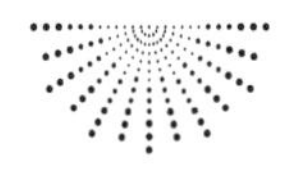

The nobles would not sacrifice their usual comforts while at sea. They each had private cabins aboard the *Silk Goddess*, and the hold overflowed with fine food, wine, and the silverware and crystal with which to enjoy them. A lounge area with crimson cushions and warm blankets had been set up on the foredeck, where they could enjoy the sea views in comfort. Jessamyn wanted the voyage to feel fanciful and special. Austerity would be unacceptable for her guests.

Mica played the charming hostess as they left the capital farther behind. She picnicked on deck with the seven nobles, all of whom seemed in good spirits—with good reason. The princess had specially chosen them to be her companions on her tour of the empire, which would raise their status substantially in the eyes of their peers.

"Let's have a toast to our effervescent princess!" Lord Dolan called, raising a glass to them all. "And to the prettiest ship on the Windfast seas!"

"To the *Silk Goddess*!" Fritz cried. "May she carry us safely west!"

"The *Silk Goddess* and Princess Jessamyn!"

As the nobles celebrated their fortune, Mica contemplated how to work out which one was the imposter. Lord Ober's Mimic had selected one of these men or women to replace—and perhaps murder. Mica doubted she would spot flaws in the imposter's appearance. She was certain Ober would only hire a highly skilled Mimic. She would have to scrutinize their actions, their words, their moods. She would seek out discrepancies in the little snippets of information that only the true individuals could know. And she would have to do it fast. This journey would be perilous enough without an assassin in their midst.

At least no one paid any attention to Myn Irondier the cultural advisor, apart from a few glances at the disfigurement visible above her veil. Jessamyn was free to walk the ship in safety, Banner close by her side, while Mica entertained her noble traveling companions.

The hours glided by as swiftly as the water beneath their hull. When it grew dark, the steward lit candle lanterns around the lounge, and the lords and ladies dined beneath the stars. Attendants rushed back and forth, bringing hot chowder, bread, olives, mature cheeses, fresh oysters, and bottle after bottle of wine. The mood became festive with little prompting. The lords and ladies told stories and enthusiastically discussed the destinations they'd visit on their voyage. The careful sophistication they cultivated at the imperial court faded bit by bit.

Mica kept a close watch for the enemy in their midst, trying not to relax despite the crisp breeze in her hair, the warm food in her belly, and the sea rolling gently beneath her.

This isn't a holiday for you, she reminded herself. *You are on an assignment.*

Amber Island slipped past, almost invisible beyond the ring of light. They would be sailing north up the Amber Coast for two days before veering to the west and crossing the Heart Sea to Pegasus Island, where Lady Wendel's family lived.

"I hope the weather will cooperate," Lady Wendel said as she lounged at Mica's side, slurping oysters from their shells. "I can take you all riding in the countryside."

"I'd love that," Mica said. "I've heard the Pegasus countryside is stunning."

"Don't you remember your last visit?" Lady Wendel sounded hurt. "My cousin Aren chased us through a pasture, pretending to be a lion, and you fell into a pile of sheep dung."

Mica suppressed a chuckle at the image of pretty little Princess Jessamyn covered in dung. She had neglected to share that memory.

"Forgive me. I forgot all about that delightful incident."

"My cousin will be happy to see you again," Wendel said. "Aren hasn't visited court in a long time. He doesn't like feeling confined in the big city."

"I am looking forward to the wide-open spaces *ever* so much." Mica raised her drink to Lady Wendel. "To Pegasus!"

The noblewoman smiled. "I just can't wait to be home."

Their glasses clinked, and Wendel drank deeply. Mica only pretended to sip her own wine, studying Wendel over the crystal rim.

She looks like herself so far. Wendel's mannerisms were the same as always, and even her newly crooked nose was the right shape. Mica would have to verify the details about her cousin with Jessamyn later.

This is harder than I thought.

She called for more wine for all the nobles, hoping some feature would slip or some stray phrase would betray the imposter. But Elana still simpered. Ingrid still made biting remarks. Riven still talked about his accomplishments. Mica was most worried about Caleb and Fritz, who were her favorites among the seven. They acted as easygoing as ever, and she dearly hoped that meant Ober's Mimic hadn't gotten to them.

As for Lord Dolan, he held court as if he'd already been named the princess's consort. If he was the imposter, he had captured Dolan's creepiness perfectly. After the meal, he moved over to sit close beside Mica, pressing her hand and regularly refilling her wine—which she spilled on the deck whenever he wasn't looking.

"May I say your gown sets off your exquisite features in the most . . . inviting way."

"You are too kind."

"I have always said you would be a great beauty." He smiled, revealing wine-stained teeth. "Even when you were little."

"That's very . . . uh . . . perceptive."

Dolan's every word made Mica's skin crawl, but she had her orders to accept his courtship, and she tolerated his compliments as much as possible.

Then the real Jessamyn caught her eye and jerked her head toward the prow.

"Excuse me, my lord." Mica extracted herself gratefully from Dolan's clutches. "I must speak with my cultural advisor."

"Of course, my princess," Dolan slurred. "Unfortunate thing, isn't she, with a face like that? Wherever did you find her?"

Mica ignored the comment and stepped out of the circle of lantern light, summoning "Myn Irondier" with a wave of her hand. They strolled to the prow, the rushing wind and creaking timber hiding their words.

"You don't need to put up with Lord Dolan like that," Jessamyn said. Her voice was heated, and her eyes were bright with anger.

"Isn't he one of the top choices for your consort?"

"I've been letting him think so, but seeing the way he keeps pawing at you . . ." Jessamyn shuddered. "It looks different from the outside. Do you honestly think I should marry him?"

Mica was surprised to realize the question wasn't rhetorical. Jessamyn didn't often ask for her counsel.

"No, I think he would be the wrong choice," Mica said, "and not just because he's a creepy bastard. He has power over the merchants' guild, but he wouldn't tie you strongly enough to one of the major ruling families."

"And do you think the empire will suffer if I refuse the head of the merchants' guild?"

Mica thought for a moment. "No," she said. "They will continue about their business, because it's in their self-interest for the empire to prosper."

"I agree." Jessamyn gave a satisfied nod. "Lord Dolan has served his purpose. It will be nice not to endure his cloying attentions anymore."

Mica resisted the urge to point out that *she* had been the one actually enduring Dolan's cloying attentions lately. Sometimes it was as if Jessamyn no longer saw the difference between them. But if she had finally rejected Dolan's suit, did that mean she was taking her father's ultimatum seriously?

The lords and ladies began calling for her to join them for dessert. Mica pretended to examine the gilded figurehead and quickly filled Jessamyn in on what she had learned from Peet's note.

"And you trust the Blur?"

"I do."

"We'll have to be extra careful then." Jessamyn glanced at the nobles eating frosted cakes in the ring of light. "Perhaps I can spy out inconsistencies in their behavior. You know they have not once looked me in the eye? It's almost insulting."

Mica grinned. It would be good for the princess to see what it was like to be a commoner for a few weeks.

"I'd better get back to them," Mica said. "Is there anything else?"

"Yes." Jessamyn adjusted her veil primly over her mottled features. "You mustn't tell that Blur Elite who you really are. I know you're thinking about it."

Mica's jaw went slack, growing an inch in the process. "How on earth did you—?"

"Emir *Grayson*. Need I remind you that I have an excellent memory, Micathea *Graydier*? And I know how patronymics work, thank you very much. Your fathers are both named Gray, and you have the same wide-eyed stare when you look at fancy people."

Mica sighed. "Okay, he's my brother. I wasn't planning to tell him who I am, though."

"You had better not. I've gone to a great deal of trouble to help you get this impersonation right. It would be terribly inconsiderate of you to ruin it after everything I've done for you."

"Yes, Princess."

"Good. Now, I am going to bed. It doesn't look as if our friends have drunk their fill yet. Make sure you're the last person up. No one outlasts me."

"Of course not."

Jessamyn headed below deck, where she would sleep on a cot in the nicest cabin on the ship—which had been commandeered from Captain Pol for the princess's use. Actually, Mica would probably end up sleeping on the cot, and Jessamyn would take the bed piled high with cushions.

At least she's resting. The princess had pushed herself too hard for far too long.

Mica rejoined the party, which showed no signs of winding down despite the chill in the sea air. Caleb and Fritz—who had both indulged heartily in the wine—decided to entertain the ladies with a dramatic rendition of a courtly epic called *The Lords of Heart Sea*. They convinced Lord Riven to play a role, and he gave a passable performance as a villainous pirate, whom they fought with spoons and shields made of oyster shells. As the young lords dueled across the deck, Mica looked for any change in Fritz's scar, or Riven's height, or Caleb's stocky build, but she could see no flaws. She listened for unfamiliar tones in the ladies' voices but detected no false notes as their laughter drowned out the sighing of the wind.

Their escort, the HIMS *Arrow*, remained comparatively quiet as they sailed through the night, the soldiers ever vigilant. Mica's brother took up a post by the starboard railing, keeping watch on the darkened coast. He glanced over occasionally as the nobles giggled and drank, lolling about late into the night. Mica was aware how frivolous they must look, especially to someone used to the stark way of life at Stonefoss. She felt a little embarrassed, even though Emir didn't know it was her.

The gentle lull of the sea made her sleepy, and she was relieved when her noble guests began to bid each other farewell and depart for their own quarters. Dolan had moved his attentions to Ingrid when Mica withdrew from him, but the hawk-faced woman told him to leave her be in no uncertain terms. She paused at the ladder on her way to bed, though, casting a look back at Lord Riven. The proud, cold lord made no move to follow her below, and it was a while yet before he retired.

At last, only Mica, Fritz, and Caleb remained on deck. The Shields on duty, including Rider and Caleb's retainer, Stievson, gave the princess and the young lords a wide berth. Emir kept guard at a respectful distance, watching over the night-dark sea. Mica wished she could call him over to join them for a little while. She would love to know what he thought of Caleb.

It doesn't matter what your brother thinks of Lord *Caleb. You're not going to court him, unless you do it as Jessamyn.* There was no point in entertaining *that* thought.

Fritz had been drinking merrily all evening, and he babbled about Lady Lorna as the candles burned low.

"She has such a sweet heart. And she is wonderful with children. Her hair is as soft as a lamb's wool, and her eyes are like . . . are like . . ."

His head dropped onto his chest, and he began to snore. His features remained unchanged.

Caleb looked over at Mica.

"You can go to bed, if you like, Jessa," he said. "You don't need to prove how robust you are to me."

Mica stifled a yawn. "What are you going to do?"

"I think I'll walk on deck. My last episode was a few weeks ago, and I'm feeling more awake than usual."

Mica thought about the imposter lurking somewhere on the *Silk Goddess*. She had to narrow down her suspects—starting with Caleb. She felt as if she could meet any threat as long as he was still himself.

"Do you mind if I join you for a stroll?"

He shrugged. "It's your ship. Well, Dolan's ship, but your empire."

She touched the knife strapped beneath her skirt. She *hoped* Caleb wasn't the imposter, but she was ready if he was.

Caleb was still a little tipsy, and he hummed tunelessly as they meandered over to watch the uneven coastline drift by. Mica observed him closely for signs that he was an Impersonator.

"Watch your step." Caleb offered her his hand. "It's a bit slick here."

"I'm quite all right." Mica stepped nimbly over a puddle of wine—which she had spilled to keep from getting tipsy herself.

"Of course you are. What did Dolan call you? Effervescent." Caleb chuckled. "I thought that was a good one."

Mica grinned. "I am *delightful*, thank you very much."

"Yes, but is your hair as soft as a lamb's wool?"

"Softer."

Caleb's movements were a bit looser than usual, and he'd unbuttoned his deep-blue waistcoat, but he seemed like exactly the same person. He had always been considerate and good-humored, regardless of how ill or tired or inebriated he might be. He also didn't pose and scheme the way the other lords did. He had been too busy managing his mysterious ailment, never knowing when he would suddenly be as strong as ten men or when he might turn around a dance floor so fast he blurred. His condition made him refreshingly unpretentious—and Mica hoped it would provide the clue she needed to verify his identity.

They reached the starboard side, and Caleb rested his square hands on the railing, looking across the water at a cluster of lights on the shore. He seemed to be searching for something.

"What is it?" Mica asked.

"See those lights? I think that's the town of Gullton. I stayed there once, with Ober and Euphia."

Mica moved closer to him. She could just make out the dark shadow of the cliff on which Gullton sat. The lights were muted, half hidden in fog. That was where she and Caleb had met on a night much like this one. But Ober's Mimic would know Caleb had been there.

"What's Gullton like?" she asked.

"Busy," Caleb said. "It's the last stop on the main road before you reach Old Kings and Jewel Harbor. It's mostly inns and taverns." He glanced down at her. "Haven't you been there before?"

Mica studiously avoided his gaze. She wanted to tell him the truth, to let him know she thought about that night too. Instead, she released one of Jessamyn's longsuffering sighs and said, "I can't be expected to remember every little country town in my empire."

"Some would say you can."

"Can what?"

"Be expected to remember every little town. People need their leaders to care about their homes, even the ones in wayside places like Gullton."

Mica arched one of Jessamyn's thick, expressive eyebrows. "You're implying I don't care?"

Caleb drummed his fingers on the railing for a moment. The wind ruffled the sleeves of his linen shirt, making it billow like sea fog.

"May I speak plainly?"

"Please do."

"We've all heard the rumors of rebellion in the Twins. I don't know if they'll truly secede from the empire, but the message I've heard over and over is that the leaders of the empire care more for politics and clever schemes than for the people's needs."

Mica couldn't argue with that. Jessamyn schemed enough for three people, and she refused to show any authenticity lest it be confused with weakness. Hiding behind Mica's face was exactly the sort of deception the common people hated, exactly the sort of thing *Mica* hated.

But she wasn't here to question the princess's decisions, even if a lord she thought of as an ally was doing it.

"Tell me, Lord Caleb. Do the Pebble Islands hold similar views?"

Caleb turned to face her, moving so fast he blurred. He seemed surprised by the quick motion, as if the burst of Talent had given away more of his true feelings than he intended. And possibly his true identity.

"Are you asking me if my people would join a revolt in the Twins?"

"That's precisely what I'm asking."

Caleb paused, a thoughtful stillness replacing the Blur speed. Mica had never known anyone who, despite the erraticism of his other movements, could achieve such meditative stillness.

"The honest truth is that I don't know," he said at last. "But there are cracks in this empire, Princess, and people like my uncle are more than capable of exploiting them."

"With the help of people like you?"

"I am loyal, Jessa." Caleb sighed, brushing a hand through his wind-tousled hair. He sounded completely sober now. "You shouldn't even have to ask. But yes, if he ever perfects his potion, he could do an awful lot of damage with people who have my abilities without my side effects."

"We'll just have to find him before then." Mica paused, meeting his eyes steadily. Would Ober's Mimic talk about Caleb's multiple Talents like that? He would need to be a Mimic *and* a Blur—and he would need to have an impressive level of control. Based on the madman at the ball and Caleb's own limitations, the potion was very far from perfect. She dreaded to think what would happen if Ober got it right. This had to be the real Caleb.

But she needed more proof, something only the two of them would know.

"Do you have any more ideas for where this barren fortress might be?" she said.

"I've been thinking about that and about something Haddell said to me in the warehouse."

Mica pictured the moment, when the old potioner had feigned madness while fumbling for a bottle of poison to throw at Caleb. She barely had time to knock the deadly vial aside.

"He said I'd find the rest of Ober's operation—"

"—where you least wish it to be."

Caleb blinked. "Did I tell you that?"

"Of course you did, darling." Mica waved a hand quickly before he could work out whether or not he'd told Jessamyn this part. Mica and Caleb had been the only two people within earshot of Haddell. This *was* the real Caleb. Relief crashed over her like a summer rainstorm. "Go on."

"I would least wish Ober to be working in the Pebble Islands themselves. There's a lighthouse on the westernmost Pebble that could be described as barren."

"More barren than Timbral Castle?"

"Definitely."

She remembered the mad Talent's words: *a barren fortress, an abominable cesspit.*

"So we have two possible locations for Ober's headquarters in the West. Good thing we're sailing that way with a warship full of Talent soldiers for an escort."

Caleb raised an eyebrow. "I thought we were on vacation."

"So do a lot of people." She didn't dare look at him, afraid he would see the very Mica-like determination burning through her Jessamyn mask.

"You know, sometimes I pity people who think they can outmaneuver you," Caleb said.

Mica grinned. "So do I."

If Mica had her way, she and Caleb would be fighting Ober side by side soon. She wished she could tell him the truth. Caleb had gone into the fray at the warehouse to save a group of Talents, even though it put him at odds with his uncle. He was a good man who would choose the right course of action over the convenient one. He wouldn't betray the princess. In fact, he might be the only person she could trust right now.

Emperor Styl had said Caleb would be a good choice for his daughter's consort, despite his family's lack of influence. Mica would rather see the princess with someone like Caleb than with Dolan or Riven. Or an imposter in their place. She wondered how *Caleb* felt about Jessamyn. They were good friends, but could his fondness for the princess run deeper than she thought?

They fell silent as the lights of Gullton slipped away in the distance. It was a beautiful night, if a bit chilly, and the fog had begun to clear. Mica leaned into Caleb as if for warmth, curious how he would react. He didn't pull away, his eyes remaining fixed on the dark horizon.

She shifted closer, so her side was pressed against his arm, her arm hooked loosely around his elbow.

You're just seeing what he'll do, she told herself. Her pulse quickened, her blood running hot beneath her skin. *Your feelings aren't important here.*

Caleb's breath caught as he became aware of the way she was leaning into him, different from the way he and Jessamyn normally exchanged affection. Was there a chance he suspected the truth? Mica couldn't be sure she was hearing his altered breathing right because her own heart was pounding in her ears.

She felt lightheaded, effervescent even. She leaned closer.

You're just looking for clues.

Her control was slipping, as if her body—the part of her body that was really Mica—couldn't bear to be separated from him.

Caleb used to be able to tell when it was really Mica instead of whoever she was impersonating. She wanted that back, wanted to believe that it had meant more than just a flaw in her performance. She could barely contain the thunder in her chest. She wanted to hear her name on his lips again.

He spoke at last, his voice low. "Jess—"

Mica pulled away abruptly, as if a dose of energy potion had been forced down her throat. She couldn't do this, couldn't snuggle into him wearing this face in a body that wasn't really hers, not when her feelings for him were only growing stronger.

She gave a shaky version of Jessamyn's chuckle. "Oh, I'm practically falling asleep on my feet. I'd better turn in now. Good night!" And she darted away before Caleb could say another word.

CHAPTER NINE

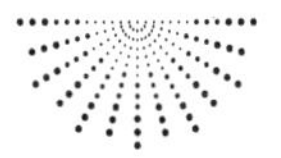

Mica knew she had danced too close to the line with Caleb. She made a point of treating him exactly as Jessamyn always had as the voyage continued. Neither more nor less affectionate. Sometimes she thought he was watching her more closely, following the turn of her steps and the pitch of her voice. Her cheeks heated when their eyes met, and she couldn't tell if she feared discovery or hoped for it. And she couldn't tell if *he* was watching her because he suspected the truth, or if he was slowly coming to see Jessamyn as more than a friend.

Jessamyn's lively mannerisms helped Mica obscure her genuine feelings. Her laughter took on a higher pitch, and her brown eyes flashed with manic energy as she focused on entertaining her noble guests—and identifying the imposter among them.

Mica's first assumption had been that the Mimic was here to assassinate the princess, but three out of the four lords were candidates for Jessamyn's hand in marriage. It was possible the imposter had something besides murder on the mind. Of course, if an assassination were carried out, Mica, not Jessamyn, would be the victim.

Mica avoided being alone with anyone as they left the waters off the Amber Coast and sailed across the Heart Sea. She and the nobles lounged in the sun, eating rare fruits and honey and playing little games to pass the time. The lords practiced fighting with wooden swords and knives, occasionally inviting soldiers over from the *Arrow* to join them in their exercises.

Lord Riven proved himself surprisingly adept with a blade, but he was no match for Caleb. He moved with an erratic sort of grace, occasionally speeding up or striking with extra force. Mica even heard Lord Riven compliment him once, a rarity for the arrogant lord.

Riven's grudging approval was drowned out by the fawning attention Elana and Wendel paid to Caleb.

"He hardly breaks a sweat," Wendel said one morning as they watched him spar with his man, Stievson, while Fritz, Riven, and a handful of sailors looked on.

"I wouldn't mind seeing him sweat a little," Elana said.

"And look at that fine pair of shoulders." Wendel sighed. "If only he were a little taller."

"Or you were a little shorter."

Wendel ignored Elana's dig, too busy admiring Caleb's shoulders. His build was stocky but well proportioned. Mica figured he was exactly the right height.

The practice blades clacked together, and Caleb retreated, adjusting his steps to the rolling of the ship. He paused for one beat. Two. Then he advanced for another attack. As his sword swung up to meet Stievson's, it suddenly moved so quickly the wooden blades shattered on impact.

Stievson laughed, and the two men went to grab new practice swords. Stievson knew about his liege's condition. Mica studied the other lords to see if they were surprised, figuring Lord Ober's Mimic likely knew about it too. Riven frowned, as if trying to work out exactly how that strike had gathered so much force. Fritz was busy sharpening the jeweled dagger he often carried, and he didn't seem to have noticed the oddity. Lord Dolan was nowhere in sight.

"Caleb's style is unique, isn't it?" Wendel said. "My uncle and cousin will want to see him spar when we reach Pegasus."

"I hope we get there soon," Elana said. "Being at sea is so *boring*."

"Shall we have some music, ladies?" Mica said quickly. "Perhaps those fine lords will join us for a dance when they've cleaned up."

They filled their days with relaxation and gossip and their nights with dancing and dining. Mica looked for odd behaviors in her traveling companions, but she couldn't tell if any inconsistencies were because she was used to seeing them at court. Spending time in such intimate quarters changed the dynamic.

Jessamyn reported her observations to Mica too, seeming to relish her role as a spy in the shadows.

"Ingrid and Elana are getting along," she said one evening as they dressed for dinner in their shared cabin. "I don't like it."

"I heard them bickering over a card game an hour ago," Mica said.

"Bickering, yes, but they aren't as cold to each other as they used to be."

"Do you think one of them is the imposter?"

"Perhaps." Jessamyn fiddled with the stack of bracelets on her wrist. "Or maybe they are finally getting over their differences."

"What happened between them, anyway?"

"Elana bought a villa in Winnow Bay that Ingrid has had her eye on for years. It finally became available, and Elana snatched it up while Ingrid was in Talon."

Mica paused in the act of buttoning up one of Jessamyn's warmer dresses. It was getting colder now that they were sailing north. "They're enemies because of a house they don't even live in most of the year?"

"That villa has some of the best views in the Bay," Jessamyn said, "and it happens to be right next to one owned by Lord Riven and his family."

"Oh, right. Ingrid has been eyeing him for a while, hasn't she?"

"Like a hawk," Jessamyn said.

"Elana doesn't seem interested in him, though." Mica resumed her work on the buttons. There had to be at least a thousand of them on this dress. "And he has been eyeing *you*. I don't get why they'd be fighting for Lord Riven's affections."

"Who said anything about his affections? Elana doesn't want the link between Talon and northern Amber Island to strengthen." Jessamyn gestured to the large map of the Windfast Empire that hung on the cabin wall. "She thinks they'll impose tariffs on the trade route between their lands if they were to marry."

"Isn't Ingrid still in love with Riven, though?"

"What in the Windfast does *love* have to do with this?"

Mica blinked. "It—never mind. So Elana didn't want Ingrid and Riven becoming friendlier on their visits to Winnow Bay, so she snatched up the villa. And now Ingrid hates her for it?"

"Yes. And then Ingrid spread some rather nasty rumors about Elana's behavior in that villa, which is why Elana hates Ingrid. Before, it was just business."

Mica rubbed her nose, making it hawkish like Ingrid's then sharp like Elana's. "But now they're getting along?"

"I heard them having a perfectly amiable conversation this morning when no one else was around," Jessamyn said. "They were talking about seagulls. Imagine! I wonder if some of their rivalry has been an act of late."

"Or one of them is an imposter who can't quite pull off the right level of animosity."

"Or that."

"Well, I'll keep an eye on them," Mica said.

"Good. And see that you pay a bit more attention to Lord

Riven at dinner tonight. I'll see how Ingrid reacts. If she's the real Ingrid, she won't like it."

"I thought you said this wasn't about love."

"The dispute between Elana and Ingrid isn't about love. But Ingrid's affections for Riven are almost certainly genuine, poor girl."

"Why—"

"Shouldn't you be finished dressing by now?" Jessamyn snapped. "We can't sit around gossiping like ninnies all night."

"Yes, Princess."

Mica pulled back her dark-red hair and hurried to the cabin door, bracing herself for another evening of duplicitous socializing. She paused at the door.

"Princess?"

Jessamyn gave a longsuffering sigh. "What is it now, Micathea?"

"Do *you* want to marry for love?"

For a moment, there was no sound but the creaking of the ship.

When Jessamyn answered at last, her voice was soft. "My life has never been about what I want."

"Do you love any—"

"Quickly now," Jessamyn said before she could finish the question. "Our guests are waiting."

Mica obeyed, unable to suppress a burst of sympathy for Jessamyn. Their relationship was strained at times, but Mica wanted the princess to have a chance at happiness. They both knew what it was like to put aside their personal feelings in the name of duty.

But as they sailed toward dangers unknown, getting no closer to identifying their imposter, they faced bigger problems.

"Ships are being raided in the Northern Channel, Your Highness." Captain Karson had come aboard the *Silk Goddess* to deliver his regular report. Every day, he sent Blur scouts out from the *Arrow* to speed across the water in light skips, rowing as fast as they ran, and survey the route ahead. Karson relayed what they said to Mica, standing in the shade of a longboat hanging above the deck of the *Goddess*. Only Myn Irondier was permitted to listen in on these private conferences.

"Most of the activity is centered between Cray and Silverfell, but at least one ship encountered trouble near Pegasus."

Mica checked to make sure the others weren't listening.

"Who is responsible?"

"We don't know yet," Captain Karson said. "I suggest we alter our route through the Heart Sea and approach Silverfell from the south. We could sail upriver to reach the city and avoid entering the Northern Channel at all."

"That would require skipping our stop in Pegasus, would it not?"

Across the deck, Wendel looked up, as if she could sense they were discussing her home even though she was nowhere near them.

"That's correct," Captain Karson said. "I believe it's the safest option."

Mica weighed this news carefully. She trusted Captain Karson's judgment. The Shield soldier had so far conducted himself with impressive professionalism. He knew the risks they faced, and he wouldn't want to take the emperor's daughter into danger if the turbulence in the West continued to escalate.

And if someone's attacking ships now, it could mean—

Jessamyn gave a demure cough, reminding Mica that it wasn't actually her decision.

"My princess," Jessamyn said. "It would offend local Pegasus custom to go back on our word after accepting an invitation."

Mica nodded in understanding. "Myn makes a good point.

We cannot alter our course, Captain. Can I trust you to be vigilant as we traverse the Northern Channel?"

"Always, my princess."

"Good." She glanced at Jessamyn, whose veil was twitching as if she was trying to communicate something else. "I want to know who these raiders are, Captain. Send a team of your best men to scout the Channel while we fulfill our diplomatic obligations in Pegasus. See if you can get your hands on a hostage."

"It will be done, Princess." Karson saluted and marched off to board the small boat that would return him to his own ship.

"Very good, Micathea," Jessamyn murmured when he was out of earshot. "You may learn to read my mind yet."

"Why is it so important to go to Pegasus?"

"I refuse to be scared away by a few troublemakers," Jessamyn said. "The Northern Channel is part of my empire. We won't solve any problems by taking detours."

"Let's hope Captain Karson can get us a hostage, then," Mica said.

"My thoughts exactly."

Mica wished she *could* read Jessamyn's mind. It would certainly make her job easier. On the other hand, the more indispensable she became to the princess, the harder it would be to break away when the time came.

Mica had not forgotten her other mission. She used her few spare moments—and the detailed map of the empire in Captain Pol's cabin—to learn more about her candidates for the barren fortress. Timbral Castle and the lighthouse in the Pebble Islands were both in remote settings, and they could easily host Ober's experiments without drawing too much attention. Her search couldn't truly begin until she caught the imposter on the *Goddess*, though. Jessamyn's identity had to remain hidden while a murderer traveled in their midst.

Mica had another, more enjoyable mission to occupy her as they crossed the endless swells of the Heart Sea: getting her brother to talk about their family. The real Jessamyn would never make small talk with a random Blur soldier in the Silver Palace, but it was easier to arrange casual interactions on the *Silk Goddess*.

"Excuse me, Soldier Grayson, would you be so kind as to settle a disagreement?"

She was lounging on the crimson deck cushions with Ingrid when she called to her brother. It had grown colder during their week at sea, and they were wrapped in thick blankets to protect them from the chill.

Emir had been watching Caleb and Fritz practice their sword forms down on the starboard deck, but he appeared at her side at once. "How can I help, Your Highness?"

"I have been telling Lady Ingrid here that more Talent soldiers ordinarily reside at Stonefoss Base than at Ironhall on Talon."

"Nonsense." Lady Ingrid sat up. The wind blew her black hair around her face in wisps, softening her hawkish features despite her indignant expression. "Ironhall is the most important base in the entirety of the Windfast."

"Its location is vital to the empire's defenses, of course," Mica said. "I don't mean to disparage your homeland, Lady Ingrid. Stonefoss simply has more men."

"That's correct, Your Highness," Emir said. "Stonefoss has about ten percent more soldiers than Ironhall, and a higher proportion of them are Talents."

"Because of the Talent residence program," Mica said. "Isn't that right?"

"Yes, Your Highness." Emir remained straight-backed and unintimidated as he spoke to the future empress and her companion. "Stonefoss offers extra housing benefits for Talents who marry each other. The goal is to encourage them to produce more Talents."

Mica smiled. "Are you from Stonefoss originally, Soldier Grayson?"

"I am. I grew up in one of the Talent houses, along with my siblings."

"Tell me about them." Mica spotted Jessamyn speaking to Banner over by the mast. She hadn't been hovering as much lately, trusting Mica not to mess up every conversation, but she edged closer now. Mica wrapped her blanket tighter around her shoulders and leaned toward Emir, wanting to hear as much as possible about her family before the princess interrupted. "Please."

"My parents are Talents, Your Highness," Emir said, his formal tone softening. "I have three brothers and one sister. My older brother, Aden, is a Muscle. He has recently been given command of his unit. My younger brothers are Shields. My sister is an Impersonator who trained at the Academy in Redbridge."

Mica pictured them all, sitting around their large pinewood table, sharing a modest meal of brown bread and roast pigeon. She could almost smell the aroma of leather and earth that permeated their home. The boys all lived in the barracks now, but they had made a point of coming over for dinner when Mica came home from the Academy on high days.

"And your parents?"

"A Muscle and a Blur. Both of them have served the empire for their entire lives."

"The empire is grateful for it." Mica swallowed a lump in her throat. "And your Shield brothers? Are they still—are they soldiers at Stonefoss too?"

"Yes. They get themselves in trouble sometimes, but they haven't been kicked out of the army yet."

Mica grinned. Wills and Rees were always cooking up tricks to play on each other—or on their brothers—knowing they wouldn't be hurt if the older boys retaliated. The twins would be turning twenty later this year, but she still thought of them as rambunctious little boys. They had teased her mercilessly as children, but they'd knock down anyone outside the family who did the same. They'd once pushed a Muscle boy into a neck-deep manure pit for making fun of Mica's less-than-elegant early impersonation attempts. The boy turned out to be the son of their father's commanding officer, and only some quick thinking by Emir had saved him a demotion. Emir had run errands for the boy for an entire year in exchange for his silence.

"It must be wonderful to have so many siblings."

"It is." Emir seemed emboldened by Mica's interest. "Your Highness, may I ask a question?"

"Of course, Soldier Grayson."

"My sister was assigned to serve a noblewoman in Jewel Harbor. It has been months since we had a letter from her. Would you happen to know whom she serves?"

"Micathea?"

Mica jumped as a voice spoke her true name directly behind her. Caleb had come up from the starboard deck while she was speaking to Emir, and she hadn't heard him approach.

"Is your sister's name Micathea, Soldier Grayson?" Caleb asked.

"That's right, my lord," Emir said. "Do you know her?"

"I do. She saved my life a few months back."

"Mica did that?" Emir swelled with pride. Mica was too busy panicking to appreciate the moment.

"She quit her position almost two months ago," Caleb said. "Are you saying you haven't heard from her since then?"

"Wait. She quit?" Emir's brow furrowed. "That doesn't sound like her."

"She must have had a good reason," Mica snapped. She had to keep them from connecting the dots. She sat up, her blankets falling to the deck. "Oh, Lady Ingrid, isn't it time for tea? Perhaps Soldier Grayson can fetch it."

But Ingrid didn't hear her, too interested in the exchange between the soldier and the lord. Jessamyn was glaring daggers across the deck at Mica, demanding her to contain the situation.

Caleb looked genuinely worried now. "Mica may have angered a powerful lord who is a known danger to Talents."

"What?" Emir blurred to Caleb's side, a hand on his sword. "Where is this lord?"

"Last I heard, he's in Timbral," Caleb said. "I'll go there at once. If she has been taken because—"

"I am sure Micathea is fine!" Mica said shrilly. "None of you will be charging off to Timbral."

Caleb spun toward her, and she could see the exact moment when realization struck him like a lightning bolt. The color drained out of his face, and his mouth opened wide. He didn't just look shocked. He looked horrified.

This isn't good.

Mica leapt up, her feet tangling in her discarded blanket. "Join me in my cabin, Lord Caleb," she said. "Emir, you will attend us as well."

Emir blinked at her for a second. She shouldn't have used his first name, but she needed him to listen. She had to talk to these two in private before they ruined everything—or before the foolish young heroes charged off to Timbral together to rescue her.

Ingrid was watching the whole display with great interest, but there was nothing Mica could do about that now. She would explain later—somehow.

Not daring to look at the real Jessamyn, Mica hurried below and marched toward her cabin, Caleb and Emir close on her heels. She ushered them inside and slammed the door.

"Okay," she began.

Before she could get another word out, Caleb had pushed her back against the wall. He held her in place, not hard enough to hurt her, but she couldn't move or fight.

"*Where is she?*" he demanded.

"Caleb—"

"Did you kill her? Strike it all. I *knew* there was something different about you. Have you been working for Ober all this time?"

"No! I've always been on the princess's side." She struggled against him, her features shifting. "Let me go!"

"Mica?" Emir said. "Is that you? Let go of her!"

He started forward, reaching for his sword, but Caleb grabbed him by the uniform and held him back, suddenly Muscle strong. Emir gaped at the young lord.

"What happened to Jessamyn?" Caleb's grip on Mica's shoulder had strengthened too, and he was nearly lifting her off her feet. *Now* it hurt. "If you've harmed her—"

Mica filled her lungs and shouted in his face. "Put. Me. Down."

Abruptly, Caleb noticed that his hands had become far stronger than normal. He released her at once and took a step back, letting Emir go too.

"I'm sorry. I—"

The door burst open so violently it cracked against the wall. The three of them spun to face it, reaching for steel.

"Don't you dare hurt her, you big dumb oaf!" The real Jessamyn stood on the threshold, her eyes blazing above her veil. "You're going to ruin everything."

Caleb stared. "Jessamyn? You're alive?"

"Of course I'm alive." She marched into the cabin, Banner close behind her. "For an occasional Blur, Caleb, you can be remarkably slow."

"But—"

"Shut the door, Banner," the princess said. "See that no one listens in."

The Shield guard obliged, though he needed to hold the door closed from the outside because the latch was cracked. Jessamyn had hurled it open so hard she might have been a Muscle herself.

She faced the three of them, her gaze thunderous. "I have

never seen such bumbling in my entire life. *Honestly*, I'm surrounded by incompetents."

"Jessa," Caleb said. "I thought you'd been murdered and replaced. Why did you tell me your Mimic quit?" He looked down at Mica, and his face fell. "Were you trying to avoid me? You could have just said you weren't—"

"No," Mica said. "This isn't about—"

"Mica, is that really you?" her brother interrupted. "You work for the princess herself?"

"Now isn't a good time, Emir," Mica said.

"That's right, Emir," Jessamyn said. "I am not done with your *shipwreck* of a sister. How hard is it to keep a simple secret, Micathea?"

"They were going to run off to Timbral because—"

"I am not deaf," Jessamyn snapped. "I heard it all, as did every other person on that deck. Now Lady Ingrid will be asking why these two thunderheads were so interested in my Impersonator, and why I felt the need to pull them down into my cabin to speak in secret. It will take me *weeks* to recover from this catastrophe even if she *isn't* an imposter. Think if even more nobles had been on deck!"

Caleb threw up his hands, motions blurring slightly. "But why is Mica pretending—?"

"Because of this!"

Jessamyn yanked off her cap and veil, silencing him at once. The full extent of her disfigurement was suddenly illuminated in the light flooding from the porthole. The melted skin, the red patches, the shorn hair.

"Jessa," Caleb said after a moment of shocked stillness. "How?"

"Your darling of an uncle," Jessamyn said. She looked oddly satisfied at the horror on her friend's face. She did love to get a reaction out of people. "He replaced my energy tonic with a particularly nasty poison. We managed to stop it from killing me, but you can see why it was expedient for Micathea to take on the role of imposter."

"Expedient? Jessa, this is grounds to declare war on Timbral and have Ober executed. Why in all the Windfast are you hiding it?"

"That's what *I* keep saying," Mica said.

Jessamyn whirled toward her. "Are you princess here or me? I will not have my decisions questioned, especially after you've made such a mess of things."

"I'm sure you have your reasons not to announce it at court," Caleb said. "But why didn't you tell *me*?"

"Caleb," Jessamyn began. "You are my dearest friend."

"Am I?" Caleb looked between her and Mica. "I trusted you—both of you—with my own secret. And you couldn't do the same?"

"The situation is delicate," Jessamyn said.

"I know a thing or two about delicate situations."

Suddenly, a knock sounded at the door. "We are about to make landfall in Pegasus Island, my princess," Banner called through the door. "Shall I tell the captain to wait?"

"No, I'll be right out." Jessamyn's eyes were still on Caleb. "Are we going to have a problem?"

"Are you asking me if I'll betray you?" Caleb said. "Don't answer that. Of course your secret is safe. May you thrive." And he strode out of the cabin without looking at either of them.

Mica watched his slumped shoulders disappear down the corridor, wishing she could say something to justify the way they'd betrayed his trust. The man had experienced more than his fair share of betrayal lately. She could only hope no permanent damage had been done between them.

"Well, Micathea?" Jessamyn clapped her hands, making Mica jump. "Don't you need to prepare for your reception?"

"Yes, Princess." Mica quickly resumed Jessamyn's face and

reached for the outfit the princess had set out for their arrival in Pegasus.

Emir was still staring at her. "You're really Mica acting as the Princess of Windfast? All the time?"

"Please don't tell anyone," Mica said. "We can talk about it later."

"I won't." Suddenly, Emir blurred forward and gathered her up in a hug. "It's good to see you, Mica."

She pressed her face into his shoulder, inhaling the earthy, leathery smell of home. "You too."

"They are waiting, Micathea," Jessamyn said.

Emir set her back on her feet, and he was out the door before the princess could yell at them again.

CHAPTER TEN

Pegasus Island was a rolling green land. Grassy pastures covered the hills as far as the eye could see, stretching all the way down to the water's edge. White and gray sheep dotted the landscape, grazing on the tough sea grasses or being chased by black sheepdogs across the verdant hills.

The hills eventually gave way to a vast river. The delta broke up most of the southern coastline, with stretches of pungent marshland spreading between the river's branches. West of the delta lay a sprawling city known as Carrow. The settlement had been the capital of Pegasus before the island kingdom joined with Amber, Winnow, Silverfell, and the smaller islands surrounding them to form the Windfast Empire.

Carrow was a city of thatched-roof houses and wooden towers. Many of the structures were built into the hills, making them blend in with the landscape. The air smelled of musk and fresh-cut grass, and it was noticeably cooler than in the Jewel Harbor.

Mica was in good spirits as she prepared to disembark in this gentle green land. Now that Caleb and Emir knew the truth, she felt certain she was almost finished with the imposter charade.

Jessamyn would realize it wasn't so bad for people to see her true face, and Mica would be free. They still had to catch the imposter Lord Ober had placed among her traveling companions, but it would be easier with Caleb and Emir's help.

Mica grinned at the nobles assembled around her on deck, dressed in their finest, warmest clothes. The fake couldn't hide for much longer.

Ingrid was looking at Mica curiously, only half listening to Elana whispering in her ear. She clearly hadn't forgotten the odd exchange she'd witnessed. Wendel stood on her toes at the railing, as if she wanted to leap overboard to get home sooner. Dolan was reviewing a piece of parchment that appeared to be a list of merchant contacts based in Carrow. Fritz was looking around, possibly searching for Caleb, who had retreated to his cabin instead of coming out on deck. And Riven was gazing at Lady Ingrid.

Interesting. None of them paid any attention to "Myn Irondier" at the princess's side, which was all that mattered right now.

The *Silk Goddess* moored alongside a roughhewn dock, where a small welcoming party awaited the visitors from the capital. Pegasus Islanders crowded the waterfront, eager to get a glimpse of the future empress. The murmur of their voices mingled with the lowing of cattle and the sigh of the wind over the hills. Everyone was dressed in wool, giving the place a cozy, intimate feeling that was welcome after the opulent silks and jewels that had surrounded Mica for the past few months.

Captain Pol barked the final orders, and the sailors let down the gangway. The nobles disembarked one by one, all a little unsteady after a week at sea. They paused to regain their balance as the welcoming party approached.

The lord governor of Pegasus, Lady Wendel's uncle Gordon, was the first to greet them. He was a robust man with a red face, jowls, and thick black hair.

"Princess Jessamyn! So good to see you again!" He pumped

Mica's hand up and down so hard her teeth rattled. His jolly manner more closely resembled that of a country innkeeper than a direct descendant of the ancient Pegasus kings. "It has been too long since you last graced our shores."

"Thank you, my lord," Mica said. "I am *ever* so pleased to be back."

"It's a shame your imperial father couldn't make it. He enjoyed our locally brewed ale a great deal on his last visit."

"He sends his regards," Mica said, trying to picture the grave Emperor Styl drinking ale with this ebullient man. "He was sorry not to see you at the anniversary ball."

"Alas, I couldn't leave in the midst of shearing season, but I hope my niece represented us well."

Lord Gordon gave Wendel an affectionate squeeze around the shoulders, and she beamed at him. Mica sincerely hoped this wasn't an imposter faking such a warm homecoming.

"Lady Wendel is a delight to have at court."

"That is good to . . ." Lord Gordon trailed off as the HIMS *Arrow* sailed up to the mooring beside the *Silk Goddess*. The galleon looked even bigger from the docks, dwarfing the other ships in Carrow's small harbor.

"Our escort," Mica explained. "Captain Karson wishes to resupply in Carrow before heading out to scout the Northern Channel ahead of the next stage of our voyage."

"A wise decision," Lord Gordon said, though he didn't look especially happy to have a warship in his harbor. "We have had reports of unusual activity in the Channel."

Mica and Jessamyn exchanged glances.

"What kind of unusual activity?"

"There will be time to discuss it over supper. Come along." Lord Gordon swept his arms wide to take in the entire party. "We have prepared a roast to welcome you to our hall. Join us to break bread and drink ale!"

"Break bread and drink ale!" Wendel echoed.

The other members of the welcoming party, many of them sharing Wendel's dark hair and height, repeated the call as they surged forward to greet their guests.

"Break bread and drink ale!"

The group strolled from the dock to a broad, grassy avenue leading into the middle of the sprawling city. Faces gathered at the windows of the earthen dwellings to watch them pass. Though interested in the princess's arrival, the people seemed less frantic and excitable than in Jewel Harbor. Mica already felt more at home here, despite the hints of trouble to come. She walked alongside Lady Wendel, while Lord Gordon fell back to chat with the lords. He congratulated Fritz on his upcoming wedding with a hearty thump on the back. Dolan hovered on his other side, eager to begin discussing his business interests in Carrow. Ingrid and Elana followed more slowly, as if they couldn't bear to part with the luxurious ship. Elana's sharp nose wrinkled, and she whispered something about the stench of sheep. Ingrid snickered in response.

Wendel ignored their derision, extolling the virtues of Pegasus wool as they continued through the city on foot.

"Pegasus wool is softer than any other variety. We treat it with potions to keep it from being too scratchy."

"Is that right?" Mica was pretty sure Jessamyn knew all this information already, but that didn't dissuade Lady Wendel from promoting her home's primary export.

"Yes, my princess. Pegasus wool blankets are a must for every manor house and cold palace hall. We dye the wool to be—"

"Wendel!"

Mica breathed a sigh of relief as the tall noblewoman's recitation was interrupted. A man galloped toward them on a fine black stallion, onlookers parting before him like sheep. The Shield guards stepped forward as the stranger charged, but they fell back at a word from Lord Gordon.

"My oldest son and heir," he said, a note of pride creeping into his voice. "Making an entrance as usual."

"Late as usual," Wendel said.

The newcomer pulled up just short of the group, his horse's hooves kicking up dirt and clumps of grass. He vaulted off the horse and joined them in a few long strides, immediately sweeping his cousin into a hug. He was one of the tallest men Mica had ever seen, making even Lady Wendel look petite. He had long black hair pulled back in a tail, rugged features, and a deep tan. He wore simple woolen clothes that wouldn't be out of place in a country inn.

"Aren, you smell like a barn," Wendel said.

"Why thank you, cousin. But I hear you've broken your nose. Are you sure my stench is that bad?"

"Oh, be nice." Lady Wendel smacked him on the shoulder with one hand, trying to hide her newly crooked nose with the other.

Aren let out a laugh as broad and rolling as the hills around the city. "It suits you, Wenny. You shouldn't hide a good battle scar."

Mica stared. The lord and lady were acting like her soldier brothers. What happened to all the pomp of the nobility?

"You could have been on time to greet us, you know," Wendel said as she dragged her cousin over to meet her traveling companions.

"I watched you sail in from the hilltop," Lord Aren said. "That's a mighty fancy ship."

"What do you know of ships?" Wendel said. "You haven't sailed in a decade."

"Why would I want to do that? Even the finest ship is no match for a good horse."

Lord Aren winked at Lady Wendel and turned to the rest of the nobles. "Welcome to Pegasus! Thank you for bringing my prodigal cousin home."

He greeted everyone with hearty handshakes much like his father's. As he made his way through the group, Mica distinctly heard Elana whisper to Ingrid, "He can bring *me* home anytime."

The ladies were entranced, and Mica could see the appeal. Aren had a vigorous, outdoorsy manner, with just a hint of refinement that suggested he wouldn't embarrass himself at the imperial court. As Aren clasped Lady Ingrid's hand warmly, Lord Riven gave him a particularly cold and calculating glare.

Is that jealousy? Very interesting. Mica turned to catch Jessamyn's eye and was surprised to see the princess staring intently at Lord Aren, her expression perplexed and maybe a little repulsed. Mica wondered if she was remembering when Aren had chased her into a pile of sheep dung.

Against all convention, the tall lord greeted Mica last. He looked down at her with a twinkle in his eye before sweeping into an elegant courtly bow.

"It's a pleasure to see you thrive, Your Imperial Majesty. You will see I haven't forgotten the bow you made me perfect on your last visit."

The real Jessamyn snorted softly. Mica wasn't sure what to make of that, so she simply acknowledged the young lord with a regal nod.

"Thank you for your kind welcome, Lord Aren."

Aren's smile faded, as if that wasn't the response he was expecting from the princess. Mica wondered if she should have said something more playful or biting. Jessamyn hadn't filled her in on whatever history she had with Wendel's cousin. Come to think of it, the princess had been decidedly vague about the man when she was educating Mica about the people she would meet in Carrow.

"Make haste, friends," Lord Gordon called out over the babble surrounding his son. "The roast will get cold!"

They followed Wendel's uncle to a large manor built into a grassy hill in the heart of Carrow. The smell of roast lamb and wood smoke welcomed them into the earthen hall. A fire was burning in the huge stone hearth at one end, and a wooden banquet table stretched most of its length. Wool blankets and cushions spread across the benches around it, many of them filled with more members of Lord Gordon's sprawling family. They rose to greet the guests, calling out that it was time to "Break bread and drink ale!"

The food and warmth quickly overcame any reservations the nobles had about the rough setting. Soon, even Lord Riven was knocking back hefty portions of ale and digging in to the hearty country fare. Lord Dolan proposed trade deals left and right, apparently desperate to make this trip worthwhile now that the princess had stopped responding to his amorous advances. If he wasn't going to be her consort by the end of this voyage, at least he would be richer.

Caleb still hadn't joined them as the feast got underway. He must have had to lie down after that brief burst of Muscle strength during the tussle in the princess's cabin. Mica had been surprised at his strong reaction, however unintentional, and it made her uneasy. The way he'd pushed her against the bulkhead wasn't like the calm, easygoing young man she knew, and she couldn't help thinking about the hints of madness that appeared in others with multiple Talents. Surely that particular side effect of Ober's potion would have manifested by now if it was going to at all.

He was just alarmed. He's perfectly sane.

She pushed aside her worries about Caleb and focused on Lord Gordon and Lord Aren, who sat on either side of her. The mood at the banquet table was becoming increasingly merry, but Mica had business to discuss. As soon as a suitable number of pleasantries had been exchanged, she addressed her host.

"Tell me more of the activity in the Northern Channel, my lord."

"Ah. Yes." Lord Gordon lifted his ale tankard for a refill from the single servant casually lurking by the earthen wall. "We have always dealt with piracy in the Channel, but attacks at sea have grown more frequent of late."

"My scouts have reported the same thing."

"We are still trying to find out why it's getting worse," Lord Gordon said.

Lord Aren leaned in on her other side. "We think rebels from the Twins could be raiding the ships."

Mica arched an eyebrow. "Rebel pirates?"

"Now, son," Lord Gordon said, "we don't know for certain—"

"I think the insurgents in Dwindlemire and Cray are snatching up supplies. They could be preparing for an all-out war," Lord Aren said. His face became animated, and anger tinged his voice. "They're financing their secession from the empire by stealing from loyal imperial subjects."

Lord Gordon set down his tankard with a thump. "Let's not trouble the princess with talk of secession."

"I've already heard the secession rumors, my lord," Mica said. "I have come to address the people's concerns and prevent any further violence."

"It may be too late for diplomacy."

"We have to try," Mica said. "The Obsidian King *will* take advantage of our divisions if we fight amongst ourselves."

"I won't argue with that," Lord Gordon said. "However, I fear for your safety in the Northern Channel, my princess. I believe it would be wiser for you to return to the capital."

"I can't turn back," Mica said. "It's my duty to defend the empire against *any* threats, even those from within."

"Princess Jessamyn," Aren said, a hint of respect entering his voice. "Have you brought that warship to put down the rebellion yourself?"

"I hope it will not come to that," Mica said evenly.

Lord Gordon frowned. "If something were to happen to you—"

"The finest Talents in the Windfast are protecting me." Mica glanced over to where Emir was keeping watch by the hall doors, then she put a reassuring hand on the older lord's arm. "I may still have a chance to resolve the problems in the Twins, Lord Gordon."

He sighed heavily. "I hope you are right, my princess."

"If anyone can charm them," Lord Aren said, "I reckon you can."

"You are too kind, my—" She turned back to him just in time to see him lean in and steal a piece of bread off her plate. She stared at him, stunned at his brazenness. He winked.

"You were saying, Princess?"

"I—" Mica shifted in her seat, a bit flustered. Aren looked at her blandly, chewing on her bread.

He and Jessamyn had to have some kind of history. *Not even Caleb would tease her like that.*

"I will need all the information you can give me on these piracy incidents," Mica said, gathering her thoughts at last. "Captain Karson of the HIMS *Arrow* is scouting ahead as well."

"I will have reports drawn up." Lord Gordon raised his tankard of ale to her. "I must say, I admire your bravery."

"Princess Jessamyn isn't afraid of anything," Aren said. Then he whispered under his breath, "Except maybe sheep dung."

Mica suppressed a chuckle, and Aren grinned, seeming delighted that she responded to the reference with mirth. The real Jessamyn probably didn't look on the memory so fondly.

The princess herself wasn't within earshot of their conversation. She had been seated far down the table, making it difficult to consult her. In the Silver Palace, she would have hovered behind Mica's chair, as Mica had done in various servant guises for her, dropping hints of important information wherever necessary. Lord Gordon's hall was too informal for such an arrangement, leaving Mica to make decisions on Jessamyn's behalf. She was becoming used to the responsibility.

The seating arrangements also meant Mica couldn't seek the princess's approval when Lord Aren invited her to go for an outing in the country the following day.

"It will be a hard ride, lacking in creature comforts, but the views will be well worth the inconvenience."

"I'd love to go," Mica said. "I'm eager to see more of the countryside and meet the fine men and women of Pegasus." Jessamyn might focus on charming the local nobility, but Mica figured she could spend time getting to know the commoners too. And she wanted to discover more about the dynamic between Jessamyn and Aren.

"I think it's a fine idea," Lord Gordon said. "That ought to give your Captain Karson enough time to scout the Channel."

"It's settled then." Lord Aren raised a tankard of ale to his lips and paused, studying her over the rim. "You seem different, Princess. We might become friends yet."

Later, when she and Jessamyn retired for the evening, Mica relayed all the conversations she'd had at dinner. They were in a cozy, candlelit guestroom with a large bed piled high with sheepskin pelts. Jessamyn had already claimed the bed for herself, and Mica would sleep in the adjacent servant's room.

Jessamyn reclined on the bed with her legs covered in pelts and wool blankets and dissected every detail of Mica's report. "You don't know what you've gotten us into," she said when she heard about the plan to go riding in the country. "This won't be a simple turn about the pasture."

"You could skip it, you know," Mica said. "I'm sure I won't mess up too badly if I go riding without you. Why don't you take it easy?"

"Ha! Oh, you're serious? No, Micathea, I cannot allow that. Gordon and Aren may act like simple country lords, but they are incredibly powerful, and they have astute political instincts. You should see the instructions Gordon sends Wendel at court to make sure she's making the most of her time there. They know what they are doing."

"You're saying the warmth is an act?"

"No, that's genuine. But there is more going on beneath this sweet, pastoral surface."

Mica considered this as she combed her dark-red hair, sitting on a stool at the princess's feet. She was growing tired of the duplicity. Could no one be simple and uncalculating anymore? "Maybe it's best I don't keep trying to represent you then. Isn't it time you resumed your position?"

"Mica."

"I'm serious. Telling Caleb wasn't so bad, right?"

Jessamyn snorted. "Did I miss the part where he celebrated my condition in between staring in horror and bolting from the cabin?"

"Okay, I guess it was pretty bad. But that's only because you didn't trust him."

"Perhaps." Jessamyn twisted her veil, wringing the silk with her discolored hands. "Caleb understands my actions better than most. He'll come to see the wisdom of this scheme. I can't say the same for everyone else."

"I don't see why everything has to be a scheme," Mica said. "If you would just tell the truth—"

"Truth is a tool," Jessamyn said. "I have told you again and again that I will reveal it when the time is right."

"I don't believe you anymore," Mica blurted out. "I think you're afraid of what people will think of you now that you're not beautiful anymore, and you're using this secret plan as an excuse to keep hiding."

"Are you finished?" Jessamyn's soft tone might have had Mica cowering a few months ago, but she knew better now. The princess had learned that scary, quiet voice from the emperor.

The more Mica saw the seams in her façade, the less frightening she became.

"No, I'm not." Mica stood and tossed the comb onto the stool with a thud. "Have *you* thought that maybe the rebels in the Twins have a point about the nobles in Jewel Harbor? It's all complicated strategies and subterfuge. You've wrapped yourself up in so many lies that you don't know who you really are, and no one else does either."

"You are treading on dangerous ground, Micathea Graydier."

"Oh yeah? Well, I'm willing to take a few steps further. In fact, maybe I'll just walk away and see how you fare when you have to face the world in your own flawed skin. It might be the greatest service to the empire I could perform."

Fear flickered in Jessamyn's eyes for the first time, and her veil crumpled in her hands. "You can't leave."

"I have to eventually," Mica said. "Someone needs to stop Lord Ober."

"And how do you expect to do that?"

"Well, I need to find his barren fortress. I have a few leads already."

Jessamyn raised a scarred eyebrow. "And then?"

"And then . . . Well then . . . I guess I'd—"

"Stab him with the knife you keep under your skirt? After you sneak into this fortress where he may or may not be hiding? Or maybe you could try giving him a self-righteous lecture about being true to himself."

"I'll gather intelligence," Mica said. *How had the princess managed to turn this back on her again?* "I trained to be a spy, remember?"

"So you'll use your spy powers to find him, analyze his defenses, and then storm the fortress with . . . what army?"

"I . . . Well . . . Captain Karson—"

"Answers to me," Jessamyn said. "That fine ship of his is under *my* authority, not yours. You need me just as much as I need you. I will take your advice under consideration, but you are not going anywhere."

Mica and Jessamyn stared at each other, the candlelight flickering in their matching eyes. Mica looked more like Jessamyn now than Jessamyn herself, but it was easy to forget that she was actually nobody, and the princess held all the power.

Of course, few people knew that. It occurred to Mica for a single, transparent moment that if she really wanted that power, all she had to do was take it. She could supplant the princess, take Caleb as her consort, and have all the might of the Imperial Army at her disposal.

"I know what you're thinking," Jessamyn said softly. "I can read you like a book, Micathea. I'm surprised it has taken you this long to consider taking my place for good."

"I am no traitor."

"I didn't think you were. But know this: we have the same goals. It may seem we are not aligned, but if you trust me, we will both get what we want in the end."

Mica stared at the princess. Did she trust her? Her good intentions maybe, but she trusted her judgment less each day. But they were still heading in the same direction—at least for now.

"I'll do what's right for the empire," she said at last.

"Good." Jessamyn waved her veil at Mica. "Now, Pegasus ale makes me rather drowsy. Run along, unless you have anything else to add."

"No, I don't think—Oh, what's the story with you and Lord Aren?"

"Story?"

"You didn't fill me in on your history, but he seems to like you. If he is as powerful as you say, could he be a good choice for your consort?"

Jessamyn stared at her in shocked silence. Then her answer came in a flurry. "Don't be ridiculous, Micathea. You'd better get your beauty sleep. Goodnight." And she yanked a wool blanket up to her chin and rolled over with her back to the room.

Now I know *there's something between them.* In all their months together, the princess had never once wished Mica goodnight.

Mica burrowed beneath her own blankets in the servant's room, but sleep was slow to come. Jessamyn was right. They needed each other if they were going to accomplish either of their goals. Still, she wondered what would happen when their paths diverged. And she couldn't help imagining what it would be like if she were the one making all the decisions.

CHAPTER ELEVEN

Lord Aren followed through on his offer to take the visiting dignitaries riding in the countryside the following morning.

"I have it all planned," he announced over a hearty breakfast of fried eggs and mutton porridge. "I shall lend you my gentlest horse, Your Highness. She will keep you safe."

"I'm not afraid of horses, my lord," Mica said. "I can handle any mount as well as you."

Lord Aren grinned. "Things *have* changed."

Mica raised an eyebrow, and Jessamyn carefully avoided her gaze. So there was another weakness she refused to reveal. Mica had seen Jessamyn ride many times, but she had never let on that her skill hadn't come easily.

"Who else would like to accompany us?" Aren asked. "The country air will do you good."

"I'll join you," Caleb said. He had appeared for breakfast looking somewhat the worse for wear and taken the farthest seat from Mica and Jessamyn at the breakfast table. Lady Wendel had spent the morning plying him with healthy Pegasus tea. "I could use the fresh air."

"How about you, ladies?" Aren asked.

Elana and Ingrid practically fell over themselves to decline the invitation.

"We need rest after the difficult sea voyage," said Lady Elana.

"I'm sure we'll get plenty of fresh air right here in Carrow, thank you very much," said Lady Ingrid.

"I will stay behind as well," Lord Riven said with a glance at Lady Ingrid. She smoothed back her dark hair, a blush creeping across her severe features.

Lord Dolan muttered something about meeting with his merchant contacts, and Fritz wanted to search Carrow's famous handicraft market for a gift for his bride. In the end, only Caleb and Wendel joined Mica and Aren when they departed Lord Gordon's hall. Well, them and two dozen servants and guards to make sure they weren't endangered on their journey—or inconvenienced in any way. Jessamyn would be riding among the guards and baggage, with Banner and Emir protecting her.

The sky was cloudy, resting upon the hilltops like a pile of Pegasus wool. The cold lingered on the border between refreshing and uncomfortable, but it was sure to warm up throughout the day. Mica wore a thick woolen cloak that Lord Gordon had presented to her that morning, and Jessamyn had wrapped the matching scarf around her head like an enormous, fluffy cowl.

They followed the river inland, heading north from Carrow, and the green countryside swallowed them up. The denser settlement gave way to farmhouses and fields, dotted liberally with sheep, and the occasional sleepy village. The grassy Pegasus landscape was tamer than the rock-strewn region around Stonefoss, where the farmers had to fight for every sprout and bloom. The air smelled of sheep musk, manure, and fresh-turned earth, with just a hint of the sea.

At Lord Aren's request, they stopped at villages along their way to speak with the farmers and shepherds. Aren knew many of the shepherds by name, and his rugged features were right at home among their sun-darkened noses and weathered cheeks. Many of the men also sported the same long hair tied back in a tail.

The local children were thrilled to meet a princess. They gave Mica little gifts of pretty stones, drawings on rough parchment, and handmade dolls. She did her best to be as charming as Jessamyn would have been. Aren was almost as popular with the children as she was. He hoisted them into the air on his broad shoulders and let them tie winter flowers in his hair. Mica admired the way he interacted with the commoners, and she was glad Elana, Ingrid, and Riven were not there to scoff.

"Please excuse their humble circumstances," Lady Wendel said as they waved farewell to a thin-faced family outside a rundown hovel. "We experienced a plague several years ago. The sheep population was reduced by more than half."

"Those were hard times," Lord Aren said. "Many good folks suffered."

"Production has bounced back better than ever, though, thanks to a subsidization program Aren designed," Wendel said.

"I'd love to know more about this program," Mica said.

Aren reined his stallion closer to her. "That's not the sort of thing that would have interested you in the past, Princess."

"A leader should care for the needs of their humblest subjects," Mica said. "It's my responsibility to make sure *all* imperial subjects prosper."

Aren gave her an appraising look. "I couldn't agree more."

Mica could feel Jessamyn's gaze on her back. She couldn't tell if she approved of the conversation. But the princess listened as Aren described the work he'd been doing to help the shepherds get back on their feet, and she even paused to speak with the next group they passed, shaking hands with the shepherds without flinching at the dirt on their skin.

They rode deeper into the countryside, the lords and ladies

mingling freely with the guards and servants in a loose group. Caleb hung back from the rest, more subdued than usual. His head nodded occasionally, and Stievson rode beside him, ready to catch him if he toppled from the saddle.

Mica pulled up her horse, ostensibly to watch a pair of lambs frolicking beside the road, and leaned in to speak with him.

"Are you all right?"

Caleb rubbed a square hand over his face. "Could have used another few hours of sleep, but I'll pull through."

"The Talent again?"

"Afraid so."

Mica frowned. "You should have stayed in Carrow."

"Banner told me about the imposter," Caleb said. "A ride into the wilderness would be the perfect time for them to strike."

"Most of the nobles aren't even with us."

"They could have set a trap." Caleb gestured at the countryside, where sheep and cattle grazed on dandelions beneath billowing clouds. The gently rolling hills didn't look as though they could hide an ambush, but Caleb surveyed them as if they were battle trenches.

"She's at risk without proper protection," he said. "Everyone in this party would move to protect you instead of her."

"That would be unfortunate," Mica said, her voice flat.

"That's not what I—"

"It's all right. I get it. Look, four of us know who she really is. You, me, Banner, and my brother. We'll look out for her. Besides, any attackers would kill me first."

"That's no good either," Caleb said. "I'd never forgive myself if you were hurt. Either of you." His voice became heated. "My uncle almost killed her already, and I had no idea."

"You couldn't have done anything." Mica wanted to reach out and touch him, even just to rest a hand on his arm, but there were too many people around. "Are you still mad at us?"

"No." Caleb sighed. "But Jessamyn needs help, Mica. She shouldn't be playing this game alone."

"I agree," Mica said. "I've been trying to talk her into revealing what happened."

"Have you thought of quitting? Your presence is enabling her. If you could influence her to—"

"I'm her servant, not her friend."

"You know that's not completely true," Caleb said. "You care about each other. And she trusts you. Otherwise, she would never let you speak for her so often."

Mica recalled the brief moment the night before when it had occurred to her that she could take over as Jessamyn in truth. She had been making decisions without consulting the real princess more and more often. But the arrangement had to end eventually. And Jessamyn *was* her friend.

"I intend to keep her trust," Mica said. "Anyway, this is getting me closer to Lord Ober. I want to find the barren fortress where he's hurting Talents."

Caleb looked up, a bright spark of inquisitiveness igniting in his eyes. "I've been thinking about that too! I have a theory based on what Haddell—wait, I've been talking to you about that all along, haven't I?" He rubbed a hand through his wind-tousled hair. "It feels like we have a lot of catching up to do, but I guess that isn't true."

"We *have* gone over a bunch of theories together already," Mica said. "But I've missed talking to you. As myself, I mean."

"Really?"

"Really."

A profound sense of relief and wellbeing was flooding through Mica as she talked honestly with Caleb for the first time in months. It was a little like coming home.

Just then, Jessamyn turned in her saddle. Her veil hid her expression, but Mica got the sense that she didn't approve of Mica and Caleb leaning in close to whisper to each other, regardless of which face she wore. The princess was too far ahead to hear their conversation, but Mica lowered her voice anyway.

"If you leave to search for Ober, I want to go with you," Mica said. "We can find the barren fortress together."

Caleb met her gaze, and she swore his eyes darted to her mouth for a moment. Her heart gave an unruly tremor.

"I would love your help," he said. "But I can't just take you away. Jessamyn needs you, maybe in different ways than she thinks."

They looked up at Jessamyn in unison. She faced forward again, sitting her horse like royalty, despite her disfigured face and simple clothes. It still amazed Mica that no one had noticed the new cultural advisor's resemblance to the princess.

"Jessamyn wants to stop Ober too," Mica said, "but she and the emperor are more worried about the unrest in the Twins. Even after what Ober did to her, she thinks he's not the biggest threat right now."

"And you disagree?"

"I do. Imagine what would happen if Ober perfected his potion and gave it to our enemies. In the long run, the ability to create unstoppable Talents is a greater threat than any single enemy—and that's not even taking his methods into account." She clutched her reins tight, her voice becoming fierce. "We have to make Ober pay for what he's done."

"There's the Mica I know." Caleb grinned, and this time she was sure he looked at her mouth. "I missed having you around."

Mica flushed, but before she could answer, Lord Aren interrupted them with a shout.

"Hurry, friends!" He had crested the ridge ahead, and he stood out sharp against the rolling, grayish clouds. "You have to see this view. Princess, won't you join me?"

Caleb touched Mica's hand briefly. "Can we talk later? Just you and me?"

Mica turned her eye color from brown to hazel in a Mimic's

wink, and she was rewarded with a broad smile. Then she spurred her horse forward, galloping up the ridge to join the other lord.

She was the first to reach the top of the hill where Aren waited. The wind was stronger here, and his long ponytail streamed behind him, making him look rather magnificent. He grinned at her as she joined him and swept his arms wide.

"Welcome to Narrow Vale."

Below the ridge spread a breathtaking valley. A thin silver river sliced through the center, and trees clambered in close to the banks on both sides. Mountains rose on the horizon, purple and indigo beneath the cloudy sky. The clouds had begun to look ominous and heavy. A blurry shimmer suggested rain was already falling on the distant mountains.

"It's beautiful," Mica said.

"Not as beautiful as you are."

She looked up at Lord Aren in surprise. She felt elated after talking with Caleb as herself again. All she wanted was to ride at his side and speak to him in her own voice, so it took her a minute to respond to the other man with Jessamyn's cadence.

"My lord, you are ever so sweet," Mica said. "I . . . That is . . ."

"I've never known you to be rattled." Aren sounded pleased that he had elicited such a response. "You never cease to surprise me."

Mica glanced back at the others, wishing they'd hurry up. Wendel appeared to be slowing down deliberately to give her cousin and the princess a moment of privacy. The real Jessamyn watched them closely over her veil. Mica wished the princess had given her more explicit instructions regarding Lord Aren. He certainly seemed interested in her. Was she supposed to encourage him or not?

Then Mica's eyes fell on Caleb, and her heart beat at Blur speed in her chest. Jessamyn deserved a chance to be as happy as Mica was when she looked at him. The princess hadn't explicitly told her *not* to encourage Aren if he attempted to woo her.

Besides, if Jessamyn marries Lord Aren, she can't marry Caleb.

Mica summoned her most attractive smile and batted her eyelashes at Lord Aren. "I think you'll find I have even more surprises in store, my lord."

This time Aren was the one who looked flustered. His stallion pranced beneath him, betraying the effect the smile had on him.

The rest of their party soon joined them on the ridge, where they spent a few minutes exclaiming over the splendor of Narrow Vale. Lord Aren stayed close beside Mica, clearly more enthralled by her—or Jessamyn's—beauty than that of the landscape. She encouraged him with smiles and sultry looks. She hoped she hadn't guessed wrong about the princess's feelings for the robust Pegasus lord, or she might lose her head after all.

They rode into the valley and picnicked beside the river. The servants brought out mutton sandwiches and a barrel of ale and spread wool blankets on the ground so the nobles wouldn't get mud on their fine riding clothes. The servants themselves, Jessamyn included, sat on rocks a little way off, jumping to assist whenever someone called on them.

"You may be used to finer things," Lord Aren said as he passed Mica a tankard of ale. "But we Pegasus folk know how to have a picnic."

They lingered in the vale after they ate their fill of mutton sandwiches. Caleb stretched out on a blanket to take a quick nap, warning Stievson to wake him if they needed to fight off any kidnappers. Mica had to keep pulling her gaze away from his peaceful, sleeping face and reminding herself to pay attention to Lord Aren.

He and Wendel shared stories about their childhood in Pegasus, most of which seemed to involve their friends falling off horses and their mothers shouting at them for leaving wool coats out in the rain. Jessamyn listened with a sort of appalled fascination to his tales of a rough-and-tumble childhood hardly becoming of a noble lord.

So far, so good, Mica thought. She nodded encouragingly at him and asked him to tell her about his favorite horse.

They were in no hurry to end the idyllic picnic, but dark clouds were amassing above the mountains, and the guards kept looking at the sky and murmuring about getting back to Carrow before the storm broke. Aren had become almost giddy as Mica turned the full force of Jessamyn's charm on him, and he declared that no storm would deter him. He insisted on drawing them further into the vale.

"You must see the waterfall, Princess," he said as they mounted their horses and prepared to traverse the rocky ground beside the river. "You won't find another like it anywhere else in the empire."

But even Lord Aren's enthusiasm couldn't keep the storm at bay for good. The clouds broke open with a sudden, intense fury. Rain rolled over the valley in a wild rush, drenching them in a matter of seconds.

"It will pass soon," Aren called through the gusting wind. "Come, we are almost there."

Despite their guide's zeal, everyone else grew increasingly uncomfortable. Their damp clothes chafed their skin, and soreness from the long ride spread through their muscles. The horses tossed their heads and snorted nervously as thunder and lightning joined the rain.

"I told you not to bring us out this far," Lady Wendel grumbled to her cousin when almost an hour had passed with no sign of the waterfall. "This was supposed to be a pleasant ride through the country."

"I'm not afraid of any storm," Aren said. "You have grown soft in the capital, cousin."

But the storm was intensifying rapidly. The rain pelted down on them, and the wind whipped at their clothes and tugged on their hair. Wendel was mortified that her cousin had brought the princess out in such unpleasant conditions.

"He meant well," she said frantically. "We will find shelter soon."

"It's all right, Wendel," Mica said. She glanced at Jessamyn, who was looking grumpy and bedraggled, and suppressed a grin. "A little rain never hurt anyone."

"But it's winter!" Wendel said through chattering teeth. "You'll catch cold."

"I'm perfectly fine," Mica said. "I'm wearing a Pegasus wool cloak. You're the one who looks cold."

Wendel rubbed her crooked nose, which had gone a little blue. "I didn't expect to be out this long."

Just then, Emir reined in on her other side. He removed his oiled uniform jacket with quick hands and held it out to Wendel.

"Take my coat, my lady."

"Oh! Thank you, soldier." Wendel looked at Mica's brother as if she had never seen him before, even though he had been with them since Jewel Harbor. Since she was a noblewoman, it was possible she really hadn't noticed him. But she smiled appreciatively as he helped her wrap the jacket around her shoulders.

For her part, Mica was enjoying the riotous rush of the storm after so long spent wrapped up in silk inside the Silver Palace. She was glad of the wind in her face and the rain in her hair. She caught Caleb's eye and grinned, making her features stretch out of proportion for a brief second. He laughed, and her whole body filled with warmth. She had missed that laugh.

"I think I see the waterfall!" one of the Shield guards called out.

"It's about time," Jessamyn hissed, glaring daggers at Lord Aren's back. "This excursion was a ridiculous idea."

They rode closer to the river, which flowed about five feet below the rocky bank, and the waterfall came into view at last, spilling over a tall cliff and crashing into rapids below. The roar of cascading water was loud enough to drown out the thunder. Mica had never seen a waterfall as large and wild as this.

They dismounted on the bank above the rapids, close enough to feel the spray on their faces.

"We came all the way out here for this?" Jessamyn muttered. "*Honestly.*"

"I thought you liked pretty things," Mica said.

"Pretty indoor things."

"Don't tell me you're afraid of a little water."

Jessamyn spluttered incoherently, and Mica winked at her.

"I'd like a closer look." Mica handed her horse over to a servant and approached the bottom of the falls. Her clothes were soaked anyway, and she wanted to get a little nearer to that tremendous cascade.

"Take care, Princess," Aren called. "The rocks are slippery here."

"I have excellent balance."

"Let me come with you at least."

Aren followed Mica's lead as she picked her way to the ledge beneath the thunderous falls. The rest of the party waited by the rapids with the horses, giving them a little space. Even Jessamyn didn't try to join them.

Mica edged along the ledge and looked up through the shimmering curtain of water. Large droplets fell on her cheeks, running down her face and neck, mingling with the rain. The incredible power of the falls filled her with awe. The storm clouds blocked out much of the light, and she imagined this vale must be even more beautiful on a sunny day.

"Sometimes you can see a rainbow here," Lord Aren said, joining her on the slick ledge. "I'll show you next time you visit me."

"Don't get ahead of yourself, my lord," Mica said, the coy, Jessamyn-like tone coming naturally now. "What makes you think I'll do that?"

"Because you want to see me."

"My lord!"

"I've thought of you often since your last visit, my princess." Lord Aren stepped closer, his gaze steady on her face. "Don't you think about me, away in your Silver Palace?"

Mica looked up at him through Jessamyn's thick eyelashes, which were damp and glistening. "And if I do?"

"I don't wish to play games."

"Games, my lord? I don't know what you're—"

"Please, Jessamyn. I would speak plainly." He took another step toward her. "You have become a fine woman. I can't stand the idea that you're to sail away from me so soon."

Mica blushed at the fervency in his tone. Lord Aren's ardor was unlike anything she'd experienced from Dolan, Riven, and the other lords who had tried to claim Jessamyn's favor.

This man would be great for the princess. Mica saw it clearly. His admiration and respect were sincere, a priceless quality among the nobility. He was enchanted by Jessamyn but not intimidated. He teased her, while treating her with consideration, and they had been friendly in their youth. Most important of all, Jessamyn seemed infuriated and captivated by him in return.

She needs this kind of person in her life.

The least Mica could do was help them along.

She turned away from Aren, pretending to be shy, and undid her braid, allowing her long red hair to cascade down her back and frame her pretty face. She cast an alluring gaze over her shoulder, one she had seen Jessamyn deploy to great effect. Lord Aren cleared his throat, and Mica grinned internally. The princess was going to be *so* mad at her.

"What precisely do you want, my lord?"

For a moment, Aren looked as if he would sweep her into his arms in front of everyone—Caleb and Jessamyn included. Instead he took her hand and kissed it, first on the back then on the palm.

"I want to make you happy, Jessamyn. If you'll let me."

Mica's stomach stirred uncomfortably. The gesture felt too intimate somehow, more intimate than a dramatic smooch.

"And if I want that too?" she said softly. "What then?"

Before Aren could respond, there was an especially loud clap of thunder, followed by a flurry of movement. Several horses in their group spooked, surging in different directions.

Then someone screamed.

Mica and Aren spun around, feet sliding on the ledge, in time to see the real Jessamyn stumbling back from the spooked horses. Her back foot slipped, and she teetered, her veil whipping in the wind. Then she fell into the rapids with a terrible splash.

CHAPTER TWELVE

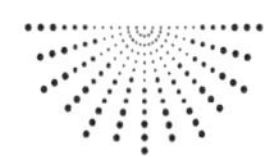

Caleb was the first to act, lunging forward to grab the princess as she fell. But he was still lethargic, and his Blur speed didn't appear. Jessamyn's hand slipped out of his reach as she tumbled into the swift current.

The princess plunged beneath the water then resurfaced, gasping and spluttering, getting farther away by the second. The rough torrent slammed her against the rocks, ignoring her efforts to grab hold of something. A shout escaped Mica's lips, though whether it was in her own voice or another's, she couldn't say.

"Someone help her!"

She sensed movement beside her, then another splash drowned out the cries. Lord Aren had leapt off the ledge and into the river. He swam after the struggling woman, his powerful arms and legs churning. But the distance between them was already too big.

The princess screamed as the water tried to swallow her whole. She tumbled over boulders, losing her cap and veil to the rapids. Mica's chest heaved, as if she were drowning too. For a moment, Jessamyn's features slipped off her face, but the others were too horrified by Myn's plight to notice.

Suddenly, Emir reappeared among them. He had been scouting their perimeter, but he took in the situation in a heartbeat. He blurred into motion, rushing downriver and out of sight.

As the current carried Jessamyn and Aren rapidly downriver, Mica and the others ran after them along the slippery riverbank.

The water is too fast. We can't catch up.

Caleb charged alongside her, moving no faster than a normal man, a look of grim frustration on his face. He'd warned Mica that his powers didn't always turn up when he needed them. Now she knew why that haunted him.

I wish I were a Blur, she thought desperately as she raced through the mud, her feet slipping and sliding, furious that she didn't have the supernatural speed or strength to help her friend.

But Lord Aren, who had no Talents at all, was closing the distance between him and Jessamyn, deftly avoiding the most dangerous rapids as he powered through the raging river. His long hair streamed behind him, flowing like a black snake in the foam.

With a mighty surge, he reached the princess and scooped her up in his arms. Jessamyn curled into him like a half-drowned kitten, her short red hair visible against his dark chest. He held her to him with one hand and used the other to protect them both from the rocks.

They weren't safe yet. The river was a furious beast, stronger than ever thanks to the storm. Aren could barely keep their bodies protected. He couldn't escape the swollen current.

But they had a Blur on their side.

As they raced around a bend in the river, Emir came into view again. He had run downriver until he found a fallen tree sticking out above the swift-moving current, his supernatural speed giving him time to position himself.

He shimmied out onto the log as Jessamyn and Aren approached, borne along by the storm-fed waters.

"Grab my hand!" he called.

Aren kept his wits, despite the battering of the rapids. As he and the princess were carried beneath the jutting log, he thrust a hand up to grab Emir's. They locked hands, fingers white and trembling and slick with river water.

Their grips held.

For a moment, the three of them hung suspended from the log, Emir fighting the pressure of the water, no doubt wishing for Muscle strength. Then he hauled Jessamyn and Aren out of the deadly current.

Free of the river at last, they scrambled along the log toward the riverbank. The rest of the group sprinted toward them, their feet skidding as they reached the bare patch of earth where the tree had fallen. They caught up as Emir helped Aren clamber down off the log, still holding the princess.

Jessamyn kept her arms wrapped tight around Aren's neck until he knelt to set her on the ground beside a mess of muddy roots the fallen tree had pulled from the dirt. He checked her for injuries, his face close to hers, his movements gentle. She gazed back at him, wide brown eyes shining. They breathed in unison, gulping down air.

Mica paused a few paces from them, not wanting to interrupt. She marveled at the tenderness in the big man's actions. Aren didn't seem to notice Jessamyn's disfigurement as he took off his lambskin coat and wrapped it around her shoulders.

He saved her.

Mica's knees shook as she realized how close she had come to losing Jessamyn again.

She could have dr—

A wordless cry sounded behind her, and Mica turned to intercept Banner before he could throw himself at the princess and reveal who she really was.

"She's okay," Mica hissed into his ear. "Remember her name."

"I know." Banner pulled free of her grasp, his usual placid demeanor absent. "Are you all right, Myn?" He dropped down beside Jessamyn and Aren, elbowing the tall lord aside. "I feared the worst."

"I'm just a little banged up." Jessamyn pulled up the collar of Aren's coat to obscure her face as the others gathered closer, anxiously inquiring about their welfare. "No broken bones, as far as I can tell."

"I'll be the judge of that," Banner said.

While the Shield fussed over Jessamyn like an anxious lover, Aren's guards moved in to check on him too. They didn't look at all surprised that their lord had dived into harm's way to save a commoner. They retrieved the picnic blankets from their saddle-bags to wrap around the pair. Both Aren and Jessamyn had some scrapes and bruises, but the cold was the greatest danger now.

The rest of them were nearly as cold and wet, even though they hadn't ended up in the river. Mica wrapped her arms around herself, shivering partly from the chill and partly from relief so intense it made her nauseous. Caleb looked a little green too. He caught Mica's eye, and she saw the shame written on his face. On another day, he might have been able to help Jessamyn as Emir had, but his Talents were unpredictable. This time, they had failed him.

Mica sympathized, but she wished he wouldn't wear his distress so plainly on his face. These people wouldn't understand why Lord Caleb was so worried about one of the princess's retain-ers. Mica wasn't acting quite like she was supposed to either, for that matter.

She turned to her brother. "Thank you for your quick action, Soldier Grayson."

"That's why I'm here," Emir said. "All in a day's work for the Blur Elite."

His steadiness helped Mica regain the concentration she needed for her impersonation. She summoned her Jessamyn voice, in control once more.

"Lord Aren!" she trilled. "You were marvelously brave. You two saved her life."

"Anything for you, my princess," Aren said. "I'm sorry I brought you all so close to danger." He didn't look up at her, too busy watching Banner help Jessamyn to her feet. The princess gave him a lopsided smile.

At that moment, Lady Wendel hurtled into their midst, her chest heaving and her hair wild around her face.

"Find us shelter, or take us home at once, Aren, before someone gets killed." Her tone indicated *she* might kill Aren for bringing them out in the storm. She had taken a tumble in her rush to catch up, and mud covered every inch of her body. Emir blurred to her side and offered his arm. She clung to him gratefully, smearing his shirt with mud.

Aren knew better than to argue with his cousin. "There is a dry cave not far from here."

They set out to retrieve their scattered horses, the guards and servants chattering animatedly about the incident. Mica still felt a little raw at what had almost happened. She might be tempted to make Jessamyn's decisions sometimes, but she had no desire to take her place permanently.

She seized her chance to talk to Jessamyn after they found the last of the horses and set off into the forest. The princess had lost her wool scarf in the river. She still wore Aren's lambskin coat with the collar turned up, but she was shaking like a scared puppy.

"Are you okay?" Mica said when she was sure no one could hear them. "I was so afraid you—"

"Of course I'm all right, Micathea," Jessamyn said through chattering teeth. "Do you think I'm that clumsy? I knew someone would save me."

"Huh?"

"I appreciate your enthusiasm for courting on my behalf,"

Jessamyn said. "But you needn't lure them in for romantic moments beneath every waterfall you see."

"You . . . you didn't jump in the river to stop him from kissing me, did you?"

"I have no idea what you're talking about," Jessamyn said airily. She flashed a triumphant grin over the collar of her borrowed coat. "I didn't expect him to leap in to save me himself. I must say he *has* fleshed out nicely since I last saw him."

She urged her horse ahead, a satisfied smile playing on her blue-tinged lips.

Mica stared after her, wondering if the poison had addled her brain as well as her face. She couldn't be serious. Jessamyn might be conniving, but even she wouldn't go that far.

Still, the princess had far too little regard for her own health and safety. That worried Mica.

On the other hand, Jessamyn must be more drawn to Lord Aren than she admitted. She had never objected to Mica engaging in romantic moments with any of the *other* lords who had courted her.

Maybe Jessamyn can have one thing she really wants when all this is over.

They left the river behind and rode beneath a dripping canopy. It was growing dark, except for the lightning forking through the clouds above the forest. Thunder shook the trees, and the smell of damp wool and horseflesh surrounded them. They were all soaked and bedraggled, and the sudden brush with disaster had left everyone with ragged nerves.

Tempers ran thin by the time they reached the mouth of a dark cave set into a tree-covered hillside.

"We can wait here until the storm passes," Lord Aren called. "This cave is used as a hunting lodge. There should be dry wood for a fire inside."

The servants cared for the horses and baggage while the nobles hurried toward the cave. Jessamyn got caught in the shuffle of activity around the horses, and one of the Pegasus guards barked at her to make herself useful. Her eyes flashed angrily, and she turned to give the man a piece of her mind. It was difficult to hear her tirade over the rumble of the storm, and the guard simply shoved a leftover bundle of food into her hands and told her to get to work.

Caleb paused to whisper in Mica's ear. "I can't believe I didn't realize it was you. You don't complain nearly as much as Her Imperial Highness."

"A little grunt work will be good for her," Mica said.

"She'll probably toss all our provisions in the river, just to spite us."

Mica grinned up at him, feeling slightly giddy in the aftermath of everything that had happened today. Caleb smiled back, and for a brief moment, she imagined the way he had kissed her after the fight in the warehouse, as if it were a promise of things to come. His face grew serious, as though he sensed where her thoughts had turned, and he reached out to touch her hand.

Lord Aren appeared suddenly between them. "Allow me to escort you inside, Princess." Aren was taller than Caleb, and he paid the other lord no mind as he claimed the princess's attention.

"Thank you, my lord." Mica took Aren's arm, wincing at the disappointed expression flitting across Caleb's face. Before she could say anything to him, Aren whisked her into the darkened cavern.

The cavern was dry and spacious, with a dirt floor packed down through regular use. The servants built a fire in a pit in the center, and they shared the last of the mutton sandwiches and ale as the thunder rumbled outside. Nobles and servants alike huddled together, with calls to "Break bread and drink ale!"

Aren sat beside Mica and regaled her with more tales of Pegasus Island life as they waited for the rain to stop. Mica wondered where he and Jessamyn would live if they got married. It was hard to picture the tall, rugged lord in the opulent halls of the Silver Palace. The princess was sure to be bored stiff at Lord Aren's country estate, though.

It's probably too soon to be planning her life with Aren. She could still choose Caleb.

Caleb and Jessamyn sat side by side now, talking quietly and occasionally laughing. It had been months since the two friends spent any time together. Caleb might have been upset that she didn't tell him the truth, but it looked as though they had patched things up in the face of her near-death experience.

Mica tried to ignore the pair, returning her attention to her hosts.

"I hope we'll have time to visit my parents' estate," Lady Wendel was saying. "We own the finest pastures on the island."

"If the weather keeps up like this, I don't think the journey would be wise," Lord Aren said.

"Oh, now you want to be wise?" Wendel shook her head and leaned closer to Mica. "My cousin can be remarkably selfish sometimes." There was no bite in Wendel's words. She seemed to have forgiven Aren for the disastrous expedition to the waterfall now that they had a warm fire crackling between them.

"Remind me where your parents' estate is, Lady Wendel," Mica said.

"Greenfield Bay, on the western side of Pegasus," Wendel said. "There's a small port on the bay, primarily used for trade with Timbral. We export our sturdiest wool for their famous carpets, and they send us wine in return."

"I'd wager the princess knows all this," Aren said. "Princess Jessamyn knows more about the empire than anyone else I've ever met. Remember when you visited as a young girl, and I would quiz you on facts about the empire?"

Mica blanched. "Why yes, wasn't that a fun game? I must get some fresh air."

She leapt up before he could start testing her imperial knowledge. She had learned a lot over the past few months, but Jessamyn's education was unmatched.

"Allow me to accomp—"

"No need, Lord Aren. Soldier Grayson can keep me safe for a few steps."

Mica caught her brother's eye, and he was at her side in an instant.

"Yes, my princess."

"We won't be a minute," Mica said.

She strode to the cavern entrance, down the sloping floor that kept the rainwater from creeping inside. Her brother stayed a few steps behind her until they neared the curtain of rain falling outside, its noisy patter obscuring the sound of their footsteps.

Mica's shoulders relaxed as soon as they were out of earshot of the others. She dropped down to sit on a rock, not bothering with a ladylike posture for once.

"I've got to say, Mica," Emir said as he sat beside her, "I never knew you were such a good actress."

Mica snorted. "Sure."

"I'm serious. You're really good."

Emir stretched his boots out in front of them, and Mica imagined they were sitting in front of the fire in their parents' house instead of watching the rain drench a foreign landscape.

"Getting the face right helps," Mica said. "People accept mistakes and erratic behavior as long as they don't suspect an Impersonator. The instant the suspicion enters their minds, it's all over."

"You and the princess seem to have a strong bond."

"We do," Mica said slowly. "She saved my life, and I . . . well, I'm trying to do my best to repay her."

She remembered what Caleb had said that morning, that she

was enabling Jessamyn to persist in this farce. Would it be better if she simply walked away, forcing Jessamyn to reveal the truth—and Ober to face the consequences? Doing the right thing was more complicated than she had thought while she was dreaming of daring adventures at school. But the imposter still lurked, and she couldn't break away until she exposed them.

"And to think," Emir said, "last time I saw you, all you wanted was to be an Obsidian spy."

Mica picked at the lining of her damp wool cloak. "I still wouldn't mind seeing Obsidian one day."

"Well, make sure you stop by Stonefoss first. You've grown up so much, the family will hardly recognize you."

Mica felt a sharp pang in her chest, and her own features flitted across her face. "I miss everybody so much—even Wills and Rees. What are they up to?"

"Causing the same trouble," Emir said. "Breaking hearts, risking court martial." He grinned. "Aden is getting pretty friendly with a certain Shield girl. I reckon they'll get married. Mention it to the parents, and they act all severe about how he should focus on his next promotion, but they get weepy if you mention grandkids. Both of them."

"Dad is going to be such a sappy grandpa."

"Not going to argue with that."

"What else?" Mica rested her elbows on her knees, feeling like a little girl hanging on her brother's every word. "How's everyone from our quarter?"

"The same, as far as I know," Emir said. "I haven't been in Stonefoss much lately."

"Too busy with your Elite duties?"

"Something like that." Emir glanced at the party silhouetted against the campfire and lowered his voice. "I spoke to Master Kiev at your Assignment Ceremony. As soon as I got home, my promotion was waiting for me."

"Master Kiev?" Mica frowned at the non sequitur. Then she

realized why he was telling her this. "You're working for the Masters Council now!"

"Don't need to shout about it." Emir grinned proudly. "Turns out you're not the only Gray offspring with dreams of serving the empire as something besides a pair of boots on the ground."

"So you're reporting directly to Master Kiev?"

"I'm observing for him, but he's away."

"What he's doing? Is he still in Obsidian?"

Emir shrugged, and Mica tossed a small stone at him.

"Come on, you can tell me that."

"I don't know his exact location."

"Fine. At least tell me what you're supposed to be observing."

"I really can't say anything more," Emir said. "But I figured since I know your secret, it's only fair you know mine."

"Thank you."

In truth, Mica knew Emir could have only one mission if he'd been posted at the princess's side. The council wanted to spy on Jessamyn herself. Lady Maren hadn't said a word about it, despite her bond with the princess. Mica found that troubling.

"Emir," she said slowly, "please don't report what the princess and I are doing until she gives the okay. She'll inform them herself when the time is right."

"My duty—"

"Is to the empire first and foremost. I think that means we need to do what the emperor and future empress want, not the Council."

Emir scratched the stubble on his chin. "Are you sure you haven't got it the wrong way around?"

"What do you mean?"

"I'd say we owe a group that stands for the good of the empire more allegiance than the imperial family. They'll always look out for the interests of the imperial family first and foremost."

"Jessamyn isn't like that," Mica said. "She serves the empire first."

"Are you sure?"

Mica hesitated. She didn't like the implication that the agenda of the Masters Council, the imperial family, and the empire itself could be at odds. But she also *couldn't* say with absolute certainty that Jessamyn and her father weren't primarily focused on their own interests. What would she do if Jessamyn's orders and the needs of the empire began to diverge?

"Jessamyn will tell everyone what happened to her after we catch the imposter," Mica said. "And then I'm going to deal with a serious threat to the empire—one that affects Talents and puts everyone in danger. Could you at least wait to report this one secret until I have a chance to do that?"

Emir fell silent, considering the request. Mica fidgeted with her cloak. She admired her brother for the meticulous way he thought through his decisions, but she wished he would hurry up.

At last, he nodded. "All right, Mica. I'll hold off on it. Master Kiev is hard to reach right now, anyway."

"Thank you." Mica glanced back at the circle around the fire. The echoes in the cave made it impossible to hear anything they were saying. "We'd better get back before Wendel starts a rumor about *you* and the princess."

Emir chuckled. "She is remarkable, isn't she?"

"Don't even think about it." Mica tried to smack Emir's shoulder, but he dodged her easily. "She is way more trouble than you think. I doubt she's any less demanding of her lovers than she is of her Impersonator."

Emir blushed. "The princess is lovely, but I was talking about Lady Wendel."

CHAPTER THIRTEEN

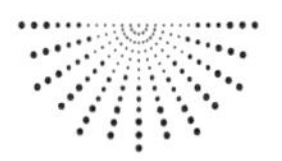

It was dark by the time the storm passed, and they rode back to the city by moonlight. Lord Aren stayed close at Mica's side, telling her of his hopes for the future and teasing her gently about her life in the city. Mica didn't mind his company, and she wondered if they might be friends when all this was over.

The warm lights of little cottages were dotted across the countryside, and they slowly winked out as the hour grew late. But as they drew nearer to Carrow, the city still glowed brightly, as if every household had a dozen lanterns burning in the windows.

"Something is wrong," Aren said suddenly. "The midnight hour is past, but—"

"My lord! Riders approach!"

Aren shifted forward, placing himself in front of Mica.

The thunder of hooves made the earth tremble as a dozen men on horseback approached from the brightly lit city.

"That's Fritz," Caleb said. He too had advanced, so that he was halfway between Mica and Jessamyn.

Mica recognized Lord Fritz's blond hair among the darker, taller Pegasus men.

"Let them approach," she commanded, and she urged her horse past her would-be protectors to the front of the group.

Fritz's eyes were bright with excitement and fear as he joined them on the hilltop overlooking Carrow.

"News came while you were away!" he called out. "The Obsidians have captured Ironhall on Talon. We are at war!"

Gasps erupted behind Mica. She leaned forward in her saddle.

"When?"

"Two days ago. Lady Ingrid is preparing to depart for her home now."

"What of the other border bases?" she asked, not daring to look at her brother. Stonefoss was almost as close to Obsidian as Ironhall.

"They haven't been attacked yet, according to the Blur's report," Fritz said breathlessly. "They're all on high alert, but no one knows where the Obsidians will strike next."

"How did they succeed in taking Ironhall?" Jessamyn had forced her way to the front of the group too. Fritz did a double take, but he was too worked up over the news to question Myn Irondier's involvement in the discussion.

"A surprise attack," Fritz said. "The fortress was caught unaware. The Obsidians came in vast numbers from the Stone Coast and overwhelmed the defenders."

"What of—the emperor?" Jessamyn said.

"Yes," Mica said quickly. "Where is my father?"

"Still in Jewel Harbor. He sent a letter for you." Fritz drew it from his coat pocket and passed it to Mica. Jessamyn's fingers twitched, as if she wanted to grab it out of her hands.

A servant moved forward with a light, and Mica scanned the brief note, written in the emperor's blocky handwriting.

"He orders me to return to Jewel Harbor at once."

Jessamyn made a sharp hissing noise, like an angry cat.

"That sounds wise, my princess," Lord Aren said. "This isn't a good time to be sailing about."

"We should stay right here!" Wendel said. "I'm not going to sea during a war."

"You are under no obligation to leave Carrow, Lady Wendel," Mica said. "But it sounds as though the Obsidians are far away from here." *For now.*

She was watching Jessamyn for guidance. The princess's eyebrows drew down in a stubborn line. They hadn't completed their missions. They couldn't just turn around.

"There's more, Princess," Fritz said. "Captain Karson has returned."

"Already?"

"The *Arrow* was in a skirmish in the Northern Channel. They came upon a merchant ship under attack. Both sides suffered losses, but he managed to take a prisoner."

"Obsidians here!" Wendel exclaimed at the same time Lord Aren asked, "Were the attackers from the Twins?"

"Not Obsidians," Fritz said. He nodded at Lord Aren. "Yes, we think he's with the secession group, but wait until you see what he can do!"

Mica and Caleb exchanged tense glances.

I hope he doesn't mean what I think he means.

"We're holding him in a cell," said one of Lord Gordon's men, who had accompanied Fritz. "I reckon you should see for yourself, Your Highness."

"Take me to him," Mica said.

They rode swiftly down the hill toward the blazing lights of Carrow. Fritz fell in beside Mica, all but bouncing in his saddle.

"Princess, I wish to carry on to Silverfell," Fritz said. "Lorna could be in danger!"

"I'm not going anywhere," Wendel said on his other side.

"I don't think the princess should go to sea right now," Aren said. He rode beside Mica still, scanning the hills as if he expected an attack at any moment.

"But Lorna!"

"I am sure Lorna will be safe in her father's city." Mica held up a hand to silence her companions. "Let us see what this prisoner has to say before we make any decisions." She couldn't catch Jessamyn's eye with the nobles crowding around her, but she hoped they were of the same mind. She wasn't ready to turn back yet.

Carrow was alive with activity, as if no one could sleep with the news of war. Faces appeared at the windows as they rode past, bright eyes and pale cheeks betraying their anxiety. Mica imagined what would happen if the Obsidian hordes made it this far into the empire. These humble houses wouldn't stand a chance against the slave armies of the Obsidian King. They had to turn back the invaders before they made it this far.

She trusted the Imperial Army to meet the threat, but Mica and Jessamyn wouldn't make any difference on the front lines. They were needed deeper in the empire.

Lord Gordon's men led the way to a cell set into a hillside on the far edge of town. Captain Karson and Lord Gordon himself waited for them outside. Torches lit the night with a reddish glare, and their faces were grave.

"The prisoner isn't saying much, Your Highness," Captain Karson said after offering a crisp salute. "He wants to talk to you. You should know there were Talent fighters among his comrades. They were well trained and—I know this may sound crazy—some of them had more than one Talent ability."

Mica clenched her fists. "Are you certain?"

"I saw it with my own eyes."

"Were they sane?"

Captain Karson blinked. "Sane, Your Highness?"

"Did these multi-Talented fighters show signs of illness or erratic behavior?"

"Not that I saw," Captain Karson said, "but I will ask my men."

He studied her with renewed respect, picking up on her lack of surprise at the news of multiple Talents. He was a sharp man, and Mica could see why the emperor had chosen him for this delicate mission.

"But no one can have more than one Talent," Wendel said. "Can they?"

Mica ignored the question, her attention on Aren and Gordon. They had exchanged a few quiet words at Captain Karson's report, their expressions uncomfortable.

"My lords?" she said. "Is there something you wish to tell me?"

Lord Gordon grimaced. "Survivors of other skirmishes have made wild claims, saying the Talents were as fast as Blurs and as impervious as Shields." He glanced at his son, whose face looked grave in the torchlight. "We had ignored them until now."

"I confess we thought the sailors were exaggerating," Lord Aren said. "No one can be a Blur *and* a Shield."

"With all due respect, my lord, it looks like you were wrong." Captain Karson gestured to the door set in the hillside. "The one we caught is one of them. You can see the truth for yourselves."

"Yes, we've had enough talk," Mica said. "Show me the prisoner."

She entered the earthen prison with Emir and Captain Karson flanking her. The cell was divided from a small guard station with iron bars. Torches burned here too, giving it a stuffy, claustrophobic feeling. There wasn't enough room for Jessamyn to come in with them. Mica would have to handle this one on her own.

She expected the prisoner to be like the madman from the anniversary ball.

The reality was far worse.

"Good evening, Princess Jessamyn." The man had a large blond beard, and his eyes were small and watery. His clothes were blackened with soot and torn in dozens of places, but he appeared to be uninjured. "So kind of you to visit."

"Good evening," Mica said, matching his polite tone. "Have we met?"

"You don't remember? I wouldn't expect you to, I suppose. You care little for people like me."

Mica approached the cell, trying to get a better look at the man in the flickering light. Suddenly, his features morphed into those of Lord Dolan: doughy skin, close-set eyes, thinning hair.

"Is that better?" he said. "This is the kind of face you'd pay attention to, an important, rich face. Or how about this one?" His features changed again, and he stared down Lord Riven's aquiline nose at her. "Or has he fallen out of favor too?" The man's features changed for the third time, and a perfect copy of Emperor Styl faced her through the bars of the cell.

"Very impressive," Mica said. "Will you tell me where we met? You've clearly seen my father in the flesh too."

"It matters little," the man said in the emperor's cold, clear voice. "Your tyranny cannot touch me anymore."

Suddenly, the man was right at the bars. Mica stumbled back a few steps, and he grinned at her with the emperor's straight, white teeth. So he was a Blur and a Mimic. The lack of injuries suggested he was a Shield too, given how roughed up his clothes were. So that made three Talents, just like Caleb. Could he have the fourth?

As if he sensed where her thoughts led, the man grasped the bars of his cell with both hands and pulled. With a steady, implacable strength, he bent the iron aside. *Muscle.*

Emir and Captain Karson were on him at once, pushing past Mica with their blades drawn. But their steel glanced right off the prisoner's skin when they tried to drive him back. The man smiled at them with the emperor's mouth. Then he turned around and walked to the cot at the back of his cell. He sat, resuming the blond, bearded face once more, and grinned up at them through the bent bars of his cage.

"You see there is no point in trying to contain me," he said. "I allowed myself to be captured so I could speak with you face to face."

"You want to talk?" Mica said. "So talk. How did you get those Talents?"

"From a benefactor who understands the needs of my people."

Ober. Mica knotted her hands in her skirt, struggling to keep her features in place.

"And who are your people?"

The blond man raised his head proudly. "The noble men and women of the Independent Republic of Dwindlemire."

"I see."

"We have sent our Talents to the Imperial Army for generations," the man said. "In return, you help us only when it suits your own ends. No more. Now, we will all be Talents. *More* than Talents."

Mica swallowed. "All of you?"

"When the time is right."

"But what about the fatigue? Do you sleep for days after using your abilities? Or have you seen hints of madness and violence among your friends? You may think you've been given a gift, but this is poison."

"I am afraid your intelligence is outdated, Your Highness," the man said. "You are describing the older model."

Mica froze. "What do you mean?"

"Our benefactor has perfected his process."

No. Please no.

"P-perfected?"

"Quite recently."

Mica believed him.

She was too late.

"Don't you know how it works?" she said, anger flaring through her like a lit torch. "This *benefactor* of yours uses Talent bones and blood to make his potions."

She thought of her friend Danil, whose leg had been chopped off in service of Lord Ober's experiments. He was from Dwindlemire, the same as the prisoner. She thought of the warehouse, with its screams and groans and jars of blood.

It isn't right.

The prisoner smiled, and for a moment, he looked at her with Jessamyn's face, somehow more grotesque for its beauty. "Sometimes the price is worth it."

"Not this time."

Mica felt the situation spiraling beyond her control. She had thought they were ahead of the game, but the attacks were coming from all sides. Obsidian. The secession agitators. And now Lord Ober was helping the rebels acquire all four Talents—perhaps without the weaknesses that had led her to believe they still had time.

But there was already a new type of Talent in the empire.

A Fifth Talent.

Mica retreated from the cell, pausing outside the door to wait for her hands to stop shaking.

"We can do little to keep him here, Your Highness," Captain Karson said. "You see why?"

"I do." Mica hesitated for a breath. "Do you think he can be killed?"

"Do you want us to try?"

A memory flashed before Mica's eyes of when she had leapt onto a man's back and stuck her knives deep into his body. She had clung to him as he died, his blood gushing over hands. That visceral moment still haunted her months later. Could she give an execution order after she knew what it felt like to kill a man? She supposed that, at least, wasn't her job.

"We have to know how to kill them," Emir said, "if we are to face more like him."

Mica looked up at her brother's face, but all she could see was the way the prisoner had ignored his sword completely. If her brother faced a Talent like that, he would be killed, despite all his elite training. The world was a very different place now.

"I want to know more about him first," Mica said. "See if you can learn his true face and name. And I want to know if he shows any signs of madness or extreme fatigue." She still held out hope that his mixed Talents weren't as flawless as they seemed.

We never should have let Ober leave Jewel Harbor.

The nobles and their retainers were waiting for her in the ring of torchlight a few paces away. The rest of her traveling companions had joined the group. Lady Ingrid, looking pale and murderous, was already dressed for travel, and Lord Riven stood close at her side, a cloak over his broad shoulders. Elana and Wendel were whispering together, catching each other up on the news—and gossip—with lightning speed. Dolan, Fritz, and Caleb formed another knot, but Caleb wasn't paying attention to the other lords. He had clearly been watching the prison door, waiting for Mica to emerge. Jessamyn had been watching the prison just as intently, and she had just happened to position herself next to Lord Aren.

One among those nobles was untrustworthy, and Mica couldn't afford to keep trying to guess who it was. The stakes were too high now. It was time to dispense with the imposter.

She rejoined her companions.

"Thank you for your hospitality, Lord Gordon. I am afraid we must cut our visit short."

"I understand completely."

"Do you intend to return to Jewel Harbor, Princess?" Fritz asked. "I must go to my bride."

Mica glanced at Jessamyn, who shook her head, confirming what Mica already knew they must do.

"I shall continue on to the outer islands," Mica said. "My father will handle the Obsidian invasion."

Fritz gaped at her. "But he ordered you to return to—"

"What my father says to me is between the two of us," Mica said sharply. "I will *not* have you questioning my decisions."

"Apologies, my princess." Fritz ducked into a low bow.

Jessamyn's eyes brightened, as if she approved of Mica's use of her angriest voice. Mica felt as if they were in sync. Their adversaries were helping each other now. Ober. The rebels. Their missions were converging. Once again, she had the eerie sensation that only one of them was real.

She turned to the others. "I will continue on to Silverfell with Lords Caleb and Fritz and my soldiers," she announced. "The rest of you may remain here or sail east, but I can no longer have you in my party."

Elana opened her mouth. "But—"

"This is not a discussion. Lord Dolan, I require the continued use of the *Silk Goddess*. You will be compensated later."

His doughy face paled. "But Princess, we—"

"We've had a delightful jaunt, my lords and ladies," Mica said. "But our journey together ends here. I cannot bring you into danger in a time of war."

Ingrid and Riven were whispering to each other, unbothered by her decree. Perhaps Riven had already decided to accompany Ingrid back to Talon. Wendel looked relieved. Only Dolan and Elana appeared distressed. So which one was the imposter?

It didn't matter now. Mica had spent enough time trying to figure out the imposter's identity. She decided to leave Rider the Shield guard behind for good measure. It wouldn't be the first time a Mimic had succeeded in securing a job at the princess's side. She refused to sail toward untold dangers with a snake in their midst. She trusted Caleb, and she knew Fritz would try to swim after the boat if she left him behind. She would have Caleb verify his identity before they set sail, but she couldn't have the others lurking at her back anymore.

"I beg you to reconsider your voyage, Princess," Lord Gordon said. "The rebels have grown too bold. The Channel is not safe."

"The agitators will have to put aside their secession ambitions when they learn of the Obsidian invasion," Mica said. "They will be the next target if the empire falls. I *must* reach them."

Obsidian might be attacking to the east, but Mica wouldn't allow the West to fall too. And she had to learn exactly how many people this "benefactor" had corrupted with his gifts.

Lord Aren exchanged a few quiet words with his father then said, "Princess, let me accompany you to Silverfell. I will contribute my best fighters to your force."

"That's kind of you, Lord Aren," Mica said, "but that won't be necessary."

"You have extra room on your ship now, Princess. Besides . . ." Aren stepped forward to take her hand. "I couldn't live with myself if you were harmed."

Lord Riven and Lady Ingrid broke off their quiet conversation, watching with interest as the Pegasus lord addressed the princess. Riven raised a dark eyebrow, as if surprised that she was accepting Aren's advances when she had pushed him aside.

"The Obsidians may be far away yet," Aren said, "but too many dangers lurk out there. Allow me to protect you."

Mica hesitated. "You'd have to travel on a ship."

"Even that would be worth it to see you safely to Silverfell."

Mica looked at Jessamyn for guidance. But instead of being ready with a quick signal for Mica, her gaze lingered on Aren and on the way he held Mica's hand as if it were a precious jewel. Mica knew what to do.

"I accept your offer, Lord Aren." He hadn't been with them when Peet warned her about the imposter—and Mica had a feeling Jessamyn was going to need him in the days to come. "We depart for Silverfell at first light."

Jessamyn looked up sharply, as if realizing Mica had made that decision without her. But she didn't object as Lord Aren began issuing orders to his retainers to prepare for departure.

Lord Dolan attempted to talk her into letting him stay on the ship, but she refused to hear his pleas as they returned to Lord Gordon's manor to gather their belongings. She planned to dump most of the luxurious foods and trappings and load up with as many fighting men as Aren could muster. She was a soldier's daughter at heart, and she'd had enough of subtlety. She was marching to war.

Mica touched the parchment with the emperor's brief note commanding her to return to Jewel Harbor. He might have thought he could send his daughter into danger, but he'd had second thoughts in the face of all-out war. Mica hoped she and Jessamyn weren't making the wrong choice by ignoring his orders.

They had to finish their missions—both of them. If the Fifth Talent potion had been perfected, Mica feared the hour had already passed when the threats could be contained.

CHAPTER FOURTEEN

They departed for Silverfell with a hold full of weapons instead of silks, their noble guests and servants replaced by additional fighting men from Pegasus. The HIMS *Arrow* set a double watch, and soldiers patrolled the decks of the *Silk Goddess* day and night. In addition to the rebel raiders, now they had to watch for stealthy advances from the Obsidian invaders. Tension quivered through the ship, from the broad wooden hull all the way to the tip of the tallest mast.

Unsettling squalls punctuated their journey, making many of Aren's retainers horribly seasick. Captain Pol grumbled about bad omens as the Pegasus men hurled the contents of their stomachs overboard.

"They will fight if they have to," said Lord Aren, who looked a little green himself as they sailed out of sight of land. "We will keep the princess safe."

"This isn't a warship, nor a healer's house neither," Captain Pol muttered, not noticing that Mica was listening in. "I'd better be rewarded for this."

"We have to restore peace in the empire," Aren said. "The princess will—"

He clapped a hand over his mouth and darted for the railing. Aren already looked thinner and less robust at sea than he did on land, but Mica believed him when he said his men would fight if the occasion arose, seasickness or no seasickness.

Silverfell was a relatively short distance from Pegasus, but the voyage felt longer than their trip across the Heart Sea. Mica and Jessamyn spent most of their time confined in their cabin. Banner insisted upon it, claiming it would be all too easy for an enemy to sail out of the mist and murder or kidnap the princess.

"Captain Karson told me about the multi-Talented prisoner," Banner said as he positioned himself in front of the cabin door, preventing Jessamyn from going out. He had lost some of his implacability since learning of the existence of what they'd all begun to refer to as the Fifth Talents. "Such an enemy could scale the side of the boat with Blur speed and immediately impersonate someone we know—even me. And then it would be all too easy for him to carry you away with his Muscle strength."

"You forgot the Shield part."

His mustache quivered irritably. "This isn't a joke, my lady."

"I know it's not, Banner," Jessamyn said. "We have set a double watch, and our Talent soldiers are not helpless. Honestly, what else can we do?"

"We can turn around and sail right back to Jewel Harbor, as your father ordered."

Jessamyn put her hands on her hips, staring fiercely up at her guard. "My father is busy with the Obsidians. We must restore order in the West before the war in the east escalates. This is why we sailed out here in the first place."

"The situation has changed."

"He's right," Mica put in. She sat on the floor, playing with the leather sheath of one of her knives, deciding whether to wear it on her ankle or hide it farther up her thigh today. The other one was already secured beneath her sleeve. "Maybe you should tell everyone about your pois—"

Jessamyn whirled around. "If you finish that sentence, I swear I will have you beheaded, Micathea!"

Mica wisely kept her mouth shut, and the princess returned to her bed to sulk. She crumpled and tugged at her veil, nearly ripping it to shreds, and didn't speak to Mica and Banner for the rest of the day.

Mica and Jessamyn soon tired of each other's company in the cramped quarters, which had begun to smell thanks to the seasick men who now crowded into the nearby cabins in place of the perfumed ladies. Mica occasionally slipped into a different face to get some air on deck, but Jessamyn didn't have that option with Banner keeping such a close watch on her. She grew increasingly moody, snapping at Mica worse than ever and criticizing every nuance in her impersonation, even though she had precious few opportunities to mess it up.

Mica had always thought Jessamyn was a step ahead of everyone else, but she seemed to be floundering a bit as news of the war reached them. She feared for her father's safety, and she began second-guessing the decisions she'd made since leaving the capital. Mica renewed her efforts to get Jessamyn to reveal her new face now that they had left the imposter behind, but the princess was even less willing to entertain her arguments than before. She still insisted that she would do it when the time was right.

As they sailed west through the Northern Channel, they received regular reports about the war from Blur messengers, who powered their little skips back and forth across the tumultuous seas. They learned that Ironhall had fallen in a matter of hours when the surprise attack hit. The Obsidians had come in force from the Stone Coast, and their dread hordes overwhelmed the base through sheer numbers. The surviving Windfast soldiers had retreated to the rocky Talon mountains, where they had already begun to wage guerrilla warfare on the invaders. Despite their efforts, the Obsidians had gained a toehold in the empire. It wasn't yet clear whether they'd set their sights on Amber or Pegasus Island next.

"I still don't understand why Ironhall had no warning," Mica said to Emir after listening to a report one evening. She had impersonated Banner—a shorter, slimmer version of him—in order to leave her cabin, and now she lingered on the foredeck with her brother. The darkened skies made the gilded figurehead look like iron, and a cold wind was blowing.

Mica looked to the east. "Our Mimic agents in Obsidian are supposed to help prevent surprise attacks."

"The spy network may have been compromised," Emir said. "I haven't heard from Master Kiev in some time."

"He can't have been caught." Mica gripped the railing as the rough seas rolled beneath their hull. The skip that had delivered the latest report was nearly out of sight, a trail of white foam disappearing into the waves behind it. "Master Kiev is a legend."

"But if *someone* was caught, they could be sending false reports."

Mica didn't want to believe that. The Masters Council sent their very best spies into Obsidian territory. The emperor had mentioned increased troop movements, but they hadn't said anything about a full-scale invasion. And yet Ironhall had fallen.

Mica lowered her voice so she could barely be heard above that cold sea wind. "Do you think they'll hit Stonefoss next? If they haven't already?"

Emir grimaced. "It's what I would do."

They looked out at the churning waves together. Mica imagined their parents preparing to defend the base, and their brothers, who might already be fighting on the front lines. If Ironhall had fallen so quickly, would they stand a chance, even with their higher proportion of Talents?

She could do nothing to help them regardless. Mica had been the princess for months. She had ridden at the emperor's side and given orders in his name. Yet she still felt powerless against the tide of war.

The *Silk Goddess* and the HIMS *Arrow* sailed onward through the steely waters of the Northern Channel. They were always on the alert, but the days still dragged, even for those not confined to their cabins.

The noblemen passed the time by continuing to train with the sword, their drills noticeably more purposeful with real threats on the horizon. Fritz, Aren, and Emir sometimes joined Caleb and Stievson at their exercises, though Fritz was often too nervous to keep at it for long. He could think only of Lorna and their upcoming wedding, which would be much subdued now that the empire was at war.

Caleb had verified Fritz's identity before they departed Pegasus.

"I quizzed him on some our youthful adventures," he explained when Mica called him away from his exercises one afternoon to discuss it in the shadow of one of the longboats. She wore Jessamyn's face, the real princess safely confined to her cabin under Banner's watch. "I know him better than any of the others. He's definitely the real Fritz."

"Good." Mica had also ordered Captain Karson test each of his men after they departed Carrow in case another Mimic had snuck in among them. She should be relieved they had left their imposter behind, but she didn't like letting the mystery go unsolved. "Who do you think Ober's imposter was?"

"My coin is on Wendel," Caleb said. "She tried to convince me to stay in Carrow. My uncle could have been trying to get to me all along."

"Or Wendel just likes you," Mica said. "She acted so naturally with her family, I was sure it must be genuine. I had narrowed it down to Elana or Dolan. They're the ones who objected to being left behind."

Caleb brushed a hand through his hair, considering the puzzle.

"What about Riven? I saw him going into Lady Wendel's room the night before we left Lord Gordon's, after I finished questioning Fritz."

"*Wendel's* room? Really?"

Caleb nodded. "That's not like him, I know."

"Ingrid was distraught over Ironhall," Mica said slowly. "I'd have expected Riven to be comforting *her* that night."

"Riven isn't the comforting type."

"Yes, but I thought he and Ingrid were finally forming a connection." Mica made her bottom lip grow and shrink absentmindedly. She had definitely seen Riven watching Ingrid, the woman who had made no secret of her interest in him. What had possessed him to go to Lady Wendel's room instead? "Do you think they were getting together?"

"I don't know. It's just as well we left them all in Carrow." Caleb looked over at the main deck, where Aren was talking swords with Stievson. "I wish we'd left that one behind too."

"Aren? Why?"

"I don't like him."

Mica searched Caleb's face for some hint of what he was thinking. "Does your dislike have anything to do with how much Aren likes Jessamyn?"

"Huh?"

"Don't tell me you haven't noticed. He's smitten."

Caleb frowned, rubbing the back of his neck. "I'd noticed, but . . . you think it's *Jessamyn* he favors?"

"Who do you think he's had his eye on?"

"Well, *you*, of course! You're the one he has been paying so much attention to."

"As Jessamyn."

"Yes, but . . . I don't know." Caleb looked around to make sure no one was watching them too closely and seized her hand. "It's complicated, Mica. Your impersonation is good, but Jessamyn is different when you're Jessamyn. I mean . . . let me back up. Before I found out the truth, I was starting to wonder if my feelings for Jessamyn might be . . . that is . . . it's possible that what he sees in Jessamyn *now* is what I see in you."

Mica blushed, feeling almost as flustered as Caleb sounded.

"Was that a complicated way of saying you think he likes me for my mind?"

"For your mind, your spirit, for the way you throw yourself into things like you're about to draw a knife or tackle somebody three times your size." His grip on her hand tightened. "How could he help himself?"

Mica locked eyes with him, suddenly wishing everyone on deck would find reasons to be elsewhere. She almost used her princess authority to send them away.

"I never thought about it like that," she said. "I thought he and Jessamyn had a connection. They have history at least."

"Maybe they do," Caleb said. "Let's hope so, or I might have to fight him for you."

"Oh?"

He grinned, still holding her hand. "Yes. And I'm impervious sometimes, so odds are I'd win."

"I thought you didn't like to rely on that."

"I'd risk it." Caleb inched closer to her, his voice becoming husky. "For you, Mica."

The sea air was biting, but his hands were like glowing embers holding hers. Mica could feel the remaining distance between like a physical thing. She had kept him at arm's length for a long time, but now he knew her and cared for her because of who she was. How could she stay away?

She balanced on the balls of her feet, on the verge of launching herself forward.

"Cal—"

"Lord Caleb."

Mica froze as someone spoke very close to them. She and Caleb stared at each other for a breathless instant then released each other's hands.

Emir was standing beside them, his expression unreadable.

"What?" Caleb said, his voice gruffer than usual.

Emir narrowed his eyes. "Are you joining the sparring session, *my lord*?"

"Right. Of course." He bowed, his eyes raking over Mica's face one last time. "Princess."

Emir didn't move as the young lord brushed past him, heading aft to where the others waited with a barrel full of practice weapons.

"Mica," Emir said.

"*What?*"

Emir raised an eyebrow, and Mica realized her voice had sounded fiercer than she intended.

"Care to fill me in on this part of the impersonation? I thought you were trying to set the princess up with Lord Aren."

"I am." Mica brushed at her skirt, not quite meeting her brother's eye.

"Well, he saw you and Lord Caleb holding hands. If you were trying to make him jealous, it worked."

"Yes, of course that's what we were doing," Mica said, going for some of Jessamyn's breeziness. "Excuse me. I must return to my lady."

Emir grabbed her arm before she could escape, his body hiding the action from view.

"Mica," he said, his voice softer this time. "I don't want you to get hurt. These lords are all the same. They use and discard young women. Even if he means well, he—"

"You don't know anything about him," Mica said.

"I'm trying to watch out for you," Emir said. "You may look

like the princess, but I'm still your big brother."

Mica scowled at him. "I didn't object when you were making eyes at Lady Wendel!"

"Did you see me holding hands with her in front of everyone? I didn't say you can't admire Lord Caleb from afar. He seems like a decent fellow. But that doesn't make him any less a lord."

Anger boiled up in Mica's stomach. She wanted to argue with him, to tell him he didn't know anything. But after all the time she had spent playing the lady, she couldn't ignore what Emir had said about Caleb's noble status. She wasn't sure where he thought this thing between them was going, but lords who dallied with commoner women didn't tend to stay with them. Emir was right on that count.

Not that Mica would tell *him* that. She plucked her brother's hand off her sleeve.

"We are at war," she said, mustering as much imperial dignity as she could. "I have bigger things to worry about than who wants to hold my hand—and so do you."

Emir sighed. "Of course we do. Just be careful."

"I will." Mica paused. "And thank you."

He gave her an exaggerated salute. "I live to serve, Princess."

Mica stuck her tongue out at him, then she waltzed back across the deck. She made a point of winking at Lord Aren as she passed him. He stared back at her, not even noticing when Caleb whacked him hard with a practice sword.

Whether Lord Aren was jealous of Caleb or not, his affections for Jessamyn remained as evident as ever. They didn't have many opportunities to speak. Aren had to tend to his men—and his seasickness—and Mica wanted to avoid any more intimate moments. But when she made her rare appearances on deck in Jessamyn's form, Aren would pause whatever he was doing to watch her pass or dip into the elegant bow he had demonstrated back in Carrow.

Mica always responded warmly, but she couldn't bring herself to resume the conversation that had been interrupted beneath the waterfall, especially after what Caleb had said. She figured Jessamyn could continue their courtship when she was herself again.

Then, late at night the evening before they arrived in Silverfell, Lord Aren knocked on the princess's cabin door.

The *Silk Goddess* had made unusually good time with the threat of war and rebel pirates at their backs, and they expected to sail into Silverfell City's harbor shortly after sunrise. The stormy weather had calmed at last, and the wind was no more than a muted roar outside.

Still, Aren had to knock a second time before they heard him over the creaking and groaning of the ship.

"It is Aren, Princess," he called through the cabin door. "May I come in?"

Before Mica could answer him, Jessamyn leapt to her feet.

"Pretend to be asleep," she hissed.

"But—"

"Do it! And do not stir until I give you leave."

Mica flopped down on the bed and closed her eyes. Breathing slowly and deeply, she listened as Jessamyn answered the door herself.

"May I help you, my lord?"

"Good evening, Miss Myn. I'd like to speak with your lady."

"She's sleeping, my lord. She said she would slice off my ears and feed them to the fish if I woke her."

"Oh. You needn't disturb her, then. I shouldn't have called on her so late."

The disappointment in his tone made Mica wonder what he had expected to happen when he knocked on Jessamyn's door in the quiet of the night when everyone was supposed to be in bed.

Aren didn't leave right away, and she strained to hear what he said next.

"I haven't had an opportunity to ask if you are well since the river. I was worried about you."

A pause. "You were?"

"I was afraid you'd catch cold after I foolishly dragged you all into the wilderness with a storm coming."

"No, I'm quite all right." Jessamyn sounded caught off guard. "I can't get much worse." She gave a humorless laugh, and Mica imagined her gesturing to her ruined features, or what little could be seen beneath her veil.

"May I ask what happened to you?" Lord Aren said.

"I was caught in a fire as a little girl."

"That must have been awful."

"It doesn't hurt so much anymore, but it isn't getting any better, either." A note of vulnerability entered Jessamyn's voice. "I'm not sure it ever will."

"Why do you wear a veil? Is it a custom from your homeland?"

"Of course not," Jessamyn said with a snort. "My face is hideous. You saw it yourself."

"I wouldn't say it's hideous at all," Lord Aren said. "Besides, you seem like a brave and steadfast woman. That's far more important than being pretty, don't you think?"

Jessamyn was quiet for a moment, and Mica cracked open one eyelid. She couldn't see the princess's expression as she faced Lord Aren through the doorway. When she finally spoke, her voice was so soft Mica almost couldn't hear it.

"Thank you, my lord. I will tell the princess you stopped by."

Lord Aren bowed and strode away. Jessamyn watched the corridor long after he was gone.

The princess didn't say anything at all about Aren's nighttime visit. Mica allowed herself to hope that Aren's words would move her and the truth would finally come out. Mica had made too many decisions on Jessamyn's behalf lately. With the empire at war, a common Mimic from Stonefoss had no business acting as the princess.

But as the morning of their arrival in Silverfell dawned, Jessamyn put on her veil and cap as usual and handed Mica a crown.

"I expect your very best performance, Micathea. Many nobles will be staying at Silverfell right now. We mustn't give them any reason to doubt us."

Mica sighed. "Yes, Princess."

Of course she won't give up her secret just because of a handsome man.

Jessamyn fussed over the elaborate gown she had chosen for Mica's reception in Silverfell, the rich cobalt satin and silver embroidery a marked contrast to her simple tunic.

"Remember," she said, "we need to convince everyone that we have absolute confidence in the empire right now. We are not afraid of the Obsidians or intimidated by the rebels."

"Understood."

"And don't mention that Fifth Talent from Dwindlemire. That rumor will spread fast enough as it is."

"As you wish."

Jessamyn looked as if she had more to say, but they heard shouting from above, the words indistinct.

"Well, what are you waiting for, Micathea? We must have arrived. Hurry!"

Mica and Jessamyn climbed up to the deck together to get their first look at Silverfell in the early-morning light. The weather had calmed at last, and the sea reflected the shimmering blue of the sky. The island was mountainous, and its largest city was set beneath towering purple peaks.

But smoke was billowing into the clear skies, and the smell of char mixed with the briny sea air.

The city was under attack.

CHAPTER FIFTEEN

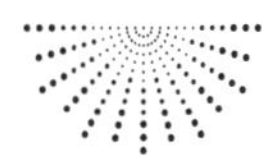

The attack had come from the sea. Enemy ships assaulted Silverfell City from the bowl-shaped harbor. Some attacked the moored vessels, while others hurled pots full of burning oil directly at the city. Fires blazed at a dozen points along the waterfront, and soldiers ran across the docks in close formation, taking cover behind piles of goods whenever arrows or fire rained down on them. Shouts rang across the water, punctuated by cracking timber and the occasional explosive splash.

The Obsidians must have beaten us here.

Mica, Jessamyn, and Banner darted to the portside railing in time to see the HIMS *Arrow* sailing toward the harbor mouth ahead of them. The long paddles scuttled like spiders' legs from the belly of the galleon, and the decks bristled with swords and arrows as their escort ship barreled down on the enemy.

"It's not safe, Your Highness!" Captain Pol shouted, hurrying over to where they stood at the rail, watching the *Arrow*. "You should get below."

"We will do no such thing," the real Jessamyn snapped.

"That's right." Mica covered for her quickly. "I cannot follow the battle from below."

"The *Goddess* was not built for battle," Captain Pol said. "We can't fight!"

"You needn't engage directly," Mica said, "but we should help the injured if we can. Hold fast at the harbor mouth for now."

Pol puffed out his cheeks as though he wanted to object. Then he gave a stiff bow. "As you say, Your Highness."

Jessamyn didn't contradict Mica's order, too busy following the battle with bright eyes. She was probably imagining herself taking up arms on the deck of the *Arrow* to save the city. Banner had placed himself in front of the princess, but he had to keep moving to shield her body while she tried to get a better look at the action.

They were still far enough away that the enemy ships hadn't noticed them. Mica hoped it would stay that way. She believed Pol when he said the *Silk Goddess* was not suited for a sea battle.

Caleb, Aren, and their men were preparing to launch the two longboats to assist the *Arrow*. Fritz was too busy shouting Lorna's name to be much use. Only his Shield guard's efforts kept him from leaping straight into the harbor. Although they weren't as efficient as Captain Karson's soldiers, the fighting men of the *Silk Goddess* were soon ready to sail into the fray.

Caleb paused in buckling on his sword to catch Mica's eye, giving her a swift, intense look. She prayed his Shield Talent wouldn't fail him. She hated that Caleb would go into battle not knowing whether or not his skin could be injured. She wanted to go to him, but she held back, aware of Emir's eyes on her. Her jaw shifted into a harder shape as Caleb climbed into one of the small boats and disappeared over the side.

Jessamyn was studying the battle too closely to pay attention as the lords and their men were lowered to the water, but she tore her eyes away to watch the back of Aren's head as he sailed into the harbor mouth, his ponytail streaming behind him. She too seemed to steel herself against what might befall him.

Haze hung thick over Silverfell City now. The surrounding

peaks contained the smoke rising from numerous fires like the bowl of a pipe. The Silverfell ships had difficulty launching while under fire, and curses echoed across the water as the captains tried to get underway. The city had clearly been taken by surprise, but Mica noticed that none of the aggressors bore the black flag with a stark white tower she'd been expecting. Come to think of it, all the ships looked as though they'd been built right here in the Windfast Empire.

They're not Obsidians, Mica realized with a jolt. *This is a whole new war.*

The rebels must have tired of looting lone ships in the Northern Channel when the ones sitting in Silverfell were ripe for the taking.

Whoever the enemies were, they didn't see the *Arrow* coming.

Captain Karson chose the ship tossing pots of burning oil at the city as the *Arrow*'s first target. The galleon shot across the harbor and crashed into the enemy ship, her steel prow ramming their hull. With a great creaking and splintering of wood, the *Arrow* ripped a hole in the other vessel.

The enemy ship was no match for one manned by well-trained imperial soldiers and powered by Muscle oarsmen. As it tried to flee, the *Arrow* rammed it a second time, and the steel prow stuck to the smaller ship like a knife in an apple. The soldiers began to leap across the gap to board the other vessel.

"That Captain Karson knows what he's doing," Jessamyn said. She was standing on her toes, her veil flying free. The morning sun shone on her waxy skin, making her look fierce, otherworldly. She reminded Mica of the gilded figurehead protruding from their own prow.

Mica had a knife in one hand, though she didn't remember pulling it from her sleeve, and she clutched the wooden railing with the other, nearly tight enough to get splinters. She wanted to join the fight as much as Jessamyn did.

She looked for Caleb's smaller boat, but it was lost in the

smoke and confusion. She leaned farther out over the water, trying to spot him through the jumble of beams and oars and fast-moving boats.

Then an arrow whistled through the air and stuck in the railing right beside her hand.

"Get down!"

"There's one behind us!"

"Quickly, to arms, men!"

Mica and the others ducked below the railing as the remaining men on the *Silk Goddess* surged into action. She couldn't tell where the arrows were coming from. The sailors were confused too, running this way and that, trying to prepare their defenses. Banner had his arms wrapped protectively around Jessamyn, who struggled like a cat as she tried to see what was going on.

The storm of arrows ceased.

Mica's heart raced, the beat loud in her ears. She waited.

When a minute had passed without the telltale thud of metal into wood, Mica risked a peek over the side of the ship.

A longboat had detached from the main battle, and it was speeding through the swells toward the *Silk Goddess*. Blurs manned the oars, and in seconds, they had reached the *Goddess*, secured grappling hooks to its railing, and begun scaling its sides.

"They're boarding us!" Mica shouted. "Look out!"

She had a sudden, vivid memory of the pale-haired Obsidians attacking the princess's pleasure barge in the middle of Jewel Harbor a few months ago. But these attackers lacked the pale hair and paler skin of their Obsidian enemies. These were Windfast citizens, trying to kill their own.

The Blur rebels swarmed up the side of the *Silk Goddess* to the foredeck. The sailors rushed to defend their vessel, wielding knives, cutlasses, and random heavy objects they found around the deck—such as the lounge chairs the nobles had used.

Captain Pol shouted orders from the helm, his face bloodless. The clash of steel and screams of men filled the deck, the gilded figurehead shaking under the onslaught.

Some of the Blur rebels were thrown back into the sea, but others gained their footing aboard the *Goddess*. Footing was all they needed to become twice as deadly.

As the Blurs swarmed the deck, Banner flattened Jessamyn beneath him, using his impervious body to protect her delicate one—despite her shrill protests. Mica crouched beside them, knife in hand, ready to fight. She was glad they hadn't stayed below, trapped in their cabin, where they couldn't see their enemies coming.

But the boarders moved too fast, and one was upon them almost before they realized what was happening.

The Blur lunged at Mica, trying to grab her in rough, sunburned hands. He had a knife in his belt, but he didn't try to use it. As his hand closed around her wrist, she realized she was wearing the wrong face. Of course their enemies would try to abduct the princess as soon as they recognized her.

She slashed at her would-be kidnapper, but he dodged the strike, still gripping her other wrist. She twisted, trying to get near enough for a slash, a bite, anything to get him off her.

Then, as quickly as she had been seized, the hold on her wrist released, and her attacker flew halfway across the deck.

A speeding figure slowed long enough for Mica to register that Emir had come to her rescue. He flowed forward, death on winged feet, and raised his sword.

The Blur rebel was no match for Mica's brother. Emir made quick work of the man, showing in an instant why he had been selected for the Elite division. The would-be kidnapper fell to the deck, gurgling his last breath almost as soon as the fight began.

"Thanks," Mica said, but Emir was already moving on to the next attacker, a blinding whirl of steel and grace.

Before anyone else spotted her—and realized what a tempting hostage she would make—Mica ripped the crown from her head and tossed it overboard. Then she trimmed the fine silver embroidery off her dress while she contorted her features to look less like a prize. Ashy blond hair replaced the red, blue chased the brown from her eyes, and her face became cute rather than beautiful. Soon, a shorter copy of her best friend, Sapphire, stood where a princess had been. Mica added a couple of scars to the look, as she had seen Mimics do when they prepared for battle. She brandished her knives, feeling more like herself than she had in a long time.

Her brother paused his deadly dance and gave her an approving nod. Then he flowed forward to confront the last of the Blur boarders. It almost hurt to watch the two men try to kill each other at supernatural speeds. The clash of their blades beat a tempo too quick to follow.

Emir sealed the victory with a vicious stab to the gut, and his opponent slumped to the deck, dying slower than he fought.

The sailors raised a cheer as Emir cleaned the blood from his blade with swift hands. Mica thought he looked like their father then, tall and slim and deadly. A fierce pride swelled through her. No enemy could take down the empire while the Gray children still fought.

"There's another boat coming," Captain Pol shouted from the helm. "Get ready!"

They had rebuffed the first assault, but the battle wasn't over yet.

Mica rushed back to the railing as the sailors prepared to use whatever weapons and Talents they had to keep the next wave of attackers at bay. Banner was still shielding Jessamyn, who looked livid at the indignity of being squashed beneath her protector.

Better angry than dead.

Mica scanned the turbulent harbor for the boat Captain Pol had spotted, expecting another longboat like the one full of Blurs.

All she saw was a little skip speeding toward them with three men aboard. Pol's men shot at the trio, but as the skip came alongside the hull, its occupants ignored the arrows raining down on them.

"Shields!" someone called. "Knock them off balance."

One of the sailors had found the *Silk Goddess*'s fancy silverware, and Captain Pol's men began throwing knives, spoons, and heavy goblets at the three Shields, attempting to distract them. The blows glanced off their skin, the attackers unfazed.

The *Silk Goddess* might not be a warship, but the sailors should have been able to keep three fighters from scaling its sides easily. The trio didn't even have grappling hooks. They scrabbled at the hull with their bare hands, as if searching for cracks in the timber.

Strange. Mica leaned out over the water, trying to see what these new attackers were doing.

Then they began to climb.

The strange Shields clung to the hull with the strength of Muscles, jamming their fingers into the tiny cracks between the beams.

"Oh no," Mica said. "They're not just Shields. They're—"

"Advance!" At the signal from their leader, the three attackers suddenly swarmed up the sides of the boat, using supernatural strength and speed to haul themselves aboard. The sailors' efforts to injure them made no difference at all. They were too strong, too fast, too invincible.

Then all three men were on the foredeck, weapons glinting wickedly in the morning sun. They paused, surveying the carnage left by their predecessors. Mere Blurs had failed to take the ship.

But these were Fifth Talents.

And they had come to the *Silk Goddess* with one mission in mind: death.

The Fifth Talents shredded through Pol's sailors with ease.

Strong. Fast. Impervious. There was no touching them. Mica couldn't tell if they were Mimics or not, but they did more than enough damage with their three visible abilities.

It was a slaughter. The sailors fled before them, any attempts to fight seeming paltry in the face of this new kind of Talent.

"Demons!"

"They can't be killed!"

"What do we do, Captain?"

But as his men called for guidance, Captain Pol fell with a knife in his belly. His first mate was next, his skull split open by a man who'd been ten feet away a second earlier. The Fifth Talent hurled the bodies aside and paused at the helm. His features morphed, taking on Captain Pol's wiry, windblown look. Then he advanced, and it was as if the *Silk Goddess*'s own captain were ripping her men apart.

That's all four Talents. And they're not slowing down.

Mica felt helpless. She cowered by the railing with the others, knowing she wouldn't last more than a few seconds if she tried to engage the attackers. It was one thing to guess what perfected Fifth Talents could do. It was quite another to see them in action.

"The ship is lost." Emir had reappeared at Mica's side. "We have to get the princess to safety before they notice her."

"I'm not giving up that easily," Jessamyn said, her voice muffled from where she was still trapped beneath Banner. "Let's blow up the ship!"

Mica looked around, wondering if these super soldiers would remain impervious if they blew the ship to smithereens. She had an awful feeling that even that wouldn't stop them.

Then the Fifth Talent impersonating Captain Pol spotted them. He started their way, cutting down anyone who challenged him.

"No time," Mica said. "Are you okay to swim, Princess?"

"Don't insult me, Micathea."

"All right, then. Jump!"

Mica grabbed Jessamyn by the tunic and with Banner's help tossed her overboard. Her indignant scream was lost in the chaos. Banner leapt after her into the waves.

Mica and her brother exchanged glances, preparing to leap over the edge together.

"On three?" Mica said.

"One," Emir said.

Then an arrow thudded into his side.

"No!"

"Jump, Mica!" Emir said, turning toward the man who had shot him, his hand going to his side. The bowman stood at the helm, looking like one of Lord Aren's men. Another Fifth Talent Impersonator?

The man was taking aim again. Mica drew back her arm to throw her knife at him. Before she could release the blade, Emir lurched toward her.

"*Don't*—" she gasped.

But he seized her by the waist, lifted her up, and tossed her over the side—just as the bowman unleashed his second arrow. Mica fell, losing sight of her brother and the arrow flying straight at his exposed back.

The world blurred.

And Mica hit the water so hard she felt as if she had run into a wall. Saltwater stung her nose, filled her mouth, and burned her eyes. She gasped and choked, the sea threatening to pull her into its cold embrace. She tried to claw her way to the surface, unsure which direction it was, her skirt tugging her downward.

Emir.

Her head broke the shell of the water.

Mica flailed, looking for any sign of her brother through salt-flooded eyes. Banner and Jessamyn treaded water nearby, struggling less than Mica as they helped each other stay afloat. Why weren't they searching? Emir had to have jumped too. She couldn't lose him like this. With an arrow in his side, in his back, he would need help. Where *was* he?

Other sailors had followed their lead in abandoning the *Silk Goddess* to the three Talents. She scrutinized the heads bobbing in the waves, some with blood pooling out from their injuries. None had that familiar dark hair, those intelligent hazel eyes.

"Emir!" Mica screamed. She was vaguely aware that she had resumed her own face, or maybe it was her mother's. But there was nothing she could do. Her brother was still on the ship.

"Look out!" called a voice she didn't know, half choked by seawater.

The great oars had begun to move. The Muscles in the belly of the *Silk Goddess* were rowing, perhaps forced by the Fifth Talents. They could do little to resist the invincible fighters.

Mica swam away from the ship to avoid the oars, her self-preservation instincts taking over. With her eyes full of seawater and tears, she could barely see where she was going. Others were swimming around her, fleeing the huge, churning oars. Then Mica caught sight of a blaze of red. Jessamyn's shorn hair. She followed it like a beacon.

The princess and Banner led the retreat as they swam deeper into the harbor, avoiding the tangle of the other ships. The battle seemed to be winding down, but they were still a long way from the docks.

The ship the Arrow had rammed was sinking. Fires blazed from its mast and upper decks as it listed sharply to the side. Another ship, likely one of the attackers, was speeding out to sea, paying little heed to the survivors struggling in the water.

Mica couldn't tell what was happening in the city itself, and she didn't much care. The *Silk Goddess* was sailing away too—and her brother was still aboard. She didn't know whether or not he lived. He could be lying bleeding on the deck. Or he could be fighting still, refusing to surrender.

No, Emir is smart, she told herself. *He has more sense than the rest of us combined. He won't keep fighting when there's no hope.*

For Mica saw it clearer than ever before. As long as there were Fifth Talents in the world, there was no hope for the rest of them.

CHAPTER SIXTEEN

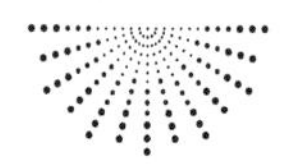

Mica struggled to keep up with Jessamyn and Banner. Either the princess was a much stronger swimmer than she had demonstrated in the river, or the adrenaline of the battle was taking over. Mica couldn't move as fast as Jessamyn could, couldn't summon the energy to battle the waves when she was leaving her brother behind.

He can't be dead.

If she hadn't paused to try to throw her knife, if she had listened to him and jumped right away . . .

He can't be dead.

It was becoming harder to hold her head above water. Mica felt as if her clothes had turned to lead and her lungs to glass. It was very cold. She couldn't keep going, couldn't swim any farther.

So cold.

Jessamyn turned then and saw that Mica had fallen behind. The princess pulled out of Banner's grasp—he was probably doing more harm than good by trying to hold her close—and swam back to join Mica.

"You haven't given up yet," Jessamyn said, "and I won't let you do it now."

Mica's every breath hurt. "My brother."

"Swim," Jessamyn snapped. "That's an order. We'll figure the rest out later."

"I can't."

A swell rose beneath them, knocking them into each other.

"Did I ask if you *could*?" Jessamyn said, spluttering as seawater filled her mouth. "Really, Micathea, it would be terribly selfish of you to drown now."

Mica glared at her, and a familiar anger bubbled up inside. With the anger came a burst of energy.

"We don't have all striking day." Jessamyn grabbed Mica's arm and squeezed hard, her nails digging deep enough to draw blood. "Now, move!"

Mica moved, forcing her limbs to churn, to carry her onward.

He has to be all right.

She swam.

He's injured. That's all.

The waves tried to push her off course, making every stroke a challenge, but she followed the princess through the water. It was the hardest thing she had ever done.

They'll take him prisoner.

She clung to that hope as if it were a life raft. Those Talents wouldn't kill injured prisoners, not when they were no danger to them. They had taken the ship far too easily to worry about one injured Blur.

Injured, not dead. He has to be.

The fight on the *Silk Goddess* came back to her in flashes as she swam. The three men swarming up the side of the ship. Captain Pol falling. Blood spattering the deck. Men screaming. The arrow flying at her brother's back.

"Help!"

Mica's reverie was interrupted by a shrill voice.

"We're over here!" Jessamyn was shouting and waving her hands above her head. "Help us!"

Banner echoed her, his usually melodious voice ragged as he too called for help.

Mica looked around, trying to get her bearings. They were still a long way from the docks. The only ships near them were in as much distress as they were. Jessamyn and Banner were trying to get the attention of a smaller boat cutting through the water ahead of them. It bobbed in and out of view as the waves rose and fell, revealing a dozen men manning the oars and one standing tall in the prow.

"Over here, you big dumb oaf!" Jessamyn screamed.

The boat made a wide turn, bringing it nearer to where they floundered, half-hidden in the swells. Mica recognized the man standing in the prow. He was searching the carnage-strewn waters where the *Silk Goddess* had been, the wind blowing his hair back from his square face.

Caleb.

His eyes were bright in the morning sun, energy in every line of his body.

Caleb is alive.

Mica felt herself drowning in relief as surely as she'd been drowning in the sea. It was an overwhelming sensation, at once painful and ecstatic. She was too relieved to join the cries for help.

Caleb is coming for us.

He spotted their waving arms and leapt into action, shouting orders to his men to turn toward the three bedraggled survivors. Mica had just enough presence of mind left to resume Sapphire's face, knowing it wasn't safe to look like the princess yet.

The boat pulled in close to the trio struggling in the swells. Caleb hauled Jessamyn aboard first, giving her his coat so she could hide her scars. Stievson helped Banner scramble into the boat beside her.

Caleb reached into the sea to rescue Mica last and lifted her onto the boat with what was clearly a burst of Muscle strength.

"Caleb," she gasped, remembering her current face. "It's me, Mic—"

Before she could get out the rest of the sentence, he pulled her into his arms and kissed her. Thoroughly.

Their last kiss had been gentle. But this one. This one was borne of desperation and relief and pent-up passion. Mica's heart was a riot of emotions she couldn't begin to name as Caleb lifted her right off her feet. Her arms locked around his neck, and she clung to him, a life raft, an anchor. As he kissed her more deeply still, her face contorted, possibly into her own face, possibly into a puddle of disparate features, and she didn't care one bit.

"I thought I lost you again," he said against her mouth—and then resumed the kiss before she could respond. She wasn't capable of a coherent response right now anyway.

"Ahem."

Mica recognized that little cough, but even that didn't matter to her now. Let Jessamyn wait on her for once. She was busy being good and kissed.

But they were still on a small boat in the smoky aftermath of a battle, so they had to release each other eventually. Caleb set Mica back on her feet and cupped her face—her real face—in his palms. They didn't say anything. Just stared into each other's eyes for a brief, burning moment.

"Are you *quite* finished?" Jessamyn said.

Mica turned and found she couldn't read the princess's expression at all. Was that anger? Jealousy? Glee? She didn't even bother trying to figure it out.

Caleb's men looked pleased, if a little confused, that their lord had plucked a random woman they had never seen before from the sea and they were already getting along so well.

"The fighting looks to be over, my lord," Stievson said. "What are your orders?"

"We'd better find the Lord of Silverfell and find out how bad the damage is," Caleb said.

"Shouldn't we keep searching for the princess?"

"Huh?" Caleb stared at Stievson, his reaction times slower than usual. Mica felt some of the same haze.

"I saw the princess being taken aboard another rescue boat," Banner said, covering for all of them. "She is probably waiting for us on the docks."

"Yes, that's right," Caleb said. "Let us check for any more survivors and then return to the city."

They sat as the boat began a wide loop around the harbor to scour the water for others who had been forced to abandon ship. While the boat rode atop the swells, Caleb and Mica sat together on a hard bench, bodies pressed close, as if they could no longer stand to have a breath of air between them.

Jessamyn took the seat opposite them. "How long has *this* been going on?" she demanded.

And for once Mica had no desire to please her. She had given up so much of herself for Jessamyn. But this moment, in the midst of carnage and death and loss . . . this moment was hers.

"*Well?*"

Mica slipped her hand into Caleb's, their fingers entwining like tree roots, and ignored the princess entirely.

CHAPTER SEVENTEEN

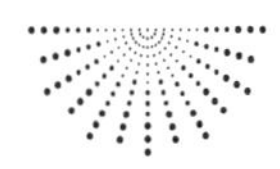

The smoke hanging over the water looked wan in the morning sunlight. It was hard to believe that it wasn't yet noon. Everything had happened so fast since Mica and Jessamyn left their cabin that morning.

They had pulled a few more people from the water, sailors who'd been at work on a civilian trading ship when the attack began. As they reached the dock, where more survivors of the harbor battle were milling about, they began to piece together what had happened from snippets of overheard conversations.

"They came out of nowhere, just before dawn."

"They had three ships at least. Maybe more."

"Aye. Never thought they'd hit the striking harbor."

"We held our own aboard the *Keith*."

"The old *Silver's Revenge* didn't fare so well."

"'Twas those fighters."

"Aye, something wasn't right about them."

The sailors murmured anxiously to each other, something about freakishly strong and fast enemies. A few city residents had come out on the docks too now that the fighting was over, looking pale and frightened. They stared, bewildered, at what was supposed to be one of the calmest and most picturesque port cities in the empire. It was still burning in places.

Mica resumed Jessamyn's face in the confusion as they came ashore. The impersonation was harder this time, as if she wanted to cling to her own self in the wake of what had just happened. She kept hearing a tinny ringing in her ears that had nothing to do with the noise of the battle. Emir had stood no chance against the Fifth Talents—and she didn't think the rest of them did either.

But she was prepared to take control once more. These people needed a leader, and while Mica was the princess, that had to be her.

Captain Karson hurried over to join them, relieved to see that the princess had survived. He kept his report quick and professional. The *Arrow* had managed to sink one enemy ship and severely damage another, but they had taken heavy losses.

"We were boarded by another Talent like the prisoner we took back in the Channel," he said. "One woman with all four Talent abilities."

"We saw some like her too," Mica said.

"More than one?"

"Three men. All with four Talents."

Captain Karson swore then immediately apologized. "No wonder the *Silk Goddess* is lost." He scanned the bedraggled group unloading from Caleb's boat. Caleb and Fritz were helping a wounded man climb onto the dock from the gently bobbing vessel. "Soldier Grayson?"

"He fell," Mica said, "saving my life. He . . . he may be injured, but I don't know for sure."

Captain Karson's mouth tightened. "He would be honored to die for you, Princess."

Mica swallowed, unable to meet his eyes.

"Where is Lord Aren?" Jessamyn said suddenly, her face still half hidden by Caleb's coat.

"I saw him organizing care for the injured, Miss Irondier," Captain Karson said. "He lives."

Jessamyn gave a brisk nod and pulled her collar up higher so Mica couldn't see her expression. But her posture showed the kind of desperate relief Mica had felt when she saw Caleb.

Around them, the docks shuddered with the cries of the injured and bereaved. Mica catalogued their features: bloodless lips, reddened eyes, bruised and broken skin. The aftermath of war was ugly. Mica hated to think what would have happened if the *Arrow* hadn't arrived. But what did the attackers want? She had thought they must be rebels from the Twins, like the man she met back in Carrow, but would Lord Ober truly have given them the ability to create invincible Talents? That seemed generous even for their supposed benefactor.

Something didn't add up. Could Ober himself have decided to deploy his perfected creations? If so, why?

Speculating was useless. She needed information so she could figure out how to meet this new threat.

News of their arrival had gone on ahead of them, and a carriage soon appeared to whisk the nobles to safety. Lord Aren was busy with a few of his men who'd been injured, and he waved for them to go ahead without him. Jessamyn looked him over once from across the dock, but she made no move to throw her arms around him or insist he accompany them. The princess had been quieter than usual since they were rescued from the water, and Mica wondered if she was still trying to decide how to react to the passionate moment she'd witnessed between her imposter and her friend and potential consort.

But when Mica paused to ask if she was okay, Jessamyn raised an eyebrow as if to say, "What are you waiting for, Micathea? I don't have all day."

They climbed into the carriage, salt water still dripping from their clothes, and settled onto cushions embroidered with silver roses. Banner joined Jessamyn, Mica, and Caleb inside, and Fritz rode in front with the carriage driver. He bounced up and down in his anxiety to see his bride, perhaps not quite believing that all the fighting had happened in and around the harbor. He had to see Lorna's face for himself.

As the carriage set off and they relaxed a bit, the cold hit Mica with a vengeance. She shivered violently, and even Caleb's hand in hers wasn't enough to keep her warm. Jessamyn fared a little better. Her simple tunic hadn't retained as much icy seawater as Mica's thick satin gown. Both of them would have to tough it out, though. They had intelligence to gather before they could retire.

Mica distracted herself from the cold by admiring the magnificent sights passing by the carriage window. Silverfell City was almost as awe-inspiring as Jewel Harbor in its own way, even in the aftermath of a deadly assault.

Silverfell was the wealthiest island in the Windfast Empire, despite its small population, and its unique prosperity was all thanks to the silver mines. The citizens had poured their wealth into beautifying their city. Where Jewel Harbor was cramped and chaotic, Silverfell City was pristine, with planned avenues, cultivated plants, and marble buildings that were elegant rather than opulent. The people all looked remarkably clean, and the air smelled of apple blossoms and pine trees beneath the layer of smoke from the harbor.

"Have you been here before?" Mica whispered to Caleb through chattering teeth.

"Yes. It's halfway to my home."

"Have 'I' been here before?" She nodded at Jessamyn, who still wouldn't speak to either of them.

"Several times." Caleb smiled. "But it's okay to gawk. There's nowhere in the world like Silverfell City."

Mica pressed her face to the carriage window as they approached their destination in the center of the immaculate city. Bont, the lord governor, lived in a large manor house that was the pride of Silverfell. The manor's exterior was refined rather than lavish, and its every line complemented the mountain peaks rising behind it. The walls bordering the grounds were made of marble cut from those mountains, and the clay roof tiles had been painted with a graceful motif suggesting hawks soaring over peaks and rivers running through mountain ravines.

The carriage entered the grounds through a pair of silver gates and delivered them to a fine marble portico at the front of the manor. The Lord of Silverfell himself was waiting for them on the steps, a silk tunic straining over his corpulent figure.

"My most gracious and glorious Princess Jessamyn." Lord Bont hurried toward her as she climbed out of the carriage, her movements stiff now from the cold. "It is the greatest honor in all the Windfast to welcome you to my home. I am devastated that you have endured such a terrifying ordeal."

"I am quite all right, my lord," Mica said. "I'd like all the information you can give me about—"

"You must be exhausted, my princess," Lord Bont interrupted, looking almost as shaken as she was by her dip in the harbor. "We have prepared our best and most elegant room to ensure your comfort. Should you want for anything, it would give me the greatest of all joys to provide it."

"I appreciate that. My lord, I understand the rebels—"

"Are you hungry, my princess?" He clutched her hand. "We have prepared an exquisite feast that is sure to delight your senses."

"Thanks. The rebel raiders—"

"Come! I am sure you wish to rest and refresh yourself after your traumatic experience, although you are vibrant and beautiful even in distress. Let me show you—"

"My lord!" Mica snapped. "The empire is at war, and your harbor has just been attacked. I do not need a nap!"

"Forgive me, Your Most Glorious Majesty," Lord Bont wailed. "I am mortified that you encountered trouble here, and I am only trying to see you spared any further inconvenience."

"Convenience is the last thing on my mind," Mica said. "We have work to do."

Lord Bont looked stricken. Mica wondered if he had been hoping he could just brush the whole harbor incident under his finely embroidered rug. She understood that keeping up appearances was important to these people, but as Jessamyn would say, *honestly*.

Captain Karson had followed their carriage on horseback after talking with the commander of the Silverfell City garrison. Mica beckoned for him to join them, hoping the stalwart soldier would provide some much-needed practicality to their discussion. Lord Aren hadn't caught up yet, but they'd have to start without him.

"Lord Bont, is there somewhere we can talk?"

"Of course. Please come inside, Your Highness."

Lord Bont ushered them in to a vast atrium just inside the doors to his manor. Man-sized vases filled with elaborate flower arrangements were spread around the edges of the room, and a marble fountain bubbled in the center, its gentle music at odds with the chaos in the rest of the city. And the rest of the empire.

They formed a loose circle by the fountain: Mica, Jessamyn, Banner, Caleb, Fritz, Bont, and Karson. Mica felt her brother's absence like a wound, but she focused on the task at hand. It was time to hold her first war council.

"Do we have any idea of the attackers' goal?" she began. "Were they trying to take the city?"

"They only attacked with three ships," Captain Karson said. "I doubt that was their objective."

"*Could* they have captured the city if you hadn't arrived with the HIMS *Arrow*?"

"They most certainly could not." Lord Bont sounded affronted. "Silverfell has never fallen."

"I agree, my lord," Karson said calmly. "Though they did

succeed in taking two ships from your waters, including the *Silk Goddess*."

"Could acquiring new ships have been their primary aim?" Mica asked.

"Doubtful," Captain Karson said. "Commandeering them out in open water is far less risky."

Mica nodded, remembering the reports she'd heard back in Lord Gordon's banquet hall. The rebels had been doing just fine as pirates. Why would they take the risk of attacking such a powerful city?

"So they were after something else?"

"Isn't the obvious answer that they wanted to take the princess hostage?" Caleb said, glancing between Mica and Jessamyn.

"That's possible," Mica said. "Rebels from the Twins could want to make demands of my father." She glanced at Jessamyn, relieved that she didn't look like herself right now. "And they sent three of their Fifth Talent fighters out to the *Goddess*."

Caleb looked up sharply. "Their *what*?"

"You didn't see any? There were fighters out there with all four Talents, like our hostage back in Carrow."

"Side effects?"

"Not that I saw."

Caleb rubbed a hand through his hair, his face grave. He knew the implications as well as Mica did. They might already be too late. On the other hand, if he hadn't seen any at all, maybe there weren't as many of them out there as Mica had feared.

"Excuse me, Your Highness," Captain Karson said. "But I'm not so sure this assault was aimed at you. They couldn't have known we'd get to Silverfell so soon. We've had the Muscles on double shifts since Pegasus, and we're here earlier than planned."

"You mean the attack should have been over by the time the princess arrived?" Caleb said.

"That's right—and by the time our warship arrived." Captain

Karson straightened a bit. “They weren’t expecting us to turn up and give them such a hard time. Trying to kidnap the princess must have been an afterthought.”

Mica chewed on her bottom lip, thinking back over the battle. The longboat full of Blurs had attacked them first, and it was only later that the trio of invincible fighters had come after them. If the Fifth Talents had gone straight for the princess in the first instance, Mica would probably be halfway to the Twins by now. Or Timbral. Or the barren fortress. They’d only known about her later in the game.

“So they weren’t here for me,” Mica said.

“They knew we—you’d see the aftermath, though,” Jessamyn said, belatedly adding, “Your Highness.”

Caleb nodded, his face grim. “They wanted to make a statement.”

“Aye,” Captain Karson said. “They showed they can intimidate one of the most powerful cities in the empire.”

“Intimidate is a powerful word,” Lord Bont cut in. He smoothed his hands nervously over his tunic. He had been looking increasingly ill as the group discussed wars and kidnappings in his atrium. “Please don’t trouble yourself so, Princess. If the emperor knew I made his daughter worry about—”

“You must remember that I am your future empress, not your houseguest,” Mica said firmly. “Nothing is more important than understanding this threat. My father would agree with me.”

Jessamyn shifted beside her. Mica had addressed the issue without looking to her for guidance. She had been doing that more and more of late, and she wondered if it made Jessamyn uncomfortable. Mica wasn’t sure how she felt about it herself.

“My apologies, Your Eminence,” Lord Bont said. “I don’t wish to allow these unfortunate events to further disturb my precious daughter’s—”

“Where *is* Lady Lorna?” Fritz interrupted. He had been standing on his toes and staring down the corridors leading away from the atrium, barely listening to their discussion. "Why hasn't she come out to greet me?"

"She should be here by now," Lord Bont said. "I told her that when the princess arrived—"

"My lord, it is a calamity!"

A steward hurled himself around a corner and ran headlong into the atrium, his feet skidding on the marble floor. He had olive skin, graying hair, and a look of deep alarm in his dark eyes.

"Lady Lorna is gone!"

"What?"

"We could not stop it, my lord! When our men went to assist the brave fighters in the harbor, those infernal scoundrels stole into the manor and abducted her."

Fritz seized the steward by the front of the tunic, his scar stretching grotesquely. "Who was it?"

"No one saw them arrive or leave," the steward said.

"What do you mean 'no one saw them'?" Lord Bont demanded, his face as white as an Obsidian's. "Where are her Shield guards?"

"Dead, my lord," the steward said. "The enemies somehow got close enough to poison them."

Gasps escaped from several members of their group, including Banner. It was rare indeed for Shields to be killed in the line of duty. Muscles could drown them or force them to consume a deadly potion—if they could catch them—but such a struggle would surely have raised alarms throughout the manor, even with all the excitement in the harbor.

But a Fifth Talent...

A Fifth Talent could use their Impersonator ability to transform into a member of the Bont household staff. That would get them close enough to force poison down the Shields' throats with their unnatural strength. And it all could have happened very fast.

Hopelessness welled up in Mica like water in a fountain. Who could stand against an enemy with that kind of power?

"There's more, my lord," the steward said. "The kidnappers left a note atop the slain body of Lady Lorna's maid. It's here in my—"

Fritz snatched the parchment from the steward's hand, ripping it in the process. He read the pieces frantically.

"My poor Lorna," he moaned. "We should have eloped in Jewel Harbor."

"Pull yourself together, my lord," Mica said, plucking the torn papers out of his hands. She read the note aloud, only just remembering to use Jessamyn's voice.

To Lord Governor Bont of Silverfell,

The people of Dwindlemire and Cray have spent years being ignored by our rulers. We are hereby divesting ourselves of any bond to the Windfast Empire. Our neighbors on Timbral Island have agreed to back our bid for independence. In return, we will defend the passage to their waters. We call on the Lord of Silverfell to join us in breaking with the empire. Each of our islands will be entirely independent, able to raise our own armies, arrange our own trade agreements, and keep our Talented sons and daughters close.

We will return your daughter unharmed when you agree to support our right to secede.

"The nerve of them!" Lord Bont said in a shocked whisper.

"There's more," Mica said.

Do not attempt to rescue Lady Lorna. We have acquired abilities from a noble benefactor that ensure we can meet any challenge, Talent or otherwise, that you send against us. You have seen evidence of our power in your harbor today.

You may approach Birdfell with a party of no more than three people to give us your assurances of support. We will send a guide to escort your representatives tomorrow at dawn.

Signed,

The Independent Republic of Dwindlemire and the Free Nation of Cray

Mica lowered the scraps of paper. "Where's Birdfell?"

"In the mountains on the western side of the island," Lord Bont said. "It is an abandoned tower—"

"Beside a pond," Caleb said quietly.

"That's right." Lord Bont glanced curiously at the younger lord. "It's a grim place. It was a mine long ago, and it has been left rather barren since its riches were exhausted. They must be using it as a base."

Barren.

Mica felt a tingling sensation in her fingertips, and it wasn't just from the cold. She felt as if she were poised on the brink of a cliff, ready to jump off into the sea.

An abandoned tower.

Mica might feel ready to leap, but Caleb looked as if he was about to keel over. He probably *was*, if he'd used his Talents out on the harbor.

She stepped toward him. "You've been to this place, haven't you?"

"Once, before I started spending so much time in the capital. It's where . . ." Caleb trailed off, and he was silent for so long that Captain Karson cleared his throat. Caleb looked up, his face gray. "Birdfell Tower overlooks a murky pond."

"More of a cesspit," said Lord Bont, his mouth twisting distastefully.

Caleb's body was still, meditative. "I nearly drowned in that pond in my youth."

A cesspit of abomination and corruption.

That was what the mad Talent had said at the anniversary

ball, when he'd screamed about the barren fortress where his suffering began, about the abominable cesspit. Could he have meant a literal cesspit?

"I should have thought of it sooner," Caleb said. "I . . . I had hoped never to visit Birdfell again."

The place where you least wish it to be.

Caleb had feared Haddell meant his home in the Pebble Islands, where Lord Ober had spent so much time. But the man had been elusive, avoiding the spies who'd searched for him in Timbral and Pebble. What if he'd been hiding out in western Silverfell all along, perfectly positioned to help the people of Dwindlemire and Cray strike at Lord Bont?

Mica still didn't know *why* Ober would want to be their benefactor, but the other pieces were coming together. Lord Ober's potions were certainly abominable, and Caleb's near-drowning could have been the exact moment when the corruption of his body occurred. Mica met Caleb's gaze, wondering if he was coming to the same realization.

His eyes were still wells, deep and dark.

The fountain burbled away beside them, adding music to the stillness.

Then another voice piped up, abruptly reminding Mica that she and Caleb weren't the only ones in the atrium. Everyone else was staring at them.

"Forgive me for interjecting, Your Highness," Jessamyn said in the humble voice of Myn Irondier. "What if the princess were to go to this Birdfell place herself and speak with the rebels?"

Lord Bont made a faint distressed noise and sat heavily on the marble lip of the fountain.

"To what end?" Mica asked.

"To persuade them to keep the empire whole."

"It's too late for that," Captain Karson said. "I say my soldiers put them down quickly and be done with it."

"It may not be quick, if they have a lot of Fifth Talents," Caleb said. He sighed heavily. "But I agree that it needs to be done."

Jessamyn shook her head, unwilling to admit that the construct she had worked so hard to preserve was failing. "The princess could make amends for the wrongs her people believe they have suffered. Maybe the rebels could even be persuaded to join us in defeating the Obsidian invaders."

"I've haven't seen any evidence that they'll listen to reason," Captain Karson said.

Mica studied Jessamyn, attempting to read her thoughts. She was no longer holding the coat up to hide her face, her disfigurement on full display. Was she going to reveal herself to help sway the rebels to their cause? Could this be the moment she had been waiting for? Or was she planning to send Mica in her place so she could investigate the barren fortress at last? Mica couldn't believe she'd found it, not in Timbral or the Pebble Islands, not even in the Twins, but hidden just a few days' ride from their current location. She *had* to go.

She opened her mouth to say as much, when Banner spoke up, inserting himself into the conversation for the first time.

"The journey would be too dangerous for the princess."

"Dangerous but necessary." Jessamyn laid a hand on his arm. "For all our sakes."

"They would never let you walk away," Caleb said then seemed to remember he shouldn't be addressing Jessamyn directly. "They already tried to abduct the princess when they realized she was on the *Goddess*. They'll kill her if she marches right up to their tower."

"Aren't you all forgetting that the note asks for Lord Bont?" Fritz said, taking the pieces of parchment back and holding them up. "If the princess goes instead, they might hurt Lorna."

"Their clever benefactor will know to chase the bigger prize," Jessamyn said. Then a beat later, she added, "my lord."

Mica figured Lord Ober would be only too happy for the

woman who had humiliated him at court and destroyed his influence with Emperor Styl to turn up at his front door. But Jessamyn clearly still believed it was worth trying, despite this risk. Mica agreed with her. They needed to end the rebellion through diplomacy for no other reason than that they couldn't defeat a large force of Fifth Talents.

"Myn is right," Mica declared. "I will go to Birdfell in Lord Bont's place and attempt to negotiate."

The lords objected immediately, talking over each other to declare how dangerous this decision was.

But Jessamyn turned on her heel and marched over to a magnificent flower arrangement by the atrium wall. Mica knew when she had been summoned.

"Excuse me for a moment, my lords."

She joined Jessamyn behind the large vase.

"Please let me go to Birdfell," Mica said before the princess could begin. "You should stay here where it's safe."

"I quite agree."

Mica blinked. "You do?"

"I was going to suggest the same course of action."

Mica couldn't believe it. She was finally being allowed to strike out on her own, when Lord Ober was almost within reach. "You trust me to conduct the negotiation with the rebels?"

"I have great faith in you," Jessamyn said impatiently, as if it were the most obvious thing in the world. "Tell the rebels about the Obsidian hordes and how they'll be the next targets if we don't work together."

"Right." Some of Mica's initial excitement faded, replaced by trepidation. She'd wanted to set out on her own for a long time, but this task might be more than she could handle. She'd been less worried when she thought she would be sneaking into another one of Lord Ober's evil workshops, not attempting to win over his allies.

Jessamyn must have sensed her nerves because she reached

out to squeeze her hand. "You know about the common people and their ways, Micathea. I am sure you can work something out with them."

"I'll do my best." Mica wasn't so sure she could do this. She might be a commoner, but diplomacy was still the most difficult part of this role. "Hopefully, I can at least get Lady Lorna back safely."

"I would expect nothing less."

Mica felt warmed by the princess's faith in her, until Jessamyn went on. "I suppose if you're killed, I will be forced to reveal myself. I shall tell the people of Silverfell that my injuries occurred while I was trying to save Lady Lorna. They will admire my bravery." She tapped a finger on her scarred lip. "Yes, it is much better for you to do this without me."

Mica's jaw lengthened as she gaped at the princess.

"Come now, Micathea, I don't *want* you to be killed. I simply need to consider every possibility."

"Okay. I guess it's settled, then."

They started to emerge from behind the flower arrangement, when Jessamyn put a hand on Mica's arm.

"Oh, I need you to do something else in Birdfell."

"Yes?"

"Get me that formula."

Mica froze. "What?"

"I gather from the meaningful glances between you and Caleb that you believe you've solved your barren fortress riddle. Some potion or process is making those invincible Fifth Talents. Now that I've seen the results in battle, I want it."

"But—"

"It's better than letting them have it," Jessamyn said, not allowing her to voice further objections. "You will go to this barren fortress, and you will bring the Fifth Talent potion back for me."

CHAPTER EIGHTEEN

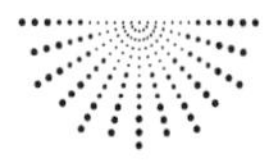

It was quickly decided that Lord Fritz would take Lord Bont's place on their journey to Birdfell.

"I cannot cave to the rebel demands," Lord Bont declared, not quite meeting Mica's eye. "Silverfell will remain loyal to the empire, and my future son will be reunited with Lorna sooner."

"I don't know if that's a good idea," Mica began.

"I must go," Fritz said. He had calmed somewhat, though he was still clutching Lorna's ransom note to his chest. "Please, Princess Jessamyn. If you are a friend to us at all."

"Very well. You will be one of the three, along with Lord Caleb," Mica said without looking at the real Jessamyn for approval. She was feeling ambivalent about following her wishes at the moment. Jessamyn couldn't seriously be contemplating using the Fifth Talent formula, not when they knew what Ober had done to perfect it, could she?

Her brother's voice came back to her, questioning whether she was certain the princess always had the empire's best interests at heart. It was getting harder to know for certain.

The arrangements for the following day made, Lord Bont at last succeeded in ushering the princess and her entourage to their rooms. Mica's teeth were chattering audibly, and Banner had a drip at the end of his long nose. Lord Bont looked as if he might collapse if the future empress were allowed to remain in such a bedraggled state for much longer.

"If you'll follow me, I think you'll find that the manor has been made still more beautiful since your last visit. If I can draw your attention to this mural of a pear orchard along this corridor. It was painted by a folk artist from the remote town of Dustwood . . ."

Mica could hardly believe Lord Bont was giving her a tour in light of everything that had just happened, but she listened patiently to the descriptions of the artwork, the architecture, and the historical significance of every sconce and window dressing on the way to her rooms. The manor smelled of fresh pine and mountain flowers, and she was sorry to trail her waterlogged satin gown across the fine floor.

"I wish to show you the utmost hospitality, Your Graciousness," Lord Bont said, tugging at the silk straining across his belly. "I'm grateful for what you're doing for my daughter. Come. You will find the views from the manor are outshone only by your beauteous face."

An elegant suite of rooms had been prepared for the princess, with a well-framed view of the mountains hiding Silverfell's famed mines. A gentle breeze blew through diaphanous curtains, carrying only a hint of smoke from the harbor. As the afternoon sunlight glittered on a silver tea set awaiting them, Mica realized she was ravenous.

"I shall have food and warm bathwater sent to you," Lord Bont promised. "I fear I must attend to other matters, but perhaps you would like to walk in the rose garden before dinner? And do let me know if I can provide anything to improve your stay in Silverfell."

"I need a new knife, actually," Mica said, drawing the only

one she had managed to save during the battle. "Preferably one about this size. I have a sheath already."

"Of course, my princess." Lord Bont bowed deeply, hiding his surprise at this request. "Anything you desire."

At last, Mica managed to shoo Lord Bont away, leaving her and Jessamyn alone to change into dry clothes.

"Finally," Mica said when she was sure he was gone. She went to the huge silver-inlaid wardrobe in the inner room and began pulling out the silk dresses and embroidered riding clothes that had hastily been prepared for them. The only thing missing was a crown.

"I don't know how you stand it, Princess," she said as she dug through the wardrobe for something more practical for her journey. "All that fawning."

"Don't be ungrateful, Micathea," Jessamyn said. "Lord Bont has gone to great trouble to welcome you."

"I appreciate the effort, but there are more important things going on here. Does that old lord have to be so . . . so . . ."

"Welcoming? Complimentary? What exactly is your problem?"

"It's all fake, isn't it?" Mica said, still sorting through the clothes. "It's the same with all these lords and ladies. They put on faces, just like Impersonators. They don't actually like us."

Jessamyn didn't reply, prompting Mica to look up from the pile of garments. The princess had gone stiff, as if she'd been slapped across the face.

Mica wished she could take back the words. "I didn't mean—"

"I know exactly what you meant," Jessamyn snapped.

"I'm sure all the nobles like you," Mica said. "But when they grovel so much, it feels—"

"I'm aware of how it feels. I have been a princess for far longer than you have been an imposter."

"I'm sorry." Mica realized she had hurt Jessamyn's feelings. "I—"

"That will be all."

"But—"

"You do not have permission to speak to me."

Mica sighed. "Yes, princess."

She changed into a simple wool dress and set aside a few things for her journey to Birdfell, trying not to disturb Jessamyn as she crept around the chamber. She supposed it wasn't the best time to broach the issue of the Fifth Talent formula again.

The princess stared out the window at the mountains, still in her wet clothes, her scarred arms folded tight around her. Mica couldn't see her face, but once she heard a quiet little gasp, as if the princess was crying—and trying desperately to hide it.

Guilt twisted at Mica's insides. She shouldn't have lashed out like that. Jessamyn had been through the same hell she had that morning, and she had just as much of a right to be delicate right now. Mica still sometimes fell into the trap of seeing the princess as the larger-than-life person she was in public instead of an *actual* person. She deserved better.

"Princess?" Mica said after a while. "Can I make you some tea?"

Jessamyn didn't answer. Mica poured the tea anyway and fetched a warm blanket from the canopy bed.

"You'll get sick," she said, holding out the steaming teacup. "That'll be no good for anyone. Please take this."

Jessamyn's shoulders slumped, and she surrendered to Mica's care at last.

"It's too much," she said quietly after she shed her damp clothes and settled in a chair, the blanket wrapped tight around her.

"What do you mean?"

"The Obsidian invasion, the rebels, the Fifth Talents. I feel like everything is blowing up around me, and I don't know what to do anymore." She sipped her tea, her brown eyes large above the rim of her cup. When she set it back on her saucer, her gaze lingered on the damaged skin on her hands.

"I wish my father were here," Jessamyn whispered. "He always said being a leader is the loneliest job in the world."

Mica curled up in the chair across from her, thinking of her own father, so close now to enemy lines. And her brothers, wherever they were.

"You're not alone," she said. "You have me. You have Caleb."

"*Lord* Caleb."

"Exactly. We're your friends, and we care about you. *You*, not just the empire. We'll help you find a way to solve all these problems."

"How?"

Mica sipped her own tea and did her very best Jessamyn voice. "I haven't the faintest idea. *Honestly*, Jessa, I can't be expected to know everything."

Jessamyn burst out laughing, and Mica realized it was the first time in ages she'd heard a genuine laugh from her. Maybe the first time ever.

The princess's laughter faded, and she sighed. "I wish . . . never mind."

"What is it?"

Jessamyn's cheeks flushed beneath her scars. "I wish I were brave."

"You *are* brave."

"Not like Caleb, who lives every day with a dangerous illness. Not like your brother and all the Talents who risk their lives to protect us."

"You don't have to be like them. You have your own way." Mica thought of Jessamyn forcing her to swim through the war-torn harbor when Emir's loss threatened to pull her underwater, of Jessamyn cracking open a man's skull with a teapot when he tried to kill her, of Jessamyn facing every day even though she'd lost what she believed to be her greatest asset. "You should let people see what you're really like, and I don't just mean your new face."

"What if they don't like what they see?"

Mica hesitated. She knew the princess had spent her entire life creating a persona for herself, one she was certain would be both enchanting and effective at achieving her goals. Mica had spent her life learning to assume different faces for essentially the same reason. But Jessamyn had been a master at it. She was beautiful while still potentially attainable. She was charming without being threatening. She made people feel special while communicating that she was the most special of all. But now she was confronted with the reality that all that might not be enough. Mica reminded herself that Jessamyn was still very young. Even though it seemed as if she was this incredible force, she was still human.

"I know it's scary," Mica said, speaking slowly as she sorted through what she wanted to say. "Everything is scary right now. Maybe they won't like the truth. Maybe they won't respond to you the same way they used to. But you can't hide forever. With everything going on, I think people need the real you more than they need what this face used to represent."

She gestured to the impersonation she wore all the time now, the face of a pretty princess who wore silver crowns and danced at starlit balls. Then she let her features contort, the skin sliding and reshaping, the hair shortening, the mouth becoming lopsided but resolute.

"I think they need *this* woman, who will fight like a hurricane to save her friends and who's willing to admit she can be wrong."

Jessamyn studied the face she had assumed, and Mica remembered when the princess had scrutinized her very first impersonations the day she arrived at the Silver Palace. Her sharp eyes filed away every detail, her lips pursed in concentration. She clearly didn't like what she saw, but she didn't turn away either, as she often did when she glanced at herself in a mirror. It was a start.

A knock sounded at the door.

"Princess?" Banner stuck his head through the doorway. "Lord Aren wishes to see you."

Mica and Jessamyn exchanged identical glances.

"Well?" the princess snapped. "What are you waiting for?"

Mica jumped, forgetting that answering was supposed to be her job. "Why don't you start with Aren? I think he's the sort of man who will look past the surface."

Jessamyn seemed to consider it for a fleeting moment, but then panic flickered in her eyes.

"I'm not ready. You talk to him."

Mica was disappointed, but she quickly reset her face and invited Lord Aren into the sitting room.

The Pegasus lord's shirt was splattered with blood, and his hair had come loose from its tail. He nodded politely to Jessamyn, who still sat, unveiled, in her chair. Then he turned to Mica and explained that he had learned the princess was heading into danger. He had come straight to her rooms to demand to accompany her.

"I reckon that going to see the rebels is the right thing to do, Princess," he said. "I trust your judgment, but I can't let you go alone."

"I've chosen my escorts already, my lord."

He shook his head with the kind of calm certainty only a man who knows his exact place in the world can convey.

"Be that as it may, I refuse to leave your side."

Mica arched one of Jessamyn's eyebrows. "You refuse?"

"Yes, my lady."

"What makes you think you can protect me better than anyone else?"

"Because I would die for you, Jessamyn."

Then Aren advanced toward her, his resolute strides suggesting he was about to give Mica a terribly ardent kiss.

Jessamyn stuck out her foot.

Aren tripped, losing his balance, and crashed hard into Mica. They fumbled for a moment, confused, and Mica managed to dodge his romantic overtures.

As soon as Mica and Aren extracted themselves from the tangle and regained their footing, Jessamyn stepped between them.

"I have something to tell you."

The princess was still wrapped only in blankets, her shoulders bare and her face uncovered. Then, despite saying she wasn't ready, despite all her fears about facing the world without her pretty mask, she looked up into Aren's eyes, took a deep breath, and finally told him the truth.

"I am the real Jessamyn. I am the girl who played with you in the fields and taught you how to bow properly. I'm the one who was afraid of horses—and even more afraid to admit it. I'm also the one you rescued from the river, even though you didn't know that was what you were doing."

"You have been Jessamyn all along?" There was something like recognition in Aren's voice, and Mica wondered—hoped, really—that some part of him had suspected the truth.

Jessamyn nodded at Mica. "This is my Impersonator, Micathea. She has been acting in my place since I was poisoned nearly four months ago."

Mica quickly scrubbed the old Jessamyn's features from her face to confirm the story. Aren looked her over for a moment, seeing her true face for the first time, then he turned back to the real princess.

"Who did this to you?"

Jessamyn's lips quivered for a moment. "Lord Ober of Timbral. I thought I could outwit him, but I was naïve. I underestimated how far he would go—and the mistake nearly killed me."

"*He* nearly killed you," Aren said. "But I am so glad he failed."

Then, without a second look at Mica, he got down on his knees before Jessamyn and took her mottled hands in his.

"Allow me to stay at your side. I swear I will do anything in my power to protect you and prevent you from being hurt again."

"Even though I look like this?"

Jessamyn's eyes welled up with tears, and Aren rose to wipe them away with a gentle, calloused hand.

"You are exquisite," he said softly, cupping her scarred cheek. "You are the most captivating woman I have ever met."

Mica quietly retreated from the pair to give the two some privacy, her heart swelling with pride and relief. The Pegasus lord was taking the revelation even better than she could have hoped. She hoped he would use the line about wanting to make her happy again. If he did, she fully expected Jessamyn and Aren to be engaged by the time she returned from her expedition.

She slipped out of the room, feeling that they'd won a little victory at last.

CHAPTER NINETEEN

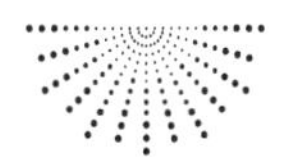

As promised in Lorna's ransom note, their rebel guide arrived at dawn the next day to escort them to Birdfell. He appeared at the gates to Lord Bont's manor wearing the grim face and dark hair of Emperor Styl.

"I think we've met before," Mica said when Bont's guards brought him up to the marble portico. She wore the old Jessamyn's face, but she felt as if the day was nearing when she would once again be nothing more or less than the princess's Impersonator.

"So now you remember," said the Styl imposter. Then the color drained out of his hair, and he became the blond, bearded man with watery eyes she had met back in Carrow. "I volunteered to be your guide when I learned *you* rather than Lord Bont would be meeting with my comrades."

Mica frowned, wondering who had carried that bit of intelligence to the rebels. She wouldn't put it past them to have spies inside the manor. She hadn't expected to travel with a true Fifth Talent, though, and it made her more nervous than she already was.

"You never told me your name."

"You may call me Ed, seeing as we're friends now."

"When did you arrive in Silverfell?"

"The same day you did, Your Highness." He offered no further explanation. Mica hoped he hadn't hurt anyone when he escaped from Lord Gordon's prison. They had known those earthen walls wouldn't hold him once he decided to leave. He could have hitched a ride on their ship as an imposter for all she knew, or gone on ahead with his Blur speed.

She introduced Ed to Caleb and Fritz, who waited beside her with packs on their backs and hands on their swords. She made sure they understood that the Dwindlemire rebel had four fully-fledged abilities, but she did not disclose Caleb's Talents.

"Lords rather than Shields?" Ed said. "Interesting choice, Princess. Shall we?"

Mica looked back at Jessamyn, who was watching them from the shadows of the atrium, Lord Aren and Banner flanking her. Jessamyn's eyes blazed with resolve above her veil. Mica trusted that she would be ready to retake her crown when the time was right. They had set out from Jewel Harbor with two different missions. Now it was up to Mica to see them both through.

The Fifth Talent cleared his throat. "Birdfell awaits, Your Highness."

Mica mounted the horse Lord Bont had provided for her and gestured imperiously to the gates. "Lead the way, Ed."

Deep-purple clouds hung overhead as they rode out of the pristine city and into the mountains. They traveled light, with a few supplies in saddlebags and bedrolls tucked behind them. They all wore cloaks and gloves to protect them from the cold mountain air—and hide their identities if necessary. Mica had a simple silver diadem in her saddlebags in case she needed it later. Lord Bont had lent her the crown, a relic from the days when his own ancestors were queens, because Jessamyn's jewels had been lost with the *Silk Goddess*.

The mountain path was misty, making it feel like twilight even though it wasn't yet noon. It was eerily quiet away from the bustling harbor and the endless rush of the sea. Mica shivered, clutching her cloak a little tighter around her. She wore the embroidered riding clothes Lord Bont had placed in her rooms, which were thick and warm, but her chill had little to do with the weather.

Every once in a while, Ed would turn in his saddle to look at her with those watery eyes. She got the sense that he was surprised she had offered to make this journey herself, and he was trying to figure out if there was a catch.

Fritz rode alongside Ed, asking him anxious questions about the road and whether they might encounter any delays. It would take them two days to travel through the interior of the island to their destination, which already felt too long. The rebels could be creating new Fifth Talents by the hour.

Fritz kept drumming an anxious rhythm on his saddle, and it only added to Mica's agitation. She hoped bringing him along hadn't been a mistake. She would much rather have her brother with her than the fretful young lord.

But at least she had Caleb.

He was a stalwart presence at her side as they climbed the rocky path overhung with trees, and he helped to keep her nerves at bay. She couldn't imagine making this journey without him.

"Can you tell me what happened to you in Birdfell?" she asked him after they crossed the first misty ridge—and she was certain their companions were too far ahead to hear them. "Why were you there in the first place?"

"I visited with my uncle one summer when I was six years old," Caleb began. "As the youngest son, I was going to be shipped away to live in Jewel Harbor in a few years. My parents wanted me to see more of the outer islands first. Ober is my mother's brother, as you know, and she especially wanted me to get to know Timbral." Caleb brushed a gloved hand through his hair, disturbing the droplets of mist that had settled on his head. "I wasn't there long when Ober and Euphia packed me up and took me traveling. We saw many different places, but I was too young to keep them all straight."

"But the purpose of the trip was to show you the outer islands?"

"As far as I knew, but I didn't spend much time thinking about it back then. It was just what we did."

Mica thought about what she had been doing at six years old, the age when Caleb was traveling the world with his uncle, preparing to become an ambassador for the Pebble Islands. She'd spent most of her time chasing after her brothers and trying to lift heavy objects. She had wanted to be a Muscle like her mother when she was little.

"Haddell the potioner already worked for my uncle then," Caleb went on. "He kept a workshop in Timbral, but he also came with us on our tour. I wonder now if it was really a research trip for their potions. Haddell and my uncle would spend hours in his cabin, reading and scribbling away in notebooks. Ober was obsessed with something, and it used to annoy Euphia when he stayed behind on the ship to work instead of going sightseeing with us."

"Was he brewing potions on board?"

"I don't know. I was too busy eating strange foods and chasing seagulls across the docks of a dozen port cities to care what kind of work he was doing." Caleb grimaced. "I was having the time of my life."

Mica touched his arm briefly. She knew Ober's betrayal still stung, and it must hurt to realize that a joyous childhood trip had been leading up to the ultimate betrayal.

"My aunt and I often explored without him, but when we reached Silverfell, Ober left the ship with us bright and early."

"In Silverfell City?"

"No, there's a small harbor closer to Birdfell. It's the nearest Silverfell port to the Twins."

"Could that be where the rebels took the *Silk Goddess*?"

"It's certainly possible." Caleb gave her a sympathetic look. Mica still clung to the hope that Emir was merely injured and that if they found the *Silk Goddess*, they would find him.

"Anyway, we left the port and rode into the mountains to Birdfell Mine. The weather was a lot like this, actually." Caleb adjusted his cloak, making the mist swirl around him. "We stayed in the tower for a few days, and Uncle Ober seemed to know the place well. He must have gone there often. Lord Bont said it was abandoned, but I believe Ober has been operating in secret there for a long time."

"And now he's letting the rebels use it."

"It seems so."

Mica glanced up at Ed, Fifth Talent and citizen of the Independent Republic of Dwindlemire. For once, she was happy Jessamyn hadn't revealed her identity after all. If Ed was leading them into a trap, it would spring on the wrong princess.

She turned back to Caleb. "So what happened with the pond, the cesspit Lord Bont mentioned?"

"Why uncle warned me to stay away from it. It was a murky thing, with red-black water that made it impossible to see the bottom." He lifted his broad shoulders in a shrug. "I wouldn't have gone near it if my uncle hadn't told me not to. Pebble Islands children learn to swim almost before they can walk, and my six-year-old pride was offended that he thought I couldn't."

"So you jumped right in?"

"It was as if I'd landed in jelly. The water seemed to cling to me, making it impossible to swim out. I flailed around, shouting for help, but no one came."

Mica could picture it. The little boy with tousled brown hair, leaping confidently into the dark waters. His confidence would turn to fear as he discovered that the murky liquid was not water at all.

"How did you get out?"

"I don't know." Caleb frowned, scanning the misty woods around them as if looking for clues that would help him understand the memory. "I slipped beneath the surface, all that murky water clogging my mouth and nose. But just before I passed out, my feet hit the bottom." His square hands tightened on his reins. "Do you know what I felt there? Stone, not mud. It was a manmade basin, with reeds planted around it to disguise it as a natural pond. The next thing I knew, I was lying on my side next to the pond, alone and covered in black scum, wondering why I wasn't dead. I cleaned myself up and never told anyone. Maybe Ober himself pulled me out and revived me as soon as I was good and drowned."

Mica shuddered, not wanting to picture that tousled-haired boy with his lungs clogged with poison.

"Do you think he meant for you to go into the water so he could try his potion on a child?"

"Haddell implied as much. Ober was eager to test his theories. Perhaps he thought his potion already worked and he was doing me a favor."

Mica felt a familiar rage simmering within her. "Still, to put any child through that, much less his own nephew . . ." She touched the cold hilt of the knife strapped to her leg.

"It was one of the more terrifying experiences of my life, but I confess I didn't connect it to my abilities," Caleb said. "When Haddell gave us that clue, I concentrated on locations where I have good memories and people I care about. I thought he meant I would least wish Ober to be conducting his experiments in those places."

"Like the lighthouse in the Pebble Islands?"

"Exactly. My brothers and I used to go there for high days,

and it's easily my favorite place in the empire." Caleb paused, looking at her with clear, deep-blue eyes. "I'd like to take you there one day."

Mica blushed, and she was glad their companions were ahead of them.

"I'd love to visit the Pebble Islands," she said, "when all this is over."

She wasn't sure what "all this" meant. Ober's schemes? The rebellion? The war with Obsidian? None of those things would make Caleb any less a lord.

They came upon a bridge over a deep ravine. The other two had already started across, their hoof beats ringing loud in the silence. As Mica prepared to follow, a flicker of movement on the opposite cliff caught her eye. Scouts, perhaps? They had to assume they were being watched as they traveled farther into the mountains.

Mica eyed the cliff as they crossed the ravine, which was filled with fog so thick it hid the river far below, but she saw no further signs of observers. She kept the cowl of her cloak pulled up just in case. She would announce who she was—or whom she represented—when the time was right.

Ed and Fritz waited for her and Caleb to reach the other side of the bridge before once more taking the lead. Mica wondered how much they could get Ed to tell them about how he had become a Fifth Talent. He certainly seemed to know the route to Birdfell well, even though he was from another island.

"Do you think you have to be drowned in the potion for it to work?" she asked Caleb, still considering his story.

"At the time, maybe," Caleb said. "But Ober has had well over a decade to improve his method, and we know he hasn't been idle."

Mica gritted her teeth, remembering the Talents in the warehouse and how they'd been tortured and sliced up and drained of their blood. She thought of the madman at the anniversary ball, screaming of suffering. How many people had Ober destroyed in order to make Fifth Talents like Ed, in control as well as invincible?

And had Ober used the potion on himself? The thought hadn't occurred to Mica before now. Would it even be *possible* to defeat him?

"We should have killed him when we had the chance," Mica said.

Caleb didn't respond for a long time. A strong wind blew through the ravine, amplifying the cries of the birds of prey swooping overhead. It had grown even colder as they traveled into the heights. It felt as if they were leaving behind the people they had been in Jewel Harbor, riding toward a new reckoning.

At last, Caleb spoke. "You are right, Mica. He needs to die. I wasn't ready before, but Ober cannot be allowed to live." He looked over at her. "And next time, I'll be wary of whom I trust. The list is pretty much down to you and Jessamyn right now."

Mica hesitated, thinking of what Jessamyn had said when they were hidden behind the vase in the atrium. She'd ordered her to procure the Fifth Talent formula, the one that had already caused so much suffering. Could Mica trust the princess not to use it?

"I don't always agree with Jessamyn," she said slowly, "but I believe she wants to do the right thing."

"I think so too," Caleb said. "But as much as she denies it, she's still human." He reached out to take Mica's hand. "If she falls, we need to be there to catch her."

Mica met his eyes, squeezing his hand tight. "Agreed."

They continued deeper into Silverfell, occasionally passing cozy villages and well-designed homes set amongst the trees. Mines were scattered all throughout the mountains, steadily drawing forth the riches of the island. As in Silverfell City, the people had used their wealth to craft large houses out of high-quality materials, even in these remote reaches.

Dwindlemire and Cray didn't have riches like Silverfell. Their mountains produced less in a year than Silverfell did in a month, which was largely why their interests hadn't been a priority at the imperial court. Mica had seen for herself how Lorna and the other Silverfell nobles had received more attention than the nobles from the Twins—never mind the commoners. *They* didn't get much attention at all, except at Emperor Styl's occasional public audiences.

I wonder if . . .

Something had occurred to Mica, a possibility that could help explain another piece of the puzzle.

She urged her horse forward to ride beside Ed the Fifth Talent, waving for Fritz to fall back beside Caleb.

"You were a petitioner, weren't you?"

"I beg your pardon?" Ed looked up, and Mica noticed his watery eyes were green above his blond beard. They'd been brown that morning and blue back in Carrow. He still hadn't mastered his Mimic ability, even though he seemed to have a knack for it.

"You said we'd met before in Jewel Harbor. Did you come to one of my father's audiences in the Silver Palace?"

"Very good, Princess. Oh, you were very kind. You smiled and nodded and agreed with your father when he refused to help my family."

Mica had attended some of Emperor Styl's audiences for commoners who didn't have privileged access to the Silver Palace. They were often an exercise in frustration. He couldn't always help those who came to him with final desperate pleas for help, though she had certainly seen him try.

"What was your request?"

"A potioner for my ailing son," Ed said. "The emperor offered me coin to buy a health tonic in Potioners Alley, fair enough, but I wanted him to send a few well-trained potioners to the Twins on a more permanent basis."

"And he refused?"

Ed morphed into the emperor again, making his stony face far uglier than the real Styl, his eyes utterly devoid of compassion.

"I traveled all that way for nothing," he said bitterly. "There he was, living in the most grotesque luxury I've ever seen, his little daughter perched on his knee in a silver crown worth more than my village. He sent me away, and when I got home, my son was dead."

Mica gasped.

"I knew it was a possibility when I left," Ed said. "That's why I wanted to bring a few potioners back with me, so others wouldn't have to travel all that way and hope their families lasted long enough for it to make a difference."

This all must have happened long before Mica came to the Silver Palace, but she still felt heartsick for Ed's child. Why couldn't the emperor have paid for a few potioners to work out in the Twins? Potions were costly, which was why people like Quinn traveled to Jewel Harbor to ply their trade, but Emperor Styl had more wealth than he could ever use. He should have helped.

"I'm so sorry for your loss."

Ed bowed his head, allowing his own features to flow into place. When he looked up, his eyes were defiant. "I learned my lesson about how meaningless it is to be an imperial subject. When I got home, I joined up with others who'd already seen the light about the empire."

"The rebels?"

"The revolutionaries."

"And then Lord Ober found you and offered you a new kind of potion?"

Ed cocked his head to the side and grinned. "I see you're not just a pretty face. No, that was years later. We tried to gather support for our cause for years before he ever turned up. It is finally time."

Mica remembered how Jessamyn and Lady Maren had been surprised that this particular secession effort was so organized, even though there had been other petty uprisings. Something had changed this time around. Lord Ober must be helping the men from the Twins refine their strategy as well as enhance their physical abilities. But she still couldn't figure out *why*.

Like Ed, Mica's friend Danil came from Dwindlemire. He had traveled to the Mimic Academy in Redbridge, hoping to serve the empire in exchange for a better life. And he had received nothing but pain at the hands of Lord Ober.

Mica felt that familiar rage, simmering away in her belly like a potioner's cauldron. Ober had corrupted the Talents, the empire's greatest strength. And for what? So he could give the power to his rebellious neighbors, who had played at uprisings for years, always falling to infighting and disagreements in the end? No, there was more to his scheme still.

Ed had legitimate grievances, and Mica couldn't defend the emperor's inaction. But Ober must be using the genuine struggles of his neighbors for his own ends, promising them the world in the form of unbeatable Talents. It was too generous—and far too easy—for him to simply give them his formula without strings. He wanted something from them. Perhaps if Mica could show them that Lord Ober couldn't be trusted, she would have a chance of swaying them to her cause.

They spent the night in a grove of trees set well away from the road, where they found a travelers' campsite with an oft-used fire pit.

"I don't reckon we should stay in an inn," Ed said after apologizing for the roughness of the accommodations. "We'd draw too much attention to your ladyship."

"I am perfectly fine sleeping on the ground," Mica said. "Someone knows we're here, though. I have seen people watching us."

"I saw them too." Ed gave her an appraising look, perhaps even a little impressed. "Still, we don't need regular Silverfell folk spotting you in a grimy mountain inn. They might decide we kidnapped you and launch a rescue."

"A wise decision to keep out of their way, then," Mica said.

They built a fire as darkness fell over the mountains. After a simple meal of bread and cheese, Fritz rolled into his blankets and fell asleep. Ed went off to scout their surroundings, perhaps looking for evidence of their shadows or to make contact with some of his comrades. Mica wouldn't be surprised to learn that their unseen escorts were actually his friends.

Mica and Caleb stayed up late, sitting on a bed of pine needles by the campfire and talking quietly. They told each other stories about their families and shared happier childhood memories than Caleb's last visit to Birdfell. Mica described her adventures with Sapphire and Danil in Redbridge, and he told her about his swordsmanship training with Stievson and his retainers. They had been with him for years, helping him to control the erratic condition his uncle had inflicted upon him.

"Stievson was the one who gave me this." Caleb touched his side, where Mica knew a puckered scar marred his occasionally impervious skin. "I got frustrated when I thought he was going easy on me. I challenged him and learned the hard way that not only was he a better swordsman, he wasn't afraid to cut me up to teach me a lesson."

"How old were you?"

"Fourteen and stupid." Caleb grinned. "Jessa teased me for a year and sent me a new flower arrangement every day because she thought my room was too ugly."

"She does love pretty things, doesn't she?" Mica said drowsily. She was so tired she could barely keep her head up, but she didn't want to retire to her own blankets yet. She and Caleb had precious little time to be alone.

When the flames began to die down, Caleb rose to put more wood on the campfire.

"I've been thinking about something," he said as he tossed a large branch onto the fire, sending sparks up to the stars. "I understand Emperor Styl wants Jessa to get married to help strengthen ties across the empire."

"She told you that?"

"She did. And it occurred to me that if she insists on keeping up this imposter charade permanently, that, well, maybe a link with the Pebble Islands could help."

Mica raised an eyebrow. "Is that a proposal, my lord?"

"I guess I'm proposing a proposal."

"Romantic."

Caleb laughed, and Mica was surprised at the joy that flooded through her at the sound. It had been too long since she last heard that rich, full-bodied laugh.

"The idea has crossed my mind too," Mica said. "Did you know you're the emperor's first choice for Jessamyn's consort?"

"Me?"

Mica grinned at the guileless surprise on his square face.

"You're nicer than her other suitors, and he said a link with the farthest islands in the empire would have symbolic significance."

"Huh. Guess I'm cleverer than I thought."

Caleb sat down beside her again, regarding her with that open curiosity that had appealed to her so much the day they met on the cliff top—and every day since, really. He took her hand.

"Couldn't something good come of all this for you and me?"

Mica's pulse quickened at his gruff, heartfelt tone.

And for the second time, she imagined what would happen if she took Jessamyn's place for good. A wedding in the Pebble Islands. A silver crown on her head. A blue-eyed lord on her arm.

She pushed away the image.

"I don't think Jessa plans to use an imposter forever." She didn't bother mentioning Lord Aren. She understood that Caleb was not talking about marrying the real Jessamyn. "In fact, I hope she doesn't."

"Oh?"

She met his gaze, surprised at the nerves that stirred in her belly. "If you want me," she said softly, "it'll have to be as myself."

"I want you," Caleb said. No hesitation, no hidden agenda. As straightforward as ever. "But if you stay the princess, it'll save us the fit my parents will throw when I tell them I'm in love with a commoner."

Mica felt as if her heart had struck up a waltz in her chest. She wanted Caleb to be hers more than she had ever wanted anything. He was within reach now, even though none of the barriers between them had actually fallen.

Mica forced her own features onto her face and crawled toward Caleb across the bed of pine needles.

She paused, hovering with her face an inch from his, savoring the way he drank in her true features, the way his breath quickened against her mouth. She got closer, closer.

"Mic—" She pressed her lips to his.

The fire crackled beside them, a sputtering flame that was no match for the heat that flared in Mica's body as Caleb's mouth moved in time with hers. After a few breathless, heated moments, they drew apart to look into each other's eyes, their heartbeats whispering into the flickering darkness. Despite the strangeness of their circumstances and the near certainty that this could never work between them, Mica wasn't sure she'd ever been happier.

"My brothers will never let me hear the end of it when I tell them I'm in love with a fancy lord."

Caleb grinned, and somehow his smile made her happier still. Then he buried his hands in her nut-brown hair and pulled her in again.

CHAPTER TWENTY

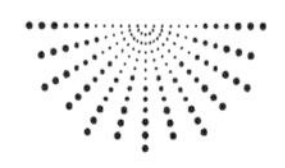

When they awoke the next morning, Caleb was too exhausted to stand. Mica had drifted off to sleep with her face pressed into his chest, his cheek resting on her head. Caleb had carried her to her bedroll and covered her face with a blanket so she would have time to resume Jessamyn's appearance before anyone saw her in the morning.

Now she knelt beside him as he fought to keep his eyes open.

"Did you use your Muscle strength last night?" she asked him quietly.

"Shield," he said. "Holding . . . Mica." Then his eyes fell shut, and he slumped back onto his bedroll.

Mica went still as she realized what he meant. As Caleb held her close in the warmth of the dying fire, his skin had become impervious, as if he was determined to shield her from all the danger and uncertainty they faced in the world.

It was very sweet, but it meant he would be vulnerable as they neared the barren fortress.

"You'll have to tie him to his horse," Mica said to Fritz and Ed, making her tone brusque.

"What's wrong with him?" Ed said.

Mica hesitated. Would the truth help him understand the cost of his precious new Talents? She couldn't count on it.

"He needs sleep," she said. "Well? We don't have all day."

Mica checked on Caleb often as they rode deeper into the mountainous western region. He always looked younger when he slept, and she couldn't help brushing his tousled hair back from his face and making sure his cloak was wrapped tight to keep him warm.

Fritz noticed what she doing, but when he started to comment, she frightened him into silence with one of Jessamyn's best death stares.

Caleb slept for most of the second day's journey, his condition slowing their progress. They had to stop often to retie the bonds keeping him in his saddle, and they couldn't ride as quickly as they had the day before. Ed grumbled that they would arrive at Birdfell later than planned, but he knew better than to suggest they leave Caleb behind.

They climbed higher and higher through remote passes and across long stretches of untouched wilderness, the cold harrying them like a beast at their heels. The mists cleared as they climbed, and the sun was a high, cold crystal above their heads.

When late-afternoon shadows again stretched across their path, they reached a crossroads marked by a faded sign. The letters looked as though they'd once been silver, but the precious metal had been dug out long ago, leaving behind deep grooves in the wood.

"Birdfell is over the next ridge," Ed said. "We'll be there by noon tomorrow."

"Wait." Mica was looking at the sign for the other fork in the path, where she'd spotted a familiar name. "Do you know anything about a place called Dustwood?"

Ed shook his head. "Can't say that I do."

"My friend told me about a sailor from there." Mica thought back to when she and Peet had chatted over bread and Redbridge cheese about the man on the docks with multiple abilities—and the cousin who kept him on.

He's from a village called Dustwood . . . spent ages telling me about their pear orchards.

"What of it?" Ed said.

"The sailor was a little strange," Mica said. "Maybe even mad."

"Lorna told me about Dustwood," Fritz said suddenly. "It's an old mining village."

Mica blinked in surprise. She hadn't expected any help from him. "What made her bring it up?"

"The people aren't right there," Fritz said. "There are some eccentric folks who come from Dustwood to work in Silverfell City. She hired a painter from there to redo her bedroom a few times. He tells strange stories about the place."

"This is all very interesting," Ed said, "but shouldn't we be moving along? We need to make camp before dark."

Mica looked at Caleb, who was still fast asleep astride his horse. She had a hunch. It wasn't much to go on, but she wanted to know for certain.

"Let's stay in Dustwood tonight," she said.

"Princess?"

"I'm sure they'll have an inn, and it won't take us far out of our way."

"What if someone recognizes you?" said Fritz.

"Then we'll tell them we're risking our lives to help their Lady Lorna. And perhaps they can tell us what it's like to live so close to Birdfell."

Ed shrugged, his beard shifting from blond to dark brown. "If you insist, Princess."

"I do."

Dustwood was strange. There was no other way to put it. Comprised of perhaps thirty cabins set amongst mature pine trees, it had an eerie, unhealthy smell, like mold, camphor, and rust. Unsettling sounds came from some of the cabins, whimpers and laughter and the crunch of breaking furniture.

As they rode past the first houses, they glimpsed swift figures flitting among the trees. They were as fast as Blurs, but their movements lacked the purposeful speed Mica was used to from Blur messengers and fighters. These people seemed to be moving very fast for no reason whatsoever.

Mica began to doubt whether they'd really find an inn as they got farther into the village. Dustwood felt forgotten, a place few travelers would visit willingly. Even the houses looked dilapidated and cheap compared to the ones they'd seen closer to Silverfell City. Her nerves tingled, as if a spider were crawling up and down her spine.

"I don't like this place, Princess," Fritz said, riding up beside her. "Why are the people—?"

Suddenly, a thunderous crash sounded behind them. Mica whirled around, and Fritz reached for his jeweled dagger. A tree had fallen directly across the road. It rested at an angle, held up by cracked branches. A tiny figure darted away from the uprooted base, disappearing amongst the run-down cabins.

"Did you see that?" Fritz wheezed. His scar stood out against his bloodless face. "Did that child push that tree down?"

"Maybe it doesn't know its own strength," Mica said.

Fritz gaped at her. "Its own . . . We should definitely go."

"Wait," Mica said. "I think we have to see this."

Something in Ed's face had caught her attention. Despite being essentially invincible, the Fifth Talent looked deeply unsettled. His head kept whipping around unnaturally fast, following the progress of those strange, aimless Blurs.

"That one was changing!"

"What?" Mica approached him warily, leaving Fritz to watch

over Caleb. Ed sounded a little frantic, and she couldn't predict what he would do if he felt threatened.

"That Blur. Its face was shifting faster than any Mimic I've ever seen."

"Like what you can do?"

"Yes, but—there it goes again!"

Mica couldn't follow whatever Ed saw, but she remembered the shifting face of the mad Talent at the anniversary ball. He *had* tried to warn them. More people had suffered at Lord Ober's hands than they had yet seen. And if her hunch was correct, they had found some of them.

"Excuse me."

Mica jumped. A woman had appeared on the path ahead, startling them and their horses. Another Blur.

The woman waited patiently as they got their horses under control. Her features (wrinkles, freckles, and a bony nose) remained unchanged. She wore a thick woolen skirt and a green scarf looped around her thin neck.

"We don't get many travelers up here." Her voice was scratchy but pleasant. Mica guessed she was in her late forties or early fifties. "Why have you come to Dustwood?"

"We seek an inn for the night," Mica said. "We're on our way to a place called Birdfell."

The reaction was brief but clear. The woman's lips thinned, and the lines in her forehead became more pronounced. She knew the place.

"Why do you want to go there?"

"My friend's lady love was kidnapped." Mica gestured to Fritz, who looked almost as spooked as the horses by the woman's abrupt appearance. "We want to rescue her."

"She will be changed," the woman said sadly. "No one comes back from Birdfell the same. If they come back."

Mica felt that cliff-top sensation again, as if she were poised to leap into greater understanding.

"Have you been there?" she said, fighting to keep her voice calm. "Can you tell us more?"

The woman went still for a moment, giving them an appraising look. Then she plucked a knife from her sleeve.

Ed whipped the sword from his belt with lightning speed, but the woman didn't flinch. She drew the knife, a plain, workmanlike blade, across her freckled arm, from hand to elbow. It didn't leave a mark.

Shield.

Then the woman walked forward to Mica's horse. Mica tensed, but the woman simply patted the horse on the neck, murmuring soothing sounds, and continued past it to the tree that had fallen behind them. She bent, her joints popping, and lifted the log as easily as if it were a bolt of cloth. She moved the tree off the path and dropped it to the ground out of the way, more branches snapping under its weight.

Muscle.

"I have been to Birdfell," the woman said. "Long ago. But I think you know what that means."

"You have three Talents," Mica said. "Can you control them?"

"Aye," the woman said. "But they cause me great pain. It is not as bad for me as for some. Come. The inn burned down last winter, but I can offer you shelter."

She turned and walked off the path into the village, beckoning for them to follow.

The Blurs continued to dance around the edges of their vision as they followed the strange woman deeper into Dustwood. Other people came out to watch them pass as news spread of their arrival, including many who moved at regular speeds. The people of Dustwood gawked at the strangers from the safety of porches and the shelter of the trees, murmuring suspiciously to each other. Mica noticed several villagers missing limbs, a hand here or a leg there. She shuddered, remembering the Talents they had rescued from Ober's warehouse back in Jewel Harbor.

"What *is* this place?" Ed demanded, still watching the shadowy figures with wide eyes.

"A place for leftovers," the woman said. "For false starts and failures."

Ed rubbed at his chin. His beard had become snowy white. "What does that mean?"

"He experimented on them," Mica said bitterly. "Your precious benefactor. His potion didn't always work so well. He had to try it out on people first."

"You mean all these people—"

"Talents are gifts," the woman said sharply. "They should have been left as given."

She led them to a small cabin and paused on the threshold.

"There's always a cost," she said. Her gaze flitted to Ed for a moment, as if she knew exactly what he was—and exactly how many people had suffered to make him so.

Then she disappeared inside.

The woman's name was Tallisa. She answered their questions willingly enough, but she wasn't what Mica would call friendly. She had lived in the shadow of Birdfell for her entire life, and she confirmed what the mad Talent had hinted at back at the anniversary ball. Many had suffered in the name of Ober's work, and they'd been left in this remote village, ignored by the empire for over a decade.

"My pains started eight years ago, after my own visit to Birdfell," Tallisa told them over mugs of weak tea, boiled pears, and food shared from their saddlebags. They sat in front of her fireplace in pinewood chairs, listening to her scratchy voice as darkness fell outside. "Sometimes the Talents work perfectly. I used the Muscle strength to build this cabin with my own hands."

"So you always have the Talent then?" Mica asked.

"Correct. My pain comes and goes. Others suffer from delusions or exhaustion." Tallisa glanced at Caleb, who was slumped on the rug in front of the fire. He hadn't even stirred when Ed carried him inside. "It took us too long to realize Birdfell was the source of these strange maladies. Some people were snatched from the mountain paths and returned with no memory of what had happened. Others went willingly to perform odd jobs at the tower."

"And you?"

Tallisa lifted her mug of tea in hands that, though wrinkled, were free of calluses, evidence of her impervious skin.

"I did not go willingly."

Mica wanted to know exactly what had happened, whether she too had nearly drowned in a murky pool of poison, but she sensed that Tallisa didn't want to go into the details. She bit her lip to keep from asking and waited for the woman to go on.

"We soon realized the source of our curse, but by then, it was too late for many of us. Victims are brought from other islands too. We take them in when they're discarded." Tallisa looked at Caleb again. "He's welcome to stay. We look out for our own."

"We're taking care of him," Mica said.

Tallisa raised an eyebrow at her aggressive tone, and Mica cleared her throat.

"Have you ever seen the tower's owner?"

"Not that I can recall. An old man with wild hair and a scarred face was there often, but I don't think he was the top authority."

Haddell.

"He was the one who oversaw my own . . . visit eight years ago, and he came here sometimes to check on the results of his work in the early days. He abandoned the tower about two years back."

"He's dead now," Mica said. "The old man."

Tallisa pursed her lips. If the news pleased her, she didn't show it.

"That may be, but a few months ago, it all started up again. Now, those who go to Birdfell do not return."

It lined up with Mica's understanding. Ober and his potioners had used the remote tower for their early experiments before eventually moving the operation to the warehouse in Jewel Harbor. Perhaps he wanted to oversee it more closely, or he knew by then that Talent blood and bones made powerful potions, and he wanted to be nearer to a steady supply. He had stopped needing the Dustwood villagers—until Mica and Caleb drove him from the capital.

Fritz raised his hand. He had been listening to the tale in shocked silence, and he waited for Tallisa to nod at him, slightly bemused, before he spoke.

"Did you ask for help from Lord Bont, ma'am?"

Tallisa snorted. "Lord Bont thinks only of profit. Our mine stopped producing long ago. He doesn't care what happens to us now." She studied them over the top of her cup, forehead wrinkling. "I can see from your clothes that you are wealthy, perhaps nobles? It has been a long time since the nobles of this empire have cared to help people like us."

"She speaks truth," Ed said. "The nobles always choose their own interests over ours. It is past time common folk like us broke away."

Mica set down her own mug with a thunk.

"How can you say that after the 'help' you've accepted from your noble benefactor?"

"He is making *us* powerful," Ed said.

"Don't you understand? All this is because of Lord Ober." Mica threw her arms wide, taking in Tallisa and the rest of the village, where strange sounds still murmured in the night. "That old man worked for Lord Ober. *This* is the cost of the help he's giving you."

"I don't believe you," Ed said.

"I think you do," Mica said. "I think you've known all along that what you can do comes at a cost, but you've never had to look it in the face before."

Ed's features changed briefly into Emperor Styl's again. "Ever the hypocrite," he spat. "You have known nothing but luxury produced by the labors of others. Don't talk to me about costs."

With that, he stood and blurred out the door. He slammed it behind him with Muscle strength, making the cabin shake.

Silence fell in his absence, except for the sound of Caleb's heavy breathing. Tallisa was grimacing as if some of her pain had returned, and she did not meet Mica's gaze.

Fritz cleared his throat delicately. "Can I pour anyone some more tea?"

Mica felt discomfited by Ed's words when she went to sleep later that night. They had been directed at Jessamyn the princess, not Mica the soldier's daughter, but she couldn't help acknowledging that he had a point. She had hoped what Ed saw in Dustwood would force him to question the wisdom of keeping Ober as an ally, but she hadn't expected to end up feeling sympathetic to the rebels. They had been empowered to fight for themselves. She understood why it was so tempting to accept his aid.

Then her gaze drifted to Caleb, sleeping on beside the fire, and Tallisa, who still sat awake in her homemade chair. No amount of power could justify the cost Ober had made others pay.

CHAPTER TWENTY-ONE

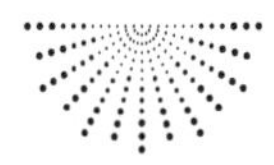

Caleb had mostly regained his strength by the morning of the third day. He was able to sit upright on his horse, his face pale and drawn, as they left Dustwood and rode at last toward the barren fortress.

Fritz filled Caleb in on what they had seen in the village. Mica caught Caleb's eye as Fritz described the residents who had suffered through the same poisoning Caleb had endured as a child. Something dangerous flickered in his eyes now. He would agree there could be no compromises when they found his uncle.

Fritz had apparently been deeply moved by Tallisa's story. The young lord had pressed his prized jeweled dagger into Tallisa's hands when they left her cabin, quietly asking her to sell it and use the money to help the other villagers.

Ed hadn't returned to Tallisa's cabin to sleep. He offered no explanation when he appeared at sunrise to accompany them out of Dustwood. He must have run ahead to tell his comrades they were on their way. He seemed subdued, and Mica couldn't help wondering if the village had had any effect on him at all.

Mica herself still felt a deep uneasiness in the pit of her stomach. She tried to ignore it and focus on the negotiation ahead. No matter what injustices the rebels had experienced, no matter what horrors the people of Dustwood had endured, a great threat was advancing to the east, advancing on her brothers and parents. If they couldn't work out an agreement with the rebels, they had little hope against the Obsidians. Despite its flaws, the empire needed to be whole.

As they got closer to their destination, scouts shadowed their path, lurking among the trees beside the road. Mica got out the silver circlet Lord Bont had given her and wore it with her hood flung back, the crown on full display.

The sun hadn't yet reached its zenith when the four travelers crested the ridge above Birdfell Tower. The fortress awaited them on the slope below, sharp and gray in the morning sunlight. It was indeed barren, perched precariously on a mountainside that had been stripped of vegetation long ago.

Instead of one murky pond, half a dozen pools surrounded the base of the fortress. Liquid filled each one to varying levels, and they mirrored the sunlight, making it difficult to discern the color of the liquid. The stones bordering some of the pools looked freshly cut, as if they'd been constructed recently.

Steel glinted on the old tower's ramparts, and a flurry of activity suggested that its inhabitants had gathered to watch their approach. A flock of birds took off from the tower and swooped into the sky, cawing mournfully.

So much for Birdfell being abandoned. Mica wondered, fleetingly, if Lord Bont knew more of what had been going on here than he'd admitted.

A party of men on foot awaited them on the steep path leading down to the tower and the mirrored pools. The men wore rough clothes of wool and cotton, beards like Ed's, and belts bristling with weapons. They formed a dense knot behind a leader with an especially long and thick beard. Lord Ober was not among them.

"Greetings." The leader with the impressive beard had a calm voice, slightly higher than Mica expected. "I am Representative Wildson of the Free Nation of Cray. None of you is the Lord Governor of Silverfell."

"Alas, he could not leave Silverfell City, though he wanted to speak with you ever so much," Mica said, doing her very best charming Jessamyn voice. "But you know who *I* am, of course." She touched the simple crown on her head.

Wildson gave the briefest nod possible. "We have not met before, but yes, I know who you are. Mica Graydier."

Mica kept her features steady.

"Micathea doesn't work for me anymore."

"Who's Mica?" Fritz said, his horse dancing beneath him. "And where is Lady Lorna?"

"I am Princess Jessamyn Styldier," Mica said, waving for the young lord to be quiet. "I come on behalf of—"

"Your impersonation is very convincing," Wildson interrupted, "but we know the truth. You don't need to keep this up, Miss Graydier."

Mica risked a glance at Ed, but he looked confused too. Apparently, he hadn't suspected that she was an Impersonator at all.

"I assure you, you have been misinformed," Mica said. "I have come to hear the concerns of my people, who—"

"We are not your people," Wildson said. "Or at least, not the princess's. We are free men now."

Mica's hands had begun to sweat. The slightest shift of her features would give her away. She had *not* expected the conversation to go like this. "I wish to discuss your complaints—"

"Miss Graydier, there is no call for this." Wildson's calm voice became a little condescending. "The *Silk Goddess* has already been brought in to the western harbor. If there was any doubt before about your identity, it was gone when we discovered your brother among our prisoners."

Emir! He's alive! Mica felt an overwhelming torrent of relief, more powerful than the wildest storm or the largest waterfall. She clutched her reins tight, fighting for control, and managed to keep her face impassive.

"I have no brother. I'm not sure what you're—"

"You have four brothers, and one of our men knows them all by sight," Wildson said impatiently. "Emir Grayson's presence confirmed what we already suspected: that the princess still has an Impersonator at her side."

"Emir Grayson was assigned to my protection detail." Mica brushed her dark-red hair back from her face, trying to draw attention to her crown. "He has nothing to do with—"

"He is your brother." An older man with curly, graying hair and a round face emerged from the back of the rebel group. Mica's heart sank.

"I am sure you remember Fair of Dwindlemire," Wildson said. "Representative Fair, I should say. I believe you and his son Danil were friends at the Redbridge Impersonator Academy. More importantly, you know what happened to Danil in Jewel Harbor and how the emperor and the authorities did nothing to help him for so long, commoner that he is."

"Danil told me everything, Mica," Fair said. "I appreciate what you did for him, but you are on the wrong side now."

"It is true," Wildson said. "You ought to join us, Miss Graydier, not continue to speak for those who failed your kind for so long. It speaks volumes that the nobles sent you instead of coming themselves."

"My people helped Danil Fairson and the others the very night the location of the warehouse was discovered," Mica said, still using Jessamyn's voice. "The investigation took longer than anticipated, but we acted as soon as we learned of their plight." She wouldn't be the one to crack first, even if Fair really had identified Emir. Mica understood why Fair would be less than enthusiastic about the empire these days, but there was another factor still in play.

She leaned toward the men. "I am sympathetic to your protests about what happened to Danil and the others, but you have allied yourselves with the very man responsible. Forgive me for doubting the rightness of your cause."

"You are referring to Lord Ober," Wildson said.

"Ed here described him as your benefactor," Mica said. "And this is his tower, if I'm not mistaken."

She gestured to the austere building behind them, wondering if Ober himself was waiting inside. More people had come out on the ramparts to watch their leaders treat with the nobles. How many of them had already taken a dip in those mirrored pools?

"Lord Ober has helped us greatly," Wildson said. "In addition to providing this tower to use as a base on Silverfell, he has offered us a weapon unlike any other."

"The Talents with all four abilities," Mica said, "what we call Fifth Talents?"

"Indeed. Their strength will allow us to achieve independence from the empire." A defiant gleam appeared in Wildson's eyes, the look of a man who finally had a chance to fight back against those who had oppressed him. "You saw them in action back in Silverfell City."

"We did." Mica pictured the three fighters scaling the *Silk Goddess* and cutting through any who stood against them as if they were little more than cobwebs. But that same frustrating question still lingered. Why had Ober chosen this cause to back? "So Lord Ober gave you the formula for his potion in exchange for what? A split in the empire?"

The faintest of mutterings spread through the group. Wildson's face remained impassive.

"Wait," Mica said, trying to interpret that reaction. "Has he not given it to you yet?"

Wildson straightened in his saddle. "He has begun to transform our men, giving us weapons unlike—"

"But you can't create the Fifth Talents yourselves?"

"All in good time," Wildson said, but he looked slightly uncomfortable.

Mica glanced at Ed, who sat his horse halfway between the two parties. They had relied on him often for a group that was supposed to have so many empowered fighters.

"How many Fifth Talents do you actually have?"

Wildson snorted. "That's hardly something we would reveal to an imperial spy."

"If you really think I'm Mica Graydier, then don't you think I'd be interested in looking out for my fellow Talents and the families of my friends? Danil's father can tell you that."

"It is true that Mica worked hard to find my son, even when the princess delayed," Fair said.

"Only a few of you have all the Talents, right?" Mica pressed. "What is it? Half a dozen? And you don't know how to use the potion to make more yet?"

No one answered, but the way they avoided her eyes was answer enough. She guessed they had fewer than ten Fifth Talents among them. There was still a chance she could convince them.

Mica's heart raced as she searched for the right words to say.

"Whether you believe I mean well or not, you have to know that Lord Ober is a treacherous man who cares only for his own ambitions. Do you really think he will give all your people these extraordinary abilities when he's your closest neighbor? That would be a terrible risk."

"He is using you." Caleb spoke up for the first time. He still sounded fatigued, but he had been tracking the conversation, and he urged his horse forward to stand beside Mica's. "Ober may be promising you the empire, but he would turn on his own flesh and blood. If he hasn't given you the means to create your own Fifth Talents, you have nothing at all."

The men behind Wildson were murmuring to each other, as

if this was something they were already worried about. As if they had known this gift must be too good to be true.

"Lord Caleb, I presume?" Wildson said. "You are on the wrong side too. The Pebble Islands are with us in the secession effort."

Caleb didn't answer, but his face drained of what little color he'd regained.

"Oh yes, your parents are keen on the idea of separating the western branch of the empire into independent nations. They've had enough of answering to a faraway ruler."

Mica shifted uneasily. She and Caleb were united in their desire to stop Ober and protect the empire, but she wished she felt a little more confident that the two of them had chosen the right side. If his family and her friends all believed in this cause, was it possible they had made the wrong choice in working so hard to support Jessamyn's schemes? Both of them had fallen under her spell in their own ways. What if their loyalty had been misplaced all along?

Caleb was frowning, the deep grooves etched in his forehead suggesting he felt conflicted too.

The rebels' cause might be understandable, but one thing at least was clear.

"No matter whose side you're on, you cannot use Lord Ober's formula without accepting his methods," Mica said. "He tortures Talents in his research. He leaves his failed experiments suffering from madness and illness. Ed can tell you."

Their Fifth Talent guard started, his face briefly taking on Tallisa's features. But he remained silent.

"He uses Talent bones in his potions," Mica said, desperate to make them understood. "You can't put up with such things for a couple of over-powerful soldiers."

"To fight for our cause." Wildson met her gaze steadily. "Some would say the ends justify the means."

"I wouldn't," Mica said.

"Then what justifies your pandering to the nobility, Princess?

You only pay attention to the special interests of those who have your ear at court. You will always favor the concerns of the powerful over the rest of us. You are culpable too."

Mica opened her mouth then closed it again. He was right, of course. Jessamyn and her father had become so wrapped up in their political games that they had neglected the needs of the common people. They might not be using their bones for potions, but they were not blameless in other kinds of suffering. She thought of the audiences she had witnessed, the desperate people—like Ed—who came to the emperor for help. Such audiences took place only once a month. Meanwhile, the nobles engaged in endless frivolous socializing in the Silver Palace—and they got what they wanted more often too.

Mica studied the rebels, who faced her against the backdrop of the barren fortress, where so much pain had originated. Wildson, leading his band of bearded men. Fair, with curly hair just like his son's. Ed, whose shifting features suggested the uneasiness within. None of them were innocent, but she had more in common with them than with the nobles of Jewel Harbor. She had grown up in a humble little house in Stonefoss, far away from palaces and crowns and politics. She was still Mica Graydier, no matter how far away from herself she had come since she fell under Jessamyn's spell.

But she *was* still Mica Graydier, and her family was in danger. Emir lived, but her other brothers were probably already marching to defend Stonefoss against the invaders. No matter how much corruption she had witnessed in the Windfast Empire since leaving the Academy, it didn't change the fact that a vast host was bearing down upon her home.

She knew what Jessamyn would say next. *Nothing unites people like a shared enemy.*

"The Obsidian army has invaded Talon and Amber Island," she said. "Did you know that?"

Wildson blinked, as if he hadn't expected the conversation to go in that direction. A few of his men exchanged uncomfortable glances.

"We have had reports."

"They will reach you here eventually," Mica said. "You may not care about the eastern islands, but make no mistake that the Obsidians will not leave you alone. You are making it too easy for them to advance through the empire by splintering it. They'll be at your door soon enough."

"The Fifth Talents can stop the Obsidian host," Wildson said.

"I think you're right, but only if you have enough of them." Mica glanced at the mirrored pools filled with potions the rebels didn't know how to use. "You had half a dozen when you attacked Silverfell City, and you still lost a ship and dozens of men. Unless every single one of you is already a Fifth Talent, you could still be overwhelmed when the Obsidians come."

"Lord Ober will create more fighters."

"And if he doesn't? You will have destroyed the empire for nothing."

Mica felt that lingering question again, the final puzzle piece dangling just out of reach. She didn't believe Ober's help had been freely given, but why, *why* had he chosen this band of bearded rebels?

"Ober wouldn't want to lose to the Obsidians either." Wildson was looking unsettled, as if he'd lost control of the discussion or he wasn't as certain of their benefactor as he claimed.

"No, but would he do all this just so he can rule the tiny independent nation of Timbral?" She frowned, looking at this desolate mountain tower, these desperate mountain men. "He is an ambitious man who once had the ear of the emperor himself. Even if the Obsidians were not advancing, do you really think he would allow you to remain independent of *him*?"

"She makes a good point," Caleb put in. "Dwindlemire and Cray offer a perfect strategic opportunity for Ober. He could control the waters around Timbral, and there is little you could do to stop him with unlimited Fifth Talents at his beck and call. Do you trust him that far?"

Wildson's men were whispering to each other, and Mica picked up on a strain of something. Anxiety spiked in her chest, and her pulse began to race.

"Where is Lord Ober now?"

Feet shifted on the mountain path, and gazes darted from side to side. No one wanted to answer, as if they sensed that something was wrong, something that worried them too.

"He's gone, isn't he?" Mica said.

"Aye." Danil's father was the one to speak up. "He left as soon as our Blur scouts confirmed you were on your way."

"Without telling you where he was going?"

"We assumed he didn't want Lord Bont to see him with us, but he could—"

"Wait, I need to think." Mica flung up a hand to silence them, mulling over this information. She felt the pieces coming together, disparate features contorting to form a recognizable face. Ober had strung these men along, promising them Fifth Talents in exchange for their help, while only actually transforming a handful of them. He had claimed to share their desire for independence, but that would give him less influence than he'd had before. He wouldn't be content with just Timbral.

Dread spooled and spun within her.

He wouldn't be content with just Timbral, the Twins, and the Pebble Islands, either.

Ober wanted the Windfast Empire.

And he had departed Birdfell as soon as he learned that Jessamyn's Mimic had left her behind in Silverfell City.

Mica seized Caleb's arm. "We need to go back."

"What are you talking about?"

"We need to return to the city at once." She turned to Wildson, Fair, and the other rebels. "Lord Ober plans to betray you. You don't have to agree with me, but I swear to you that the princess and the emperor wish to hear your concerns. You are right that I'm really Mica Graydier." Her eyes flashed hazel, and the red faded from her hair. "You are also right that there has been too much subterfuge, scheming, and corruption in this empire. It is time we put an end to it."

"Hear! Hear!" one of the men called.

Caleb caught her eye and nodded. They were united in this. Maybe they could heal the split in the empire after all.

"Emperor Styl *will* negotiate with you," she said. "He sent his daughter out to the western islands to do exactly that, knowing war was brewing, because he *does* care for the needs of his people. Ober will use your genuine concerns for his own ends. He will take the very bones of your Talents if it gives him more power." She looked at Fair, remembering the tide of horror that had risen within her when she realized Danil's foot had been chopped off. "You have seen it yourselves." She turned to Ed. "You have to stand up to him and say you won't accept his methods."

Ed's face flowed out of shape, again becoming wrinkled and freckled like Tallisa's. Mica held her breath, praying he too had been moved by her story.

Then his own features returned, and he nodded.

"I agree with the lady," Ed said to his comrades. "Wildson, you should have seen it. There's evil out there, and we're in bed with it."

Wildson was still for a moment. Then he turned to his companions to exchange a few quiet words.

Mica clutched her reins so hard it hurt as she waited for his answer. She was certain of one thing: Ober was going after Jessamyn. These men had served their purpose, and he had set his sights on a bigger prize.

She found herself staring at the barren fortress she had come so far to find, at the pools hiding their abominable contents beneath mirrored surfaces. She dreaded to think how many of his own loyal men Ober had already drowned in those pools, how many members of this new and deadly force were now speeding toward Silverfell City. There was no way Ober had done all this only for the independence of his island. He wanted it all.

The flock of birds swarmed around the ramparts of the tower, cawing at the people who'd disturbed their roosts. The wind hummed against the grim walls. Mica had found the barren fortress, but she didn't think she even had time to go inside.

At last, Wildson spoke, his voice ringing over the mountainside. "If the emperor is open to talking, then so are we."

Mica's shoulders sagged. "Good. We'll make this right, but trusting Lord Ober isn't the way." She lifted her reins, eager to fly back down the mountain once more. "I have to return to the city. Will some of you accompany me? You can meet with the real Princess Jessamyn face to face, and you'll see why she has been using me to speak for her." She surveyed her companions briefly. "Perhaps Lord Fritz and Lady Lorna can remain here with you as a gesture of good faith."

Fritz agreed at once, looking ready to dash off to the tower before the negotiations even concluded. The rebels talked amongst themselves again to decide whom to send back down the mountain.

Mica leaned in closer to Caleb.

"Is stopping Ober still our number-one priority, no matter whose side our families are on?"

"Always."

"Good."

Mica remembered her fear that Lord Ober had used the potion on himself. Were they already too late? Her horse snorted and stamped, and she forced herself to loosen her death grip on the reins.

"I understand you are anxious to depart, Miss Graydier," Wildson said at last. "Two of our comrades will accompany you back to Silverfell. We'll send Fifth Talents, as you call them."

"I'll be going back with you," Ed said, "seeing as how we're friends."

"I am glad of your company," Mica said. "We must hurry. Is my brother well enough to travel?"

"He should rest a little longer," Wildson said evenly. "He will be safe here."

Mica nodded in understanding. The rebels wouldn't let go of their leverage over her so easily. "How bad are his injuries?"

"They were grave," Fair said, "but the potioner gave him something that helped."

Mica frowned. "The potioner?"

"Yes, she's an exceptionally good one from Jewel Harbor who was already here at Birdfell when we arrived a few weeks ago. Under her ministrations, your brother should make a full—"

"Is it Quinn, from Talon?"

"That's right." Fair tipped his head to the side, and the movement reminded her strongly of Danil. "How did you know?"

"We've met." Mica hesitated. They didn't have much time, but she needed to know if Ober himself had used the potion. "May I speak with her?"

"I'm afraid she left with Lord Ober," Fair said.

Mica grimaced. "Then it is more important than ever that we return to Silverfell."

"Wait!" A young girl was hurrying up the path from Birdfell toward them, carrying a small leather-bound box. "You need to get there quickly, right? The potioner left something behind that might help."

Mica recognized Danil's little sister, Lucy Fairdier, who shared his merry face and curly hair. If she was here, Mica couldn't help wondering if Danil and Sapphire knew what had been going on with the rebels too. It had been a long time since she had seen her friends, and it wouldn't surprise her to learn they had joined this cause.

Lucy reached them, panting from her run, and opened the

leather-bound box. A set of bloodred potion bottles nestled inside. Mica recognized Quinn's signature products at once.

"These will give someone Blur speed temporarily with no side effects," Danil's sister said. "They'll get you back to Silverfell City."

"Thank you." Mica caught Caleb's eye. "I've always wanted to be a Blur."

CHAPTER TWENTY-TWO

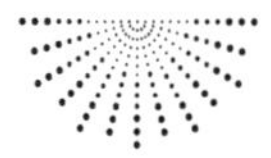

The sensation was unlike anything Mica had ever experienced. The wind whipped against her face, as cold and sharp as a dagger. Her feet barely seemed to touch the ground, and she felt as if she were falling rather than running. She didn't feel remotely in control, and only sheer luck kept her from tripping at the wrong moment and tumbling to her death. The experience was exhilarating and terrifying, and Mica could see why people paid so much to try it.

Despite the potion-induced speed, Mica still felt as if they were going too slowly. Lord Ober had specifically waited until she and Caleb left the city to set his plans in motion—and he had brought his potioner with him. The two of them were capable of doing a lot of damage. They couldn't be allowed to reach the princess.

The rebels hadn't known exactly how many Fifth Talents Ober took with him when he left Birdfell, but they believed the number was close to a hundred. That would be more than enough to take control of the city. On the other hand, if military occupation were his aim, he wouldn't have waited for Mica and Caleb to leave. He must have another scheme in mind.

Mica pushed herself to run faster, shortening her own hair so it wouldn't impede her vision. Caleb and the two Fifth Talents kept pace beside her, but they didn't have much time to talk. The wind whistled in their ears as they ran, stealing their words.

Ed and the second Fifth Talent—a younger man named Krake who was far too handsome for his looks to be natural—didn't need Quinn's potion. Caleb took some in an effort to hold off the side effects of his own condition. The artificial Blur speed didn't give Mica and Caleb endless stamina, and they occasionally had to slow down to rest or take more of the potion.

Still, they made excellent time, passing the turn-off to Dustwood, the campsite where they'd slept, then the bridge over the ravine. The journey flashed by, their newfound speed making a mockery of their three-day ride to Birdfell. The cold was their constant companion, and before long, the mists rose up to welcome them back.

They reached the ridge overlooking Silverfell City as darkness fell on the very same day they had awoken in Dustwood. Krake waited under the shelter of the trees, while Mica, Caleb, and Ed crawled forward on their bellies to assess the situation below.

Mica worked to slow her breathing and calm her racing heartbeat. The rocks were sharp beneath her elbows as she peered down at the wide avenues, marble walls, and shimmering tile roofs of Silverfell City.

"There are more ships than there were three days ago," Caleb said, his attention on the bowl-shaped harbor. "More wedding guests?"

Mica snorted. "Too bad the bride and groom are both missing."

"The nobles probably wanted to get as far from the Obsidian invaders as they could," Caleb said. "But I'll bet a lot of ordinary traders are seeking shelter here too."

Ed stroked his beard, which was currently red and wiry. A few pine needles had gotten caught in it during their run.

"A lot of powerful people in that city right now," he muttered.

"Do you think Ober will attack it?" Mica asked.

Ed shrugged, his nose briefly taking on Ober's prominent shape. But Caleb shook his head.

"No. Take a look at that center mooring. Recognize anything?"

Mica squinted at the harbor, where the last of the evening light sparked across the water. Lanterns were coming on along the waterfront, casting strange shadows across the decks of the ships. She leaned closer to Caleb so she could follow his line of sight to a familiar vessel. A beautiful woman trimmed in gold graced her prow.

"It's the *Silk Goddess*."

"One and the same."

A few people moved on the deck of the *Goddess*, but Mica couldn't see them well enough to say whether or not she knew them. The HIMS *Arrow* rested at its own mooring farther down the dock, undisturbed by the return of its erstwhile traveling companion.

"So Ober sailed here openly?"

"Remember most people don't know about his crimes."

Mica grimaced. "Jessamyn saw to that."

"Also, *we* know he's the rebels' benefactor, but no one else does." Caleb scrubbed a hand through his tousled hair. "Lord Bont probably invited him to the wedding."

"I didn't think of that."

The wind stirred, carrying the briny smell of the ocean up to their vantage point. Lights had begun to come on around the city, candles burning in a hundred costly windows. All evidence of the attack on the harbor a few days past was gone. It certainly didn't look like a city at war.

They retreated from the ridge to discuss their next move in the shelter of the trees, brushing little stones from their clothes.

"So what's the plan?" Krake asked.

"We have to approach carefully," Caleb said. "My uncle has been here for at least a day, probably with a bunch of Fifth Talent retainers, and we don't know what traps he may have set in that time."

"No breaking down Lord Bont's door, then?" Ed took on the corpulent lord's shape for a moment. He really did have a knack for impersonation. "A pity."

"The most important thing is to get to Jessamyn," Mica said. "I think it's best if I sneak in and see what the situation is before we make any plans."

Caleb shook his head. "You can't go alone."

"It'll be easier if I do."

"If you have to fight—"

"Then I'll fight." Mica flicked a knife out from under her sleeve. The other was strapped to her ankle. She might not be the best fighter among them, but these blades had drawn blood before. "It has to be me. I'm the only Mimic Jessamyn will trust."

Caleb looked at their companions, as if seeking a reason to contradict her. Ed and Krake the Handsome could do a lot of damage, but they'd be less effective in speaking to the princess—if they could even find her in the large manor. His own abilities weren't reliable enough to get him to the princess's side either, and Ober would probably be watching for him. Caleb's brow furrowed as it became clear to him that Mica was right. It had to be her.

"Maybe we can create a diversion," he said. "Pick a fight with the local watch or something."

"That would only alert Ober that something's going on. I can be invisible." Mica squeezed his hand. "You have to trust me."

"That's not the issue," Caleb said obstinately. "He could have control of the manor already, with a hundred Fifth Talents at his back. I don't want you to get hurt."

Mica smiled gently at him, then she contorted her face to

another one altogether. Freckles spread across her cheeks, her hair brushed her shoulders, turning as black as jet, and her eyes became large and fierce.

"*I* won't even be there."

Caleb studied her impersonation, conflict in his deep-blue eyes. For a moment, she thought he was going to keep arguing. Then he sighed.

"All right, Mica. See if you can talk to Jessa, but don't let anyone else see you."

Mica rose up on her toes to kiss his cheek, not caring that the two Fifth Talents were watching.

"I'll be back before you know it."

Mica crept into Silverfell City under cover of darkness. The face she wore was one of her regular impersonations, the "city woman" she had developed when she first moved to Jewel Harbor. The look was unassuming, not pretty or unusual enough to stick in anyone's memory. Fortunately, she still wore the embroidered riding clothes Lord Bont had provided, so she could pass easily for a Silverfell resident. Flitting unnoticed through the broad streets was easy, but she was nervous about getting into the manor.

I doubt I can walk in through the front gate.

She was wrong on that count, to her great surprise. It was still early in the evening, and Lord Bont's home bustled with activity. Servants dashed about the grounds, attending to the many lords and ladies staying in the manor, and no one paid any heed to one more woman slipping inside the marble walls. Mica looked like just another maid hurrying across the garden to do her lady's bidding.

She picked up snippets of conversation as she traversed the grounds, hoping to find out what had happened while she was in

Birdfell. The manor certainly didn't appear to have been taken over by a hundred invincible soldiers.

Maybe we still have time.

Most people Mica listened in on were still talking about the rebels and the raid on the harbor.

"I hear they're preparing another attack. They want to capture the whole island. Isn't it mad?"

Mica slowed, taking shelter behind a thorny hedge. The speaker was a young gardener with blemishes on her face and dirt under her nails. She was cutting roses from a bush and handing them to an older woman with pearly-white hair. Both women wore smocks with the Silverfell sigil, a silver rosebud crossed with a pickaxe.

"Dwindlemire and Cray aren't organized enough for that," the older woman said, adding the latest rose to the bundle in her arms. "I wouldn't lose sleep over it."

"It's different this time," the younger woman insisted.

"They say it's different every striking time."

"I don't understand why they're not happy to be part of the empire like the rest of us."

The older woman gave a sticky cough. "You're young yet."

The young woman handed over another rose, her nose wrinkling. "Don't *you* think we're better off as Windfast subjects?"

"Perhaps. That's enough, I think." The old woman straightened, her back creaking. "I'll take this up to the princess's chambers. Remember His Lordship wants another bouquet for her spot at the table."

The other woman sighed. "At this rate, we won't have a single rose left. It's going to take a year for the garden to recover."

"The princess gets what she wants."

The older gardener walked off toward the manor, while the younger one continued snipping roses as reluctantly as if she were being forced to remove a friend's fingers.

Mica bounced on the balls of her feet, still hidden behind the hedge. Something about what they had said rang like a false note in her mind. What was it?

Then it hit her. The princess was supposed to be off saving Lorna from the rebels. Had Jessamyn decided to reveal herself to more people than Lord Aren in Mica's absence? Why would she do that?

Mica caught up with the older gardener when she was almost to the manor's side door. She checked that no one else was near, then she slipped the knife from her sleeve and crept up behind her.

"Stop. Don't make a sound," she hissed in the woman's ear, laying cold steel against the sagging skin of her neck. "I won't hurt you or anyone else if you give me your roses and your smock."

"You can have them," the woman said stiffly. "It's on your head if the princess throws a fit."

"She'll still get her roses." Mica considered the gardener's smock for a second. It was open on both sides, and it would show too much of her embroidered riding clothes. "You'd better give me your dress too."

A few minutes later, Mica was hurrying through the manor with a bouquet of roses in her arms and pearly-white hair framing her face. She paused a few times to listen for information, but no one mentioned Lord Ober or the return of the *Silk Goddess*. The stewards and servants were busy preparing for a feast the following evening. Despite the absence of the bride and groom, Lord Bont still needed to feed those who had traveled all this way for his daughter's wedding.

Mica wasn't entirely sure how to get to the princess's rooms from the side entrance, so she wandered until she found the atrium with the marble fountain at the center. So far, no one had stopped her, and she had seen no sign that Ober or his invincible men were even in the manor. She paused to get her bearings, listening to the gentle bubbling of the fountain. The man-size vases were still spread around the room, but the flowers had begun to wilt.

Strange. I wonder why Lord Bont hasn't had those replaced.

Mica felt uneasy. Something definitely wasn't right here.

Sure of her location once more, Mica hurried down a wide corridor from the atrium, following the murals she remembered from the day she arrived.

She hadn't gone far when she turned a corner and walked directly into Quinn.

"Oh! Excuse me, ma'am."

Mica quickly bent over the roses in her arms, relieved she'd adopted the elderly gardener's features. Quinn had seen her city-woman face often.

But the potioner didn't even look at her.

"Sorry. My fault." Quinn gave Mica a brusque nod, her severe dark hair swinging around her chin, and set off down the corridor. She seemed distracted, and she was barely watching which direction she was going.

Mica waited until Quinn turned a corner before adjusting the roses in her arms and continuing on. She felt a dull pounding in her chest, a drumbeat of dread. If the potioner was a guest here, that meant Ober probably was too.

Mica's palms were sweating and her features were threatening to shift out of shape by the time she reached the corridor where the princess was staying. What she saw only increased her apprehension.

Banner was not standing at his usual post. Two men she didn't recognize were guarding Jessamyn's door. Neither wore the Silverfell sigil.

"I brought roses for the princess," Mica said in the gardener's age-thinned voice.

One of the guards (black hair, blunt chin, an old scar splitting a thick eyebrow) held out a hand for them.

Mica's arms tightened around the bouquet. "I need to deliver them myself."

"No one enters the princess's chambers."

"I was ordered to—"

"Are you daft, woman?" The guard swiped the roses from her arms so fast he blurred. "There are Mimics everywhere. His Lordship is taking no chances."

"His Lordship?" Mica had a sneaking suspicion they weren't referring to Lord Bont.

"You want to speak to him yourself, fine. No one goes into the princess's rooms."

Mica hesitated. If these men were Fifth Talents, she didn't stand a chance against them. She had already seen one of them Blur. She had to know for sure.

"I understand," she said in her reedy, old-woman voice. "Let me fix that bouquet before you take it to her, though. She'll be upset if it isn't perfect."

Mica rearranged the bundle of roses in the man's arms, making fussy humming noises as she worked. The guard rolled his eyes.

He has that old scar, but he could have been given impervious skin more recently.

As she moved a rose from one side of the bouquet to the other, she pressed down hard on the thorny stem, scraping it along the guard's arm. It didn't break the skin.

"I'm sure that's good enough," the guard said.

Blur speed. Impervious skin. That was enough evidence for her.

"Of course. Excuse me." Mica bobbed her head, backing away from the Fifth Talent.

The other guard, who was younger and thinner, with close-cropped auburn hair, had been studying her silently. She saw a hint of suspicion flickering in his hazel eyes. The eyes became green then black. She turned around.

The men murmured to each other behind her, watching her go. She kept her steps stately, unhurried.

"You there!" the younger one called, his voice raspy and harsh. Mica picked up her pace. "Who told you to bring the flowers to this room?"

She kept going, reaching for the knife in her sleeve.

There was a blur of motion, a gust of air. Then the younger guard was in front of her, and his Muscle-strong hands were closing around her throat.

CHAPTER TWENTY-THREE

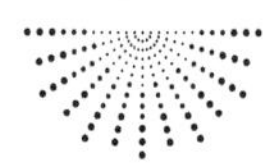

"It is about time you returned, Micathea. I *loathe* waiting."

"Jessa?"

Mica rubbed her eyes blearily, becoming aware of a familiar voice. Her head ached, and spots danced across her vision as she attempted to get her bearings.

She was lying on the floor of the atrium. A woman with short red hair was sitting on the stone lip of the fountain, wearing a red gown trimmed in gold. She came into focus slowly. Rosy lips. Arched, expressive eyebrows. Bright brown eyes. Perfect skin.

"What's going on?" Mica sat up, feeling the cold marble floor beneath her hands. Her neck felt bruised and raw, and her headache worsened every time she moved.

"You could have come openly to me, you know," the red-haired woman said. "There was no need to sneak past my guards."

Mica remembered the mural-lined corridor. The Fifth Talents at the princess's door. The bundle of roses. Those few frantic seconds when she thought she might have a chance to escape.

"Who are you?" she said. "Where's the princess?"

"Keep up, Micathea. It's me."

It *did* look like Jessamyn. The woman was beautiful, with the glowing skin and bright eyes Mica had worked so hard to perfect. Her hair fell just to the tips of her finely sculpted ears, and she was wearing a silver crown set with rubies that Mica knew had been in a jewelry box on the *Silk Goddess*.

"You're good," Mica said. "Do you work for Lord Ober? Where is he?"

"I do not work for anyone but myself and the empire." She gave a shimmering laugh. "Do you think I'm an Impersonator? How marvelous!"

The beautiful woman stood and walked toward Mica. Her stride was perfect too, that lively, confident walk that the real Jessamyn had to suppress while she was acting as Myn Irondier.

Mica shifted her position, gathering her limbs beneath her. Her fingers brushed the leather sheath attached to her ankle beneath the gardener's dress. Her second knife was still there! She could pull it and cut this woman's throat before the guards lurking around the edges of the room reached her. Two were in view now, which meant more would be hiding among the vases.

But Mica hesitated. The woman had Myn Irondier's hair, not the long locks for which the princess was famous. *Could* this be the real Jessamyn? Mica couldn't take the risk. Leaving the knife in its sheath, she stood to confront the other woman.

That face was the same one that had stared at Mica out of mirrors and water basins for the past few months. She had long since gotten used to Jessamyn's scars, and it felt strange to look at the old version of her.

"I don't have all day, Micathea." The woman put her hands on her hips. "Tell me what you learned in the mountains, and I shall fill you in on the developments here."

"I'm not giving my report to anyone but the real princess." Mica took a deep breath, surprised to feel tears pricking her eyes. "If . . . if she's still alive."

"Mica! You're not afraid I've been killed and replaced, are you? That's sweet. I can see you will require proof."

She brushed a hand through her hair, the dark-red locks slipping through her flawless fingers. Mica remembered clutching those fingers and praying the princess would survive the poisoning. There was no sign of her ravaged skin now.

"Let me see. When you arrived in my chambers on your first day in the Silver Palace, I broke something. Do you remember?"

Mica nodded.

"It was a vase full of yellow roses," the woman said. "Sent to me by Lord Riven." She snorted. "He claimed he picked them himself, as if I don't know how much trouble it is to cultivate long-stemmed roses."

"Brin was there too," Mica said. "Are you the same Mimic who—"

"Ah, no, that is true." The woman tapped a finger on her rosebud lips. "Let's see. We rode alone in my carriage to the harbor cruise, and I quizzed you about your identity as Lady Rowena of Obsidian. I chided you for answering the questions like someone who'd only read about Obsidian in books. We were the only ones in the carriage." She paused. "And later that same night, I killed a man who was trying to hurt you."

Mica looked into those bright-brown eyes, still not understanding how the skin around them was whole and unmarred. But no one else living had been there in the bowels of that vessel with her and Jessamyn.

"That's all true," Mica said at last. She looked around the atrium. Guards still lurked in the shadows amongst the marble columns and flower arrangements. None had the lanky form and drooping mustache of the princess's most loyal Shield. "But if you're the real princess, where is Banner?"

A flicker of genuine sadness appeared in those beautiful eyes.

That was when Mica knew they were in a great deal of trouble.

"Jessamyn? What happened to Banner?" Mica felt panic rising, her features threatening to slide out of shape. Nothing short of death would keep Banner from the princess's side. "And why do you look like that?"

"I am afraid we experienced some complications while you were away," Jessamyn said sadly. "I believe this will be better for the empire in the long run."

"What will?"

A deep male voice answered. "Our new partnership."

Mica whirled around at the sound of the familiar voice. A distinguished older man with iron-gray hair and an appealingly prominent nose stepped out of the shadows. Lord Ober.

The last time Mica had seen Caleb's uncle, he had been spitting mad at the princess for humiliating him in front of the court and thwarting his plans. Now he looked calm. Triumphant.

Mica stepped in front of Jessamyn instinctively, but she didn't reach for the knife at her ankle yet. She would only have one chance to use it.

Jessamyn patted her on the shoulder as if she were an overeager guard dog. "It's all right, Micathea, although I appreciate your enthusiasm for protecting me. Lord Ober will not hurt me. Quite the opposite, in fact."

Mica looked back at Jessamyn, at her beautiful, flawless skin, and a frisson of horror ran through her.

"What did you do?"

"You mean this?" Jessamyn touched her rosy cheek. "Lord Ober has a very talented potioner in his employment."

"What did you promise him in return for that face?"

"This isn't about my face. Honestly, do you think I'm that shallow? The face is merely a perk."

"The princess is a wise woman," Lord Ober said, striding over to join them by the fountain. He still had the energetic mannerisms and natural charisma that had made him such a powerful political force at the imperial court. "When I paid her a visit yesterday, she was quick to see that an alliance between us would benefit the empire far more than any further animosity."

Mica stared as Lord Ober offered the princess a gallant bow. Jessamyn couldn't seriously be choosing to work with this man who had done such horrible things to her.

"He *poisoned* you," Mica said.

A faint grimace crossed Jessamyn's face, gone in an instant. "The survival of the empire is more important than my personal grudges."

"But—"

"Perhaps this will help things make more sense."

Jessamyn withdrew a tiny scroll from her cleavage and handed it to Mica. She took the parchment, hands shaking, and began to read.

Stonefoss has fallen—

"Stonefoss?"

"I am afraid so," Jessamyn said. "I know you must be worried for your family, but the whole of the empire is my family. Keep reading."

Mica's hands were trembling so hard she could barely see the scratchy writing. She pictured her parents, her brothers, all the people who lived at the base, all those who must have fallen to defend it. She steeled herself and read on.

Stonefoss has fallen. The Obsidians hold Talon and all of Amber Island east of the Ridge Mountains. There are too many of them.

Mica looked up at Jessamyn, silently begging her to say it wasn't as bad as it seemed.

Jessamyn shook her head. "Without Ironhall and Stonefoss, our two strongest border bases, I am not sure my father will succeed in holding off the Obsidian horde much longer."

"I didn't expect them to advance so quickly."

"Neither did I." Tension lines appeared around Jessamyn's perfect mouth. "Something has gone terribly wrong with our intelligence network in Obsidian."

"But with my help," Lord Ober interjected smoothly, "and the help of my groundbreaking potion, the Windfast Empire still has a chance to turn back the invasion."

Mica turned to the man she had crossed the empire to find. He wore a smug expression on his distinguished features. Deep hatred expanded rapidly within her, and it was an effort to keep her voice calm.

"Y-you want to use the Fifth Talent potion on Windfast soldiers?"

"You've seen the results yourself, I believe," Ober said. "It is our only chance against the Obsidians."

"And what do *you* get in return?" Mica folded her arms, trying to hold the torrent of hatred inside. "I don't believe you're just here to save the day."

"There would be little point in saving the empire for someone else's gain." Ober smiled the engaging politician's smile that had fooled nobles and servants and Talents alike. "But for my new bride and our future children? Not to mention the restoration of my influence at the imperial—"

"Your bride?" Mica felt as if she'd been punched in the gut. *No, no, no. Don't let it be—*

Jessamyn raised her perfect hand, and the light caught on a silver ring set with a bloodred stone. "You did tell my father I'd choose a consort, didn't you?"

Mica's features convulsed, her jaw expanding and contracting like a gasping lung. This couldn't be happening. Even if Jessamyn thought she could save the empire from the Obsidians by accepting Ober's hand, it wasn't *right*.

"He bought you?" Mica said bitterly. "What did he offer?"

"Everything." Jessamyn's voice was as bleak as wintertime in

Talon. "Quinn will repair my face permanently. The Fifth Talents will save the empire from Obsidian. And the rebels will be put down. Lord Ober's men are even now rooting them out from their hiding places in the Twins. The group you met at Birdfell will soon be the last holdouts of the secession movement. And I will be powerful, beautiful, and unstoppable."

Mica couldn't believe it. All along, Jessamyn had refused to reveal the truth. She had been afraid to show her less-than-perfect face, afraid to reveal her weaknesses. But this deal with this evil excuse for a man meant she didn't have to do any of that. And because she had kept her poisoning a secret, everyone would be perfectly willing to accept her engagement to Ober. They might whisper about the age difference, but in the end, even the emperor himself would accept Jessamyn's decision. Mica couldn't believe she had trusted her to do the right thing.

"You can't use the Fifth Talents." Desperation bubbled up in her, drowning out the hatred and rage. "You know how they're created, Jessa, how many people are left with horrible side effects."

She thought of Tallisa, of those strange flitting figures in Dustwood, of the mad Talent at the anniversary ball.

Of Caleb.

He was her only hope now, the only one who wouldn't accept Ober's methods no matter how beneficial his potion had become. Could she get word to him before things got even more out of hand?

"The experiment phase is finished now, Miss Graydier," Ober said. "That was a necessary evil in the name of progress, but there will be no further mistakes."

Mica's jaw set in a thicker, blunter shape. "Does the potion still require Talent bones and blood?"

"This is science, not magic."

"Meaning?"

"It requires certain ingredients," Ober said, "but after the transformation, our loyal soldiers are far stronger than the Talents used in their making. The results are well worth it."

He sounded calm, almost friendly, like the man who kept hundreds of books in his antechamber and invited common Talents to join him for a relaxing drink. Mica despised him for it.

She turned back to Jessamyn. "You can't agree with him."

"We must make sacrifices in wartime."

"*You're* not sacrificing anything. Talents are."

"And if we do not use this potion, more Talents will die." Jessamyn gave a longsuffering sigh. "Stonefoss has already fallen. Your brothers—"

Mica slapped the princess hard across the face. "Don't you dare talk about my brothers. You—"

Two guards tackled her before she could get another word out. They had blurred across the atrium so fast she didn't see them coming. She engaged in a brief but fruitless struggle with them and their Fifth Talent advantages. Any illusion that she was just having a friendly chat with the princess was over now.

"I trusted you!" Mica shouted at Jessamyn as twin iron grips locked around her arms. "I defended you. I honestly believed you would do the right thing."

"I am doing the *necessary* thing." Jessamyn's voice sounded sad. She hadn't so much as rubbed her cheek when Mica slapped her. "This is the only way we can save the empire."

Mica glared at her, the expression as hostile as she could make it, with reddened eyes, bared teeth, and a stretched and misshapen brow. She couldn't believe she had been helping Jessamyn all this time, only for the princess to turn on her when it suited her aims.

"Please know that I still think of us as friends," Jessamyn said as she watched Mica ineffectively try to pull free from the two Talent guards. "You will come to see the wisdom of this new alliance."

"Banner was your friend too," Mica spat. "Ober killed him to get to you, didn't he?"

"That wasn't necessary," Ober said. He had been watching their exchange with mild interest, making no move to interfere. "My men really are very strong. However, I *did* have him killed later. He reacted to the news of our engagement even worse than you have."

Mica felt a sob rising in her throat. The princess's expression remained stoic, empty.

"What about Lord Aren?"

Had she discarded him too, the man who had offered her happiness with a kiss on the palm?

Before Jessamyn could answer, the doors at the far side of the atrium opened, and another pair of Fifth Talents entered.

They were dragging Caleb between them.

CHAPTER TWENTY-FOUR

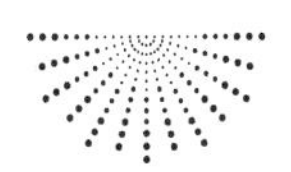

Caleb could barely stand as the guards hauled him across the atrium floor. He was bleeding from a slash to the arm, and he looked on the verge of falling asleep. He had clearly used his abilities, and he was paying the price for it. Mica's stomach churned at the sight. Caleb had been her only hope, the only one left who might still stop the evil these two were about to unleash on the world.

Ober showed only the faintest surprise when his nephew was dragged before him, a tightening of the eyes here, a twitch of the fingers there.

"Report?" Lord Ober said.

"We found spies lurking outside the city, my lord," said a guard with curly brown hair and sunburned skin. "They put up a fight, but they were no match for us."

Caleb's captors wore the same uniforms as the two Fifth Talents securing Mica. His second guard (unusually handsome face, dark skin, mustache) looked at her curiously. Mica made her face unbearably ugly for a moment, and he jumped.

Caleb lifted his head for just long enough to catch Mica's eye, his expression bleak. Her face faded back to normal, but she couldn't summon a smile. Despair threatened to pull her under. However hard Caleb had fought, it hadn't been enough against these Fifth Talents. And where were Ed and Krake? Had they fallen, despite their own supernatural strengths?

Lord Ober strode closer to his nephew and the two guards, blocking the princess's view of the newcomers.

"I am glad to see you yet live, son," Ober said quietly. "I think I can finally offer you a solution to your condition. I have always hoped to right the wrong done to you."

"By you."

Ober flinched. "I thought I was giving you a gift. My conclusions were . . . premature."

"That's one way to put it." Somehow, Caleb's voice sounded even wearier than before. His head drooped, and the guards had to hoist him up so their master wouldn't have to bend down to address him.

"I believe we can put this behind us," Lord Ober said. "My new potioner can remove your limitations and give you the strengths I intended you to have the first time around. With the dedication you have shown to your swordsmanship training and your head for strategy, you could become truly formidable."

Fear seized Mica, constricting her throat. Was she to be betrayed by every noble she thought was good tonight?

But Caleb shook his head after barely a pause.

"It's no use, Uncle," he said. "I won't touch anything you created."

"You cannot go on like this," Ober said. "Let me heal you. We need strong men like you to lead the charge against our enemies."

"My answer is no."

Mica's heart swelled with fierce pride. Caleb wouldn't be bought so easily. He understood the cost of creating the Fifth Talents better than most. They couldn't allow this evil to spread in the world, no matter what benefits came with it.

Lord Ober sighed. "I am sorry my own nephew doesn't appreciate my vision. I have accomplished something that will change the world forever."

"For the worse," Caleb said.

"That remains to be seen."

"Caleb, darling, you've missed a few things." Jessamyn elbowed past her betrothed, attempting to take charge of the situation once more. "The cost of *not* using the Fifth Talents is greater than you think."

Jessamyn quickly filled Caleb in on the fall of Stonefoss, the Obsidian advances, and the agreement between her and Ober. Mica had thought he would react with more vehemence, but he had trouble staying awake as she told him all that had changed since they rode into the mountains. He allowed the news to crash into him, a sea cliff in a storm.

Don't give up. Not yet.

Mica gave an experimental tug in case her captors had relaxed their grips, but Ober's guards held her as firmly as ever, not even glancing at her. Her arms must be turning red by now, and they ached almost as badly as her head. Only Caleb's dark, mustached captor paid her any attention, stealing glances at her as if he expected her to make the ugly face again. She bared her teeth at him.

When Jessamyn finished telling Caleb what she had told Mica, he looked blearily between her and his uncle.

"So you're engaged? But where is Euphia?"

Ober blinked. "What?"

"My aunt, Lady Euphia. Your wife."

Mica had forgotten all about Lord Ober's wife. She hadn't seen the simpering older lady since the pair fled Jewel Harbor months ago.

"What happened to her?" Caleb pressed.

Ober straightened his fine coat, his expression unreadable. "I am afraid she passed away."

Caleb's eyes widened, shock painting his face white, and he struggled to form a response. He looked as if he might finally lose consciousness. Mica didn't think Caleb had been close to his aunt, but he still appeared deeply troubled, as if he couldn't believe his uncle would pursue his ambitions so relentlessly that he would murder his wife.

That's exactly the sort of thing he would do. They had seen this man's evil behavior again and again. They had to stop being shocked by it sometime.

"You killed her, didn't you?" Mica demanded hoarsely.

"No, I did not," Ober said. "Poor Euphia died years ago of natural causes. The woman who has been at my side over the past few years is an Impersonator—a rather good one. I have no wife."

Caleb swore, and both Mica and Jessamyn jumped.

"Is *anyone* their actual selves anymore?"

Ober ignored his nephew's outburst. "You've met my Impersonator friend in other guises, you know," Ober said. "She was the one who uncovered the rather interesting result of my attempt to poison the princess." He gave Jessamyn a polite, apologetic shrug, as if it had all been a simple misunderstanding. "I had concluded that Jessamyn didn't drink my little gift at all, until my Impersonator reported back."

"Is Quinn the Mimic?" Mica asked, not sure if the timeline made sense.

"Guess again," Ober said.

Irritation flashed through Mica at his condescending tone, but she forced it down, trying to think. Peet had warned them that Lord Ober had stationed an Impersonator on the *Silk Goddess* when they left Jewel Harbor. But they had left most of the nobles behind—and none of them knew about Jessamyn's face. Had the intelligence about the spy posing as a *noble* been wrong all along?

Caleb was frowning, as if he too was trying to work out this puzzle. "She was with us on the ship?"

"All along," Ober said.

Mica felt a stab of dread as another possibility occurred to her. *Not Emir. Please, don't tell me I mistook a Mimic for my own brother.*

Before Mica could voice that terrible thought, the sound of steady footsteps sounded down the corridor. Someone was approaching the atrium with a strong, confident stride.

Anxiety spun within her. *Not Emir. Please.*

The thud of footsteps grew louder, drowning out the gentle babbling of the fountain. Mica strained to see past her captors, to see which face was attached to that gait.

Then Lord Aren of Pegasus Island strode into the atrium. He marched across the marble floor toward them, looking robust, confident, and handsome. He was exactly the right man to sweep the calculating princess off her feet. Jessamyn couldn't accept Lord Ober's suit over Aren's, no matter how many Fifth Talents he promised her.

He'll stop this madness.

Mica looked back at the princess, hoping she had come to her senses. But Jessamyn's expression was unmoved at the appearance of the man she had once gazed at with such warmth. She looked carved from cold marble, the resemblance between her and Emperor Styl suddenly apparent. No hint of affection shone in those brown eyes now.

Caleb drew in a sharp breath, and Mica whipped her head back around to see what had startled him.

As Lord Aren crossed the atrium toward them, his features had begun to morph. He shrank steadily, gaining a voluminous bosom and wider girth as his height diminished. His manly ponytail changed color, from rich black to a brassy, artificial shade not quite hiding gray roots. By the time the Impersonator reached the end of the hall, Lady Euphia stared haughtily back at them.

No.

"Hello, Caleb, dear," the Mimic said in that familiar simpering voice, the one Mica had thought sounded put-on when she first met Euphia. "It has been marvelous to spend so much time with you of late."

Caleb went a little green, looking nauseated rather than fatigued now.

"*You* were our imposter?"

"I went to a great deal of trouble to bring the princess and Lord Ober together," the Mimic said, switching to a female voice Mica had never heard before, low and self-assured. Then she contorted her appearance again, becoming tall and male once more. But this time instead of looking like Aren, she assumed the black hair and proud, fine-boned face of Lord Riven.

"He—she has been with us since Jewel Harbor," Mica said, the pieces clicking into place at last. "But as two different people."

"Indeed. I set out from the capital as Lord Riven, hoping that his status as the princess's suitor would give me a chance to secure a position of influence at her side. I was disappointed to learn that Riven had little or no hope of becoming the princess's consort, much less her confidante."

"And you saw a better opportunity when Lord Aren came along."

"The princess was quite taken with him." The Mimic dropped Riven's cold features for Aren's broad smile and sun-kissed skin. "I'd have chosen Aren too."

It was a clever move. Mica hadn't taken the possibility of a switch into account. She thought she'd done away with the imposter by leaving the nobles behind in Carrow.

"What happened to the real Aren?" Caleb asked.

"I killed him shortly before we departed Carrow," the Mimic said, "after getting him and Lady Wendel to tell me enough about his childhood friendship with the princess to make the impersonation plausible."

"It was a convincing performance, wasn't it?" Jessamyn said.

Her cold mask slipped to reveal a gut-wrenching flash of grief and dismay, gone in an instant. "I was certainly fooled."

Mica felt some of the princess's sadness. She remembered how Aren had teased Jessamyn about their childhood games, how he had saved her from drowning in the rapids, how he had admired her for all her qualities that had nothing to do with her looks. But he had been dead before their romance could properly begin.

Poor Jessa.

Mica glared at the mysterious Mimic. "It was you who came to our cabin the night before we arrived in Silverfell, wasn't it?"

"That's correct. Myn Irondier wouldn't let me in to see the princess. I didn't realize I was speaking to the real thing."

"And then . . ." Mica swallowed hard. "And then I convinced her to tell Aren the truth about her poisoning."

The Impersonator smiled, her lips becoming plump like Euphia's, stained a shade too bright. "That was a great help to us." She laughed Euphia's laugh, and Mica cringed at the affected sound. This illusion had layers upon layers. She had underestimated Euphia for her frivolous manner. She had figured out too late that the frivolity hid this woman's calculating nature. But she still hadn't understood the half of it. Euphia. Riven. Aren. Who *was* this Mimic?

"When we learned the princess's secret," Lord Ober said, "all we had to do was wait until her loyal Mimic left her side and then offer her everything she desired."

"Ober played his hand well," Jessamyn said. Her hands remained tightly folded, her face granite. "The empire will be stronger than ever."

I still can't believe it. Even with the grief Jessamyn must feel over Aren, even with the threats bearing down on her from all sides, Mica still couldn't believe the princess had yielded.

She tried to catch the Jessamyn's eye, seeking some hint that all was not as it seemed.

Please. Show me this isn't what you want.

But the princess refused to look at her, keeping her gaze trained on Mica's boots. Sour betrayal roiled in Mica's stomach.

Please.

Then the quick tap of footsteps sounded on marble. A Blur messenger entered the atrium and sprinted toward them.

"The men are moving into position, my lord. We should have control of Birdfell within the hour."

"Very good." Lord Ober exchanged glances with his Mimic, not quite hiding his gleeful anticipation. "See that there are no survivors."

Caleb convulsed, trying to pull away from his captors. "You're betraying them too? Your allies?"

"They served a purpose, but leading a band of rebels from the mountains is hardly my endgame. I don't need them now that I shall have all of the imperial army at my command."

"You're just . . . eliminating them?" Mica thought of all the people waiting for her return at Birdfell. Emir. Danil's family. Fritz and Lorna. Wildson and the rebels. Mica had promised that Jessamyn would hear them out. They had believed her when she said the princess had their best interests at heart. They had all been betrayed.

Jessamyn betrayed us—betrayed me.

"Birdfell is only the beginning," Ober said. He paced in front of the marble fountain, hardly able to contain his excitement. "Jessamyn and I shall announce our engagement tomorrow night. And then we will begin steeping our soldiers in the Fifth Talent potion."

"Starting with the fine men of the HIMS *Arrow*," Jessamyn said.

Mica felt as if she were spinning around and around inside a whirlpool. Her headache had become so powerful it was taking on a life of its own. Pins and needles spiked along her arms. The more Fifth Talents were created, the more impossible it would be to stop them. She couldn't let Ober and Jessamyn make any more. She had to act.

Ober was addressing the Blur messenger, giving further instructions for his murderous mission. Jessamyn still refused to look at Mica, no matter how much she squirmed in her captors' arms. The princess watched her future consort without expression, revealing nothing of her thoughts.

Why is she letting this happen? Why isn't she fighting with her last breath?

Caleb was still secured between the two Fifth Talents. Like Mica, it was impossible for him to move. They locked eyes for a moment, and she saw the same naked urgency in his gaze. He knew what a terrible decision the princess was making, what a terrible betrayal. They couldn't allow her to go through with this, even if it meant turning on the one person they had trusted unequivocally.

They might already be too late. They had to act *now*.

Mica thought of the knife strapped to her ankle, the weapon her captors had missed. She scanned the atrium. A Blur messenger. An anonymous Mimic. A murderous lord. A faithless princess. Two Fifth Talents holding Mica and two holding Caleb.

Could Caleb summon enough energy for one more burst of Talent? Mica glanced at the two guards holding his arms.

And to her great surprise, one of them gave her a Mimic's wink.

The Fifth Talent still had curly brown hair, sunburned skin, and unfamiliar features, but his eye was shifting rapidly from blue to green to black to white to blue again. He was trying to tell her something. The unusually handsome mustached guard was watching her too.

Ed and Krake are here!

Mica changed her eye color from hazel to bright blue and back again, acknowledging that she understood. She was not alone after all—and she was ready. The curly-haired guard squeezed Caleb's arm, and he gave a faint nod in response.

Ober sent the Blur messenger speeding out of the atrium. He turned, about to speak to his Mimic again.

Caleb coughed twice.

The two guards dropped him and hurled themselves at the Fifth Talents holding onto Mica. The rebels wrenched Ober's loyal guards apart, leaving Mica staggering in the middle. The two pairs of guards hit the ground, shouting, wrestling for control.

Mica grabbed the knife from her ankle sheath and spun toward the others. Jessamyn met her gaze, naked fear flaring in her eyes. Her perfect lips parted in surprise. Mica hurled her knife.

The weapon arced through the air between them, flashing brilliantly.

And the blade struck the Euphia Impersonator dead center in her chest. Her eyes widened in shock as she stared at the knife hilt sticking out of Aren's tunic. Blood spread from the wound in a rapidly widening teardrop. The Mimic fell, features contorting wildly, her large body shifting between male and female. The color drained out of her hair until it was slate-gray and coarse, leaving a mature-looking older woman who bore no resemblance to any of the roles she had played.

Lord Ober gave a wordless cry at the sight of his dying partner.

Caleb had gotten to his feet. He scrambled around the Mimic's body, boots slipping on marble, showing no sign of fatigue now. Then, as quick as a Blur, he closed the distance between himself and Lord Ober and snapped his uncle's neck with Muscle strength.

The crack reverberated through the room.

Caleb released Ober's head as quickly as he had seized it, and the body crashed into the marble fountain with a terrible splash.

A shocked stillness filled the atrium, as even the wrestling Talents paused their contest. Caleb stood rigid above his uncle's body, which slumped beneath the water, one leg splayed over the lip of the basin.

Mica hoped for one breathless moment that they had won.

Then Jessamyn started screaming.

"Traitors!" she shrieked. "Guards! There are traitors in our midst!"

The two pairs of Fifth Talents resumed their struggle, locked in an impossible contest between invincible foes. Impervious, fast, and strong, none could gain the advantage.

Caleb stumbled away from his uncle's body. He grabbed Mica's hand, his eyes clouded with pain. This was it. They had said stopping Lord Ober was their primary duty, even if it meant betraying the empire itself. They had done what they had to. Now, all they could do was run.

Jessamyn screamed for backup as they sprinted away from the fountain. Her true enemies lay dead on the floor, but still she called for Mica and Caleb's capture. Called them traitors. Murderers.

Mica blocked out the sound, holding tight to Caleb's hand.

And they ran.

But they didn't get far.

Caleb stumbled in the first corridor, his body giving way. Mica tried to hold him up, to keep moving forward, but guards swarmed them, blurring in from all directions. The Fifth Talents were inescapable, assured of their inevitable victory.

Caleb and Mica were wrenched apart and led away.

CHAPTER TWENTY-FIVE

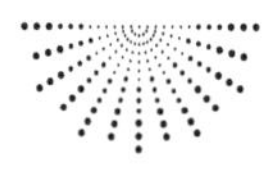

Mica practiced her impersonations in the cell beneath Silverfell Manor. She cycled through her regular rotation of faces, which were a little rusty after she'd spent so much time in a single guise. She became the doe-eyed cowherd's daughter. The mischievous lad. The lean old soldier. The Obsidian beauty. The humpbacked crone. She shifted her eyes through a dozen colors, her hair through a hundred shades and lengths. The shape of her face contorted, cheekbones rising and lowering, nose growing and shrinking, lips filling and deflating and changing in turn.

She still wore the old gardener's shapeless dress, which the Fifth Talents had ripped as they searched for more hidden knives before tossing her into this cell. It was actually a wine cellar, full of stacks of barrels stamped with the symbols of wineries from across the Windfast islands. A single lantern hung from the ceiling, its weak light casting deep shadows across the stone floor.

Mica had been sitting on one of the barrels for hours, waiting to learn her fate. The longer she sat here, the more certain she became that she would be sentenced to death for her actions.

The scene in the atrium was a blur. Jessamyn's screams. The

blood blooming around the knife in the Mimic's chest. The sharp snap of Ober's neck. He hadn't been impervious after all. Despite his confidence in his formula, he hadn't been brave enough to use it on himself.

Mica knew she and Caleb had done the right thing, even though they had gone against Jessamyn's commands. She had dared hope that Jessamyn would thank them for dealing with Lord Ober and releasing her from the terrible bargain she had struck. Instead, she'd had them taken away by Ober's men, refusing to look either one in the eye.

The princess had truly betrayed them, just as Ober had betrayed the rebels from the Twins. Mica had believed Jessamyn was better than that, and the truth stung.

Now, Mica wasn't sure whether her actions would make a difference. Ober had gotten what he deserved, but they hadn't finished saving the empire. The princess controlled the Fifth Talent potion, and she could still decide to use it.

Maybe it'll all be for nothing.

Mica wished she could talk to Caleb. They had been hauled off to separate prisons after the Fifth Talents subdued them. Silverfell Manor's dungeon only had one cell, which was why Mica was being held in the wine cellar, and she'd lost track of how long she'd been alone down here. The heady smell of wine, which had been overpowering when she was first thrown down here, barely registered now.

Maybe they'll just leave me here until the war's over.

As she waited to learn her fate, Mica couldn't help thinking about Stonefoss. She adopted her mother's face. Her father's. Her brothers', one by one. They could all still be alive or none of them. Not knowing whether they had perished was worse than knowing her home had fallen.

Mica wondered if her family would think she and Caleb had done the right thing. They had always been loyal to the empire, serving in the army without complaint. But the future ruler of the empire had taken a dark path. Would Mica's brave and noble family have done Jessamyn's bidding without question if they had been given the same choice? For Mica's part, there was no choice at all. She had seen the suffering Ober caused, the blatant disregard for Talent—and human—life. He deserved death.

As Mica practiced her faces in the flickering lantern light, her thoughts turned to Ober's Mimic. She had known the woman as Euphia, as Riven, and finally as Lord Aren. She wished she'd gotten a better look at her true face. She'd only glimpsed the coarse gray hair and older-than-expected features at the end. What had prompted the woman to serve at Ober's side for so long, despite what he was doing to Talents like her? Mica would probably never know.

She relaxed into her own face at last, every muscle stretched and weary. It had to be almost morning. She hoped Jessamyn would let her see Caleb one last time before she executed them for the murder of her new fiancé.

That's what working Talents get for being loyal to their lords and ladies.

Mica shouldn't have allowed herself to believe it would be different with Jessamyn. The nobles didn't care about people like her. They never had.

Then the cellar door opened, and Jessamyn entered. Mica was so surprised to see the princess herself that she nearly toppled off her barrel.

"Jess—"

"Just a moment, Micathea." The princess addressed an unseen figure beyond the door. "I wish to speak with the prisoner in private. I will be perfectly safe. See that we're not disturbed."

Voices murmured beyond the door, then it slammed shut, leaving Mica and Jessamyn alone.

Mica tensed as the princess strolled forward into the flickering light. She wore the same red gown she'd had on the last time Mica saw her, and she looked tired. Clearly, neither of them had slept that night. A subtle sloping and mottling had returned to Jessamyn's face too, as if whatever Quinn had done to restore her beautiful features hadn't been designed to last.

"Princess," Mica began.

Jessamyn flung up a hand, revealing the patchiness returning to her exposed skin. "I don't want to hear anything you have to say, Micathea."

"If you'll let me ex—"

"Now is not the time." Jessamyn stopped out of Mica's reach, as if she feared Mica might lunge at her, no matter what she had told the guards. She wasn't wrong to be cautious.

"Listen carefully," the princess said, her tone low and urgent. "Lord Ober left instructions that if he were to be killed, the Fifth Talent formula would be delivered to the King of Obsidian."

"What?" Mica vaulted to her feet. "The King of Obsidian has—"

"Be quiet until I am finished," Jessamyn snapped. "You have already messed things up enough for one night. I was aware he had this failsafe in place. I needed time to find his chosen messenger *before* I moved against him."

Mica's jaw lengthened as she realized what Jessamyn was saying. "You were only pretending to partner with him?"

"I had hoped you could find the messenger when you returned from the mountains. You didn't trust that I was doing the right thing, and now you may have condemned us all."

"But I thought—"

"You thought I threw my lot in with a monster for a new face." Jessamyn's voice dripped with cold fury. "After everything we've been through, I thought you knew me better."

Mica gaped at her. Had she really gotten it so wrong? It was hard to think straight. The only rest she'd had in the past twenty-four hours was when the guard knocked her unconscious, and she had lurched far past the point of exhaustion.

"I thought you'd really agreed to work with him. With Banner and Aren gone—"

"That's why I needed you more than ever." Jessamyn's voice cracked, and she turned to study the casks of wine lining the walls of the cellar. She refused to meet Mica's eyes, but vulnerability showed in the tightness of her shoulders and the way her hands clenched her skirt. "You and Caleb were my last hope. I had no choice but to accept Ober when he arrived with a hundred Fifth Talents in tow. I needed time to plan how to move against him." She drew a wavering breath. "But you didn't have faith in me. You . . . you betrayed me."

Mica slumped down to sit on the barrel again.

"I am so sorry, Jessa."

She hadn't believed it at first. She had looked for some sign from Jessamyn, but the princess had played her role too well. Besides, a part of Mica could understand why Jessamyn would agree to cooperate with Ober upon learning how far the Obsidians had advanced. *Stonefoss. Talon. All of Amber Island east of the Ridge Mountains.* She could see the argument for working with her enemy in order to halt the invasion.

On the other hand, Jessamyn had tried to play games with Lord Ober before, waiting for her moment, believing she could outwit him in the end. It had only led to pain.

Mica looked up. "Actually, let me clarify," she said. "I am sorry for not trusting that you had a plan, but I'm not sorry we killed Ober and his Mimic."

"I beg your pardon?"

"They're too dangerous, and they've done too much damage. I'm not sorry for killing them at all."

Jessamyn put her hands on her hips, no longer avoiding Mica's eyes. She looked more like her old self now than she had in the atrium, energetic rather than cold, angry rather than calm. Her skin appeared to be slipping out of shape again too.

"Do you understand you're declaring yourself an unrepentant traitor to the Windfast Empire?"

Mica got to her feet. "I am a traitor to anyone who would hurt the empire, including you. I stand by what I did."

Mica and Jessamyn faced each other, the flickering lantern casting shadows over their features. Mica refused to look away. She had stopped fearing the princess, stopped viewing her as a superhuman force. She felt guilty for not waiting to hear her plans, but she was certain Ober had a worse fate in mind for her.

So she continued to stare down her friend, hoping Jessamyn would understand, but no longer regretting what she had done. Mica had sometimes felt as if her needs and opinions and conscience were being absorbed by the princess. But in this, at least, Mica knew what was right.

She stood her ground.

The shadows danced around them, and no sound interrupted the stillness.

Jessamyn was the first to look away.

She sighed, the sound resigned rather than self-pitying. "I can never forgive your lack of trust in me, Mica, but I know what Ober is. He would probably have strangled me the moment I bore him a son if I went through with the agreement."

Mica couldn't argue with that. "Does that mean you're letting me go?"

Jessamyn snorted. "Not quite. Let's not forget that you and Caleb destroyed a fragile alliance in front of witnesses—witnesses who are loyal to Lord Ober and supernaturally Talented."

"Oh." It hadn't occurred to Mica that Ober's men might object to the murder of their lord. She supposed the people who followed him *did* seem exceptionally dedicated.

"It is vital that I take control of the Fifth Talents Ober has already created before they lend their power to another cause. Over sixty are still in the city now, with the rest out there doing Ober's bidding." Jessamyn glanced at the door and lowered her voice. "I must make them believe we were *both* betrayed so they will transfer their allegiance to me. Otherwise, none of us will survive the week."

"You intend to use them?"

"The ones already in existence, yes."

Mica's stomach plunged as she remembered what else those Fifth Talents were supposed to be doing while she was busy being captured.

"What happened to the people at Birdfell?"

Jessamyn hesitated for a beat. "They were rebels. We're out of time for diplomacy."

"I told them you would listen."

"I wanted to," Jessamyn said. "Truly, I did."

"Are they all dead?" Mica thought she might be sick on Jessamyn's fine red gown. "Ober said no survivors."

"I sent another Blur to say I wanted as many prisoners as possible after all," Jessamyn said. "But . . . I can't imagine they'll all come quietly."

Mica bowed her head, thinking of Wildson and Fair, of the motley band of bearded men who had wanted their voices to be heard. Of Emir. He had been injured. She could only hope he would allow himself to be taken prisoner once more.

"What are you going to do with the extra Fifth Talent potion Ober created?"

"I don't know, Mica," Jessamyn said. "The Fifth Talents may be our only hope against the Obsidians. We may *have* to use it."

Mica thought again of her family, who might yet be alive and in need of backup. The temptation to send super soldiers to their aid was powerful indeed, especially if they were following Jessamyn's orders directly instead of Ober's. Mica allowed herself to picture every soldier from the *Arrow* blurring to meet the Obsidian horde, impervious, strong, victorious.

That's how it starts. You can't forget the cost.

They couldn't use the Fifth Talents in battle even once, not after everything she'd seen in the mountains. It would be all too easy to use them again.

"Jessa," Mica said, "I have to tell you about a place called Dustwood."

She kept her description as brief as possible, aware of the Fifth Talents just outside the doors. She understood Jessamyn's fears. Too many of these dangerous soldiers had already been born from the mirrored waters of Birdfell. The princess needed to tread lightly in the days to come. But controlling them by creating yet more Fifth Talents was not the answer. Mica had to impress upon her what Ober had done to open this door.

Jessamyn listened carefully as Mica described the flitting figures, the fallen tree, the woman named Tallisa whose abilities caused her pain, the stories about the mysterious happenings at Birdfell. Mica begged her not to use it, not to allow this evil to spread.

"Thank you for telling me," Jessamyn said when Mica finished. "I will think it over. I cannot promise anything more than that."

"But—"

"Do not press me on this, Micathea. I don't need any further reminders that you don't trust my judgment." She waved off Mica's objections and went on, her face a dispassionate mask once more. "Now, listen. This has already taken too long. The Fifth Talent formula is on its way to the Obsidian King with Ober's messenger. I need you to go after it and destroy it."

Mica blinked. "Me? There are already Windfast agents in—"

"Would you rather rot in this cellar? I can't trust anyone else to destroy the formula. It must be you."

Mica was momentarily at a loss for words. She felt as if she were being tossed about in a storm at sea, never entirely sure where she stood. Had she and the princess reconciled or not?

When she didn't answer, Jessamyn raised her eyebrows,

where the scars were slowly emerging again. "Well? I don't have all day."

"Of course I'll do it," Mica said quickly. "I'm guessing you'll tell those Fifth Talents you want to follow you that I've been executed for my part in Ober's murder?"

"Naturally." Jessamyn pursed her lips, which were no longer rosy and smooth. Her beauty was dripping away, her poison-marred features reasserting themselves. If Quinn really could fix her face permanently, she hadn't done it yet. "I am sending Caleb with you. You two traitors deserve each other."

"Really?" Mica felt a swell of hope. "Thank—"

"You should know this is a suicide mission," Jessamyn snapped.

"Understood."

"Good. I will send instructions shortly."

Jessamyn marched back to the door, where she paused to brush a hand through her short hair, partially hiding her face—and whatever emotion she might be feeling.

"And Micathea?"

"Yes, Princess?"

"If you somehow manage to destroy the formula and escape Obsidian, don't come back."

EPILOGUE

Mica and Caleb boarded the aging schooner as the early-morning commotion surrounded them. Sailors shouted at each other, boots thudded on wooden decks, and seagulls bickered over refuse. The aroma of fish and fresh-cut timber from a dozen building projects had overwhelmed the smell of smoke from the previous week. In addition to repairing the damage from the battle, Silverfell was reinforcing its defenses, preparing for war. The Obsidian invasion was advancing more rapidly than anyone had predicted, and it was only a matter of time before the dark horde reached these shores.

Mica sported a brand-new face, a plain one with dull blue eyes and mousy hair that wouldn't make anyone look twice. Caleb had acquired a wide-brimmed hat to cast his features in shadow. Both wore simple clothes and carried sturdy packs with a few days' worth of provisions. They had taken passage on one of the few vessels willing to carry them east, toward the front lines.

Caleb had said little since they were reunited. Mica knew fatigue wasn't the only thing causing his somberness. He had killed his uncle, who he'd been close to for most of his life. His best friend had declared him an imperial traitor and a murderer and stripped him of his former life. Overnight, he'd lost friends, relatives, admirers. Only Mica and Jessamyn knew he had saved them all when he snapped Ober's neck. Still, Caleb was a good and kind man, a true noble, and he wouldn't bear the weight of his actions easily.

Mica squeezed his hand briefly as they stood on the deck of the schooner, staying out of the way of the sailors. She started to release her grip, but Caleb held onto her hand even though they were surrounded by people, entwining his fingers with hers.

They had a perilous journey ahead of them, but at least they had each other. They even had the same social status now: they were exiles.

Exiles with a mission.

"Do you think Quinn was telling the truth about the messenger?" Caleb asked, his voice as quiet as possible amidst the cacophony of the harbor.

"Quinn is from Talon," Mica said. "She wouldn't want the Obsidians to get the formula."

The potioner had been the one to release them from their cells and give them the little information they had about the messenger Ober had charged with delivering the Fifth Talent formula to Obsidian if he died. Despite the friendship Quinn and Mica once shared, her manner had been distant and even brusquer than usual.

"As long as you're sure," Caleb said. "We don't want to go chasing after a lie."

"She was wrong to work with Ober," Mica said, "but she's not so vindictive that she would want that formula to reach the Stone Court."

Quinn had also given them a box of potions that would help them on their journey—and she had assured Mica that Emir would make a full recovery. Mica held out hope that she wasn't all bad.

Caleb adjusted his hat, pulling it lower over his face. "I wish she'd stopped the messenger before he departed in the first place."

"Or she," Mica said. "All we know is the formula is with a Mimic. We can't make any assumptions."

Quinn had informed them the messenger was definitely a Mimic—and not the one Mica had killed. The person they sought had a small build and had left Silverfell on a ship called the *Keith*. Quinn suspected the Mimic was an Obsidian native. Beyond that, she had given them precious little to go on.

Despite how they'd left things, Mica was glad Jessamyn believed they could actually find this person in time. Mica herself wasn't so sure they could pull it off. Finding a small Mimic who might or might not be from Obsidian would be no easy task, especially in the midst of a war.

As the schooner eased away from its mooring, Mica looked up the elegant avenues of Silverfell toward Lord Bont's manor. She imagined a red-haired woman standing on the marble portico, watching her departure from afar. She hoped the princess hadn't meant what she'd said about not returning. Mica hated that things weren't right between her and Jessamyn. They had let each other down in profound ways. Even now, Mica couldn't be sure what the princess would do with Quinn and the Fifth Talent potion after she was gone. She trusted Jessamyn with it more than the Obsidian King, though.

If Mica saved the empire from having to face a multi-Talented army, Jessamyn would have to welcome her back. She even dared hope that the princess would allow her to serve at her side once more.

Wind gusted across the deck of the ship, carrying the first hints of spring, and the schooner picked up speed. Gulls swooped around the mast, calling out a raucous farewell.

Mica held Caleb's hand a little tighter and looked to the east. She would worry about Jessamyn later. Keeping the Fifth Talent formula out of their enemy's hands was her assignment now. Her and Caleb's.

She was going to Obsidian at last.

ACKNOWLEDGMENTS

I have been lucky to have an extraordinary support network throughout my writing career. My family and friends encourage me by asking about my progress, reading my books, providing feedback, and even printing out my drafts when I can't make it to the print shop.

My family's support was in evidence more than usual during the writing of this book. They loved the first book in the series, which was all the motivation I needed to write the second. They helped me see the forest for the trees when the early drafts were difficult to write. Then, when our grandpa died shortly before I was supposed to write the final draft, they helped me get the work done—and reminded me when it wasn't the most important thing.

In Hong Kong, I am grateful to my stalwart writing friends, especially Willow, Amanda, Sarah, Brooke, and Rachel, who listen to my venting and offer all the inspiration I need.

Thank you to my publishing team, including the folks at Deranged Doctor Design, Susie and Lynn at Red Adept Editing, and my agent Sarah Hershman. Thanks, also, to my intrepid publishing friends in the AC.

I'm eternally grateful to my advanced reviewer team and everyone else who has said such nice things about my books.

And, as always, thank *you* for reading.

Jordan Rivet

Hong Kong, 2018

ABOUT THE AUTHOR

Jordan Rivet is an American author of young adult fantasy and post-apocalyptic adventures. Originally from Arizona, she lives in Hong Kong with her husband. A full-time writer, Jordan can usually be found making faces at her computer in the local Starbucks. She hasn't been kicked out yet.

www.JordanRivet.com
Jordan@JordanRivet.com

ALSO BY JORDAN RIVET

EMPIRE OF TALENTS

The Spy in the Silver Palace

An Imposter with a Crown

STEEL AND FIRE

Duel of Fire

King of Mist

Dance of Steel

City of Wind

Night of Flame

THE SEABOUND CHRONICLES

Seabound

Seaswept

Seafled

Burnt Sea: A Seabound Prequel

Made in the USA
San Bernardino, CA
25 June 2020